ON A BALCONY

On a Balcony

DAVID STACTON

faber and faber

This edition first published in 2012
by Faber and Faber Ltd
Bloomsbury House, 74–77 Great Russell Street
London WC1B 3DA

A CIP record for this book is available from the British Library

ISBN 978–0–571–29579–1

Introduction

The Case of David Stacton

Might David Stacton (1923–68) be the most unjustly neglected American novelist of the post-World War II era? There is a case to be made – beginning, perhaps, with a simple inductive process.

In its issue dated 1 February 1963 *Time* magazine offered an article that placed Stacton amid ten writers whom the magazine rated as the best to have emerged in American fiction during the previous decade: the others being Richard Condon, Ralph Ellison, Joseph Heller, H. L. Humes, John Knowles, Bernard Malamud, Walker Percy, Philip Roth, and John Updike. It would be fair to say that, over the intervening fifty years, seven of those ten authors have remained solidly in print and in high-level critical regard. As for the other three: the case of H. L. Humes is complex, since after 1963 he never added to the pair of novels he had already published; while John Knowles, though he continued to publish steadily, was always best known for *A Separate Peace* (1959), which was twice adapted for the screen.

By this accounting, then, I believe we can survey the *Time* list today and conclude that the stand-out figure is David Stacton – a hugely productive, prodigiously gifted, still regrettably little-known talent and, yes, arguably more deserving of revived attention than any US novelist since 1945.

Across a published career of fifteen years or so Stacton put out fourteen novels (under his name, that is – plus a further raft of pseudonymous genre fiction); many short stories; several collections of poetry; and three compendious works of non-fiction. He was first 'discovered' in England, and had to wait several years before making it into print in his homeland. Assessing Stacton's career at the time of what proved to be his last published novel *People of the Book* (1965), Dennis Powers of the *Oakland Tribune* ruefully concluded that Stacton's was very much 'the old story of literary virtue unrewarded'. Three years later Stacton was dead.

The rest has been a prolonged silence punctuated by occasional tributes and testaments in learned journals, by fellow writers, and around the literary blogosphere. But in 2011 New York Review Books reissued Stacton's *The Judges of the Secret Court*, his eleventh novel and the second in what he saw as a trilogy on American themes. (History, and sequences of titles, were Stacton's abiding passions.) Now in 2012 Faber Finds is reissuing a selection of seven of Stacton's novels.

Readers new to the Stacton *oeuvre* will encounter a novelist of quite phenomenal ambition. The landscapes and epochs into which he transplanted his creative imagination spanned vast distances, and yet the finely wrought Stacton prose style remained fairly distinctive throughout. His deft and delicate gifts of physical description were those of a rare aesthete, but the cumulative effect is both vivid and foursquare. He was, perhaps, less committed to strong narrative through-lines than to erecting a sense of a spiritual universe around his characters; yet he undoubtedly had the power to carry the reader with him from page to page. His protagonists are quite often haunted – if not fixated – figures, temperamentally estranged from their societies. But whether or not we may find elements of Stacton himself within said protagonists, for sure his own presence is in the books – not least by dint of his incorrigible fondness for apercus, epigrams, pontifications of all kinds.

*

He was born Lionel Kingsley Evans on 27 May 1923, in San Francisco. (His parents had met and married in Dublin then emigrated after the war.) Undoubtedly Northern California shaped his aesthetic sense, though in later years he would disdain the place as an 'overbuilt sump', lamenting what he felt had been lost in tones of wistful conservatism. ('We had founding families, and a few traditions and habits of our own ... Above all we had our sensuous and then unspoilt landscape, whose loss has made my generation and sort of westerner a race of restless wanderers.') Stacton was certainly an exile, but arguably he made himself so, even before California, in his estimation, went to the dogs. In any case his fiction would range far away from his place of birth, for all that his early novels were much informed by it.

Precociously bright, the young Lionel Evans was composing poetry and short stories by his mid-teens, and entered Stanford University in 1941, his studies interrupted by the war (during which he was a conscientious objector). Tall and good-looking, elegant in person as in prose, Evans had by 1942 begun to call himself David Stacton. Stanford was also the place where, as far as we know, he acknowledged his homosexuality – to himself and, to the degree possible in that time, to his peers. He would complete his tertiary education at UC Berkeley, where he met and moved in with a man who became his long-time companion, John Mann Rucker. By 1950 his stories had begun to appear in print, and he toured Europe (what he called 'the standard year's travel after college').

London (which Stacton considered 'such a touching city') was one of the favoured stops on his itinerary and there he made the acquaintance of Basil 'Sholto' Mackenzie, the second Baron Amulree, a Liberal peer and distinguished physician. In 1953 Amulree introduced Stacton to Charles Monteith, the brilliant Northern Irish-born editor and director at Faber and Faber. The impression made was clearly favourable, for in 1954 Faber published *Dolores*, Stacton's first novel, which *Time and Tide* would describe as 'a charming idyll, set in Hollywood, Paris and Rome'.

A Fox Inside followed in 1955, *The Self-Enchanted* in 1956: *noir*-inflected Californian tales about money, power and influence; and neurotic men and women locked into marriages made for many complex reasons other than love. In retrospect either novel could conceivably have been a Hollywood film in its day, directed by Nicholas Ray, say, or Douglas Sirk. Though neither book sold spectacularly, together they proved Stacton had a voice worth hearing. In their correspondence Charles Monteith urged Stacton to consider himself 'a novelist of contemporary society', and suggested he turn his hand to outright 'thriller writing'. But Stacton had set upon a different course. 'These are the last contemporary books I intend to write for several years', he wrote to Monteith. 'After them I shall dive into the historical . . .'

In 1956 Stacton made good on his intimation by delivering to Monteith a long-promised novel about Ludwig II of Bavaria, entitled *Remember Me*. Monteith had been excited by the prospect of the work, and he admired the ambition of the first draft, but considered it unpublishable at its initial extent. With considerable application Stacton winnowed *Remember Me* down to a polished form that Faber could work with. Monteith duly renewed his campaign to persuade Stacton toward present-day subject matter. There would be much talk of re-jigging and substituting one proposed book for another already-delivered manuscript, of strategies for 'building a career'. Stacton was amenable (to a degree) at first, but in the end he made his position clear to Monteith:

> I just flatly don't intend to write any more contemporary books, for several reasons ... [M]y talents are melodramatic and a mite grandiose, and this goes down better with historical sauce ... I just can't write about the present any more, that's all. I haven't the heart ... [F]or those of conservative stamp, this age is the end of everything we have loved ... There is nothing to do but hang up more lights. And for me the lights are all in the past.

Monteith, for all his efforts to direct Stacton's *oeuvre*, could see he was dealing with an intractable talent; and in April 1957 he wrote to Stacton affirming Faber's 'deep and unshaken confidence in your own gift and in your future as a novelist'.

The two novels that followed hard upon *Remember Me* were highly impressive proofs of Stacton's intent and accomplishment, which enhanced his reputation both inside Faber and in wider literary-critical circles. *On a Balcony* told of Akhenaten and Nefertiti in the Egypt of the Eighteenth Dynasty, and *Segaki* concerned a monk in fourteenth-century Japan. Stacton took the view that these two and the Ludwig novel were in fact a trilogy ('concerned with various aspects of the religious experience') which by 1958 he was calling 'The Invincible Questions'.

And this was but the dawning of a theme: in the following years, as his body of work expanded, Stacton came to characterise it as 'a series of novels in which history is used to explain the way we live now' – a series with an 'order' and 'pattern', for all that each entry was 'designed to stand independent of the others if need be'. (In 1964 he went so far as to tell Charles Monteith that his entire *oeuvre* was 'really one book'.)

Readers discovering this work today might be less persuaded that the interrelation of the novels is as obviously coherent as Stacton contended. There's an argument that Stacton's claims say more for the way in which his brilliant mind was just temperamentally inclined toward bold patterns and designs. (A small but telling example of same: in 1954 at the very outset of his relationship with Faber Stacton sent the firm a logotype he had drawn, an artful entwining of his initials, and asked that it be included as standard in the prelims of his novels ('Can I be humoured about my colophon as a regular practice?'). Faber did indeed oblige him.)

But perhaps Stacton's most convincing explanation for a connective tissue in his work – given in respect of those first three historical novels but, I think, more broadly applicable – was his admission that the three lives fascinated him on account of his identification with 'their plight':

Fellow-feeling would be the proper phrase. Such people are comforting, simply because they have gone

6

before us down the same endless road . . . [T]hough these people have an answer for us, it is an answer we can discover only by leading parallel lives. Anyone with a taste for history has found himself doing this from time to time . . .

Perhaps we might say that – just as the celebrated and contemporaneous American acting teacher Lee Strasberg taught students a 'Method' to immerse themselves in the imagined emotional and physical lives of scripted characters – Stacton was engaged in a kind of 'Method writing' that immersed him by turn in the lives of some of recorded history's rarest figures.

*

Stacton was nurtured as a writer by Faber and Faber, and he was glad of the firm's and Charles Monteith's efforts on his behalf, though his concerns were many, perhaps even more so than the usual novelist. Stacton understood he was a special case: not the model of a 'smart popular writer' for as long as he lacked prominent critical support and/or decent sales. He posed Faber other challenges, too – being such a peripatetic but extraordinarily productive writer, the business of submission, acquisition and scheduling of his work was a complicated, near-perpetual issue for Monteith. Stacton had the very common writer's self-delusion that his next project would be relatively 'short' and delivered to schedule, but his ambitions simply didn't tend that way. In January 1956 Monteith mentioned to Stacton's agent Michael Horniman about his author's 'tendency to over-produce'. Faber did not declare an interest in the Western novels Stacton wrote as 'Carse Boyd' or in the somewhat lurid stories of aggressive youth (*The Power Gods, D For Delinquent, Muscle Boy*) for which his *nom de plume* was 'Bud Clifton'. But amazingly, even in the midst of these purely commercial undertakings, Stacton always kept one or more grand and enthralling projects on his horizon simultaneously. (In 1963 he mentioned almost off-handedly to Monteith, 'I thought recently it would be fun to take the Popes on whole, and do a big book about their personal eccentricities . . .')

In 1960 Stacton was awarded a Guggenheim fellowship, which he used to travel to Europe before resettling in the US. In 1963 the Time magazine article mentioned above much improved the attention paid to him in his homeland. The books kept coming, each dazzlingly different to what came before, whatever inter-connection Stacton claimed: *A Signal Victory, A Dancer in Darkness, The Judges of the Secret Court, Tom Fool, Old Acquaintance, The World on the Last Day, Kali-Yuga, People of the Book.*

By the mid-1960s Stacton had begun what he may well have considered his potential *magnum opus*: *Restless Sleep,* a manuscript that grew to a million words, concerned in part with Samuel Pepys but above all with the life of Charles II from restoration to death. On paper the 'Merrie Monarch' did seem an even better subject for Stacton than the celebrated diarist: as a shrewd and lonely man of complicated emotions holding a seat of contested authority. But this work was never to be truly completed.

In 1966 Stacton's life was beset by crisis. He was in Copenhagen, Denmark, when he discovered that he had colon cancer, and was hospitalised for several months, undergoing a number of gruelling procedures. (He wrote feelingly to Charles Monteith, '[A]fter 48 hours of it (and six weeks of it) I am tired of watching my own intestines on closed circuit TV.') Recuperating, he returned to the US and moved in once more with John Mann Rucker, their relations having broken down in previous years. But he and Rucker were to break again, and in 1968 Stacton returned to Denmark – to Fredensborg, a town beloved of the Danish royal family – there renting a cottage from Helle Bruhn, a magistrate's wife whom he had befriended in 1966. It was Mrs Bruhn who, on 20 January 1968, called at Stacton's cottage after she could get no answer from him by telephone, and there found him dead in his bed. The local medical examiner signed off the opinion that Stacton died of a heart attack – unquestionably young, at forty-four, though he had been a heavy smoker, was on medication to assist sleeping, and had been much debilitated by the treatment for his cancer. His body was cremated in Denmark, and the ashes sent to his mother in California, who had them interred in Woodlawn Cemetery, Colma.

From our vantage in 2012, just as many years have passed since Stacton's untimely death as he enjoyed of life. It is a moment, surely, for a reappraisal that is worthy of the size, scope and attainment of his work. I asked the American novelist, poet and translator David Slavitt – an avowed admirer of Stacton's – how he would evaluate the legacy, and he wrote to me with the following:

David Stacton is a prime candidate for prominent space in the Tomb of the Unknown Writers. His witty and accomplished novels failed to find an audience even in England, where readers are not put off by dazzle. Had he been British and had he been part of the London literary scene, he might have won some attention for himself and his work in an environment that is more centralised and more coherent than that of the US where it is even easier to fall through the cracks and where success is much more haphazard. I am delighted by these flickers of attention to the wonderful flora of his hothouse talents.

Richard T. Kelly
Editor, Faber Finds
April 2012

Sources and Acknowledgements

This introduction was prepared with kind assistance from Robert Brown, archivist at Faber and Faber, from Robert Nedelkoff, who has done more than anyone to encourage a renewed appreciation of Stacton, and from David R. Slavitt. It was much aided by reference to a biographical article written about Stacton by Joy Martin, his first cousin.

For
J. P. van KRALINGEN
and
EZRA SIMS

"Your letter is insane nonsense. You say: *They will not live for ever.* How do you know? Neither he nor you nor anyone else knows how long he will live. You should make your plans as though he were to die tomorrow or live thirty years more. Only children, political orators, and poets talk of the future as though it were a thing one could know; fortunately for us we know nothing about it."

THORNTON WILDER: *The Ides of March*

Part One

One

Thirteen eighty-six B.C. They had come up the river, that fifty years ago, he, Royal Father Ay, and the young prince. For the other two these journeys had become almost customary. He had not himself wanted to come, but Tiiy had forced him to. She wanted to know what the purpose of these travels was.

He knew now what the purpose of these travels was. And he did not like it.

Horemheb was twenty-four, the son of petty nomarchs from Alabastronpolis. He had his way to make at court, and his only means were personal. So far they had served him well.

He was short but not stocky. His hips were correctly narrow, his shoulders admirably wide. His chest was thick and square, with nipples like bronze wine stoppers, and his face luminous, though it would have been hard to say why. His complexion was brown, his voice low-pitched and deceptive. One had the feeling that he hadn't caught up with himself yet, though clearly he was a coming man. This is not to say he was an opportunist. On the contrary, he had the wisdom of those who can afford to wait, and therefore people trusted him.

He was the perfect person to teach the prince how to hunt. Unfortunately the prince absolutely refused to hunt, and since the family had been athletic for three generations, this made everyone uneasy.

Horemheb was himself uneasy. For one thing, he did not know for certain where they were. They were anchored five days above Thebes, which, since the

current was slack, meant that they had travelled a considerable distance. The cliffs closed in around the Nile
here, and were creased and bulged like the muscles of
an over-developed wrestler. As the sun set they turned
iodine in the folds, exactly as would the muscles of
someone left in the sun too long. There was almost no
shore. On what shore there was rambled the immense,
quivering ruins of an abandoned temple. It was their
third temple in two days, and thus Horemheb's
annoyance.

He looked around him, for he was by no means indifferent to the scenery. It was, after all, his country.
Where the prince might find it significant, he found it
real. For immanence is not the sole prerogative of
mystic young hysterics. A sober man may feel it just as
deeply after the noon meal, perhaps more deeply, since
he prefers not to mention it, and so cannot get rid of it.

But it was not after the noon meal. It was evening,
except that in Egypt there is no evening. The night
there falls as predacious as a hawk. The cliffs seemed to
edge a little nearer. A ripple ran over them, as they
began to exhale the heat of the day. Then it was night,
and the stars did not come out properly.

There was a sudden gust of cold wind across the
water. Horemheb felt that something was definitely
wrong, and the scream of a jackal in the distance did
nothing to help. It was careless of the prince to move
about this disturbed country without guards.

Nor was Ay any protection. A snake might lurk out
there, or a bandit. Ay would not notice anything so
simple as a snake. Ay was a man in whom a carefully
calculated indifference had become a way of life. A
great deal might go on behind those eyes, but he himself did nothing. He broke his astute silences only as
another man would crack a crab, in order to get at the
succulence they contained. His manner was avuncular.
He let other people take the trouble and then dropped

in unexpectedly to reap the benefits, with sweetmeats and toys. This might make him lovable, but it was wrong of the prince to trust him. Horemheb did not trust him at all.

In other words, something had to be done. Horemheb stood up, ran across the plank to the shore, and paused uncertainly before the bulk of the temple. It was unnatural for the night to be so dark and clamorous, and he could not quite get his bearings.

The temple was too massive to be recent, and too strongly built to support weeds. Only sand oozed up between the immense flags of the flooring. Nor was it wise to come to such places. One needed priests between oneself and the gods. Otherwise a temple was not safe. Cautiously Horemheb moved through the pylon into the outer court.

He thought he heard voices, but could not place them. Then, abruptly, the moon came out, bobbling along the vague rim of the cliffs, with each seeming spring bounding a little higher through the heat haze, until it settled into its customary place. It was not, however, its customary colour, but the angry orange of a very old egg.

Despite this its pale blue light was the same, and streamed across the court through an inner pylon to a confused heap of ruins beyond. As Horemheb walked down its path, the voices became louder.

On the other side of the second pylon most of the building had fallen in, so that what should have been the sanctuary was instead a cleared space in the rubble, open to the sky. Tall swaddled statues loomed around him up into the night, the images of long-dead gods and kings, great stone mummies of what had never been men. Pillars supported nothing, but the paint was still distinct on the carved walls. One or two blocks of stone had fallen to the pavement. On one of these the prince was sitting. He was a white blur. Ay stood in

19

front of him, and apparently the prince had been asking questions, for Ay's voice was full of the soft, furry irony with which he always answered questions. Horemheb stopped to listen.

"No," Ay was saying. "It is older than that. One of your predecessors of the 12th Dynasty, long after this temple was built, Amen-em-het, after his murder, warned his son: 'Hold thyself apart from those subordinate to thee, lest that should happen to whose terrors no attention has been given. Approach them not in thy loneliness. Fill not thy heart with a brother, nor know a friend. When thou sleepest, guard thy heart thyself, because no man has adherents on the day of distress.' "

"Yes, that is very true," said the prince. His voice was silvery and shrill. It echoed against those forgotten statues like a sistrum. "But I am descended from Ra, not from Amon. We have found out that much. It says so on these walls. Therefore darkness cannot touch me."

Ay smiled, and the moonlight made that smile less reassuring than perhaps it was meant to be. "The moon is not the sun, but in a moment you will see," he said.

Horemheb decided to join them. Among other things he did not like to be alone. "See what?" he demanded, and his own deeper voice echoed longer among these stones. "You should not linger here after dark. It is not safe." He stood arms akimbo, feeling very solid above the slim weak body of the prince.

The prince, if he had been startled, did not show it. He had courage of a sort. He peered into the shadows at Horemheb's rounded calves and saw who it was. "Sit down," he said, "and be still."

That claw of authority slipped out so seldom, that it seemed all the more sharp when it did. Ay gave Horemheb a quick look of amused mockery and gravely sat down. So did Horemheb. The moon appeared over the edge of the ruins, about a third of the way up the sky.

Horemheb felt an unpleasant prickling of the scalp, under his wig. Ay wore no wig. He sat there bald, expectant, and calm.

"When will it begin?" asked the prince at last.

"Now," said Ay.

They looked upward.

The croaking of the frogs along the river, as though old pilings had voices, sounded louder. It was because all the other restless night noises had stopped. The breeze, that had blown cold, abruptly blew warm and from another direction. Horemheb caught a glimpse of the prince out of the corner of his eye and felt uncomfortable. At twenty-three the prince had the body of an unattractive girl, the voice of a eunuch, and a face of the wrong kind of beauty. Yet there was that soft, scented, compelling, and somehow pathetic charm. One said, oh well, he will outgrow it. But one knew better. He was horribly intelligent. He knew things no prince should know, and almost nothing that a prince should. One thought he was easy to manage. And then suddenly one was up against something as brittle, but as smooth and hard, as glass. Seeing those overfull lips, pointed moistly towards the sky, Horemheb was frightened and glanced at Ay.

But Ay merely looked gently amused and raised a slim, wiry finger towards the moon.

Certainly something was happening to it. It looked tarnished, and now a shadow moved majestically across it. There was no way to stop that shadow. It had an inevitable pour.

"It is symbolic." Did the prince say that, or Ay? Horemheb was not sure. He watched. He was a military man, not a religious, but military men have their own ghosts, and stand as stiff-legged as any dog at the presence of what cannot be seen by others. It is one reason for their excellent discipline. The worse the nightmare, the firmer the will.

The prince sat there like a well-behaved guest at a particularly good funeral, well-fed, but waiting for his dinner. The powers of darkness were eating the light. But they would be forced to disgorge it, so one could watch the spectacle, except that, for a moment, despite oneself, one did not believe that the powers of darkness would disgorge it, even though one knew this had happened before. The orange rim grew narrower. The eclipse was complete. For that instant the world was motionless. It might live or die, and who could say which? The dreadful thing was not that the moon was dead and gave no light, but that though it gave no light and was dead, one could still see it, like the ghost of a world or of a city from which everyone had vanished instantaneously, so instantaneously that their voices still rang in your ears.

"It is only that a shadow comes between the sun and the moon, our shadow," said Ay. "But the sun will push us away."

If the prince was listening, he was not listening to Ay. In the utter darkness of the temple even his white linen had become invisible. He turned to Horemheb, and just as the dead grey circle of the moon began to yellow again at the edges, he spoke. Though the temple air was motionless, along the desert above the cliffs a wind was roaring. "Listen," he said. "Do you hear it?"

"Hear what?"

"The voice of silence."

As a matter of fact Horemheb did hear something. It made his skin prickle. He was aware of something out there, something urgent that was almost audible, but not quite. It made him angry, because he was frightened, and it also made him impatient with silly hysterics, princes or not. "It is only the desert," he said.

"Then you cannot hear it," said the prince. He hesitated, and Horemheb heard Ay stir in his clothes. "I can." He sounded sincere. He could always sound sincere when he wanted to. As a matter of fact, he had heard nothing at all. He was metaphysically deaf. He had turned to these religious matters only out of boredom, since if we have everything in this world, then we must take our unsatisfied longings off to the next. Yet this new game was the only plaything that had ever held his attention for so long.

He would probably have been furious, had Horemheb said he had heard it, but instead he gave his cryptic little smile.

Ay coughed.

The world was beginning to move again. The shadow was sliding away, slowly, inexorably retreating, as the light fought it back.

'Yes, it will be like that,' said the prince, and this time he was not playing. But the others did not hear him, for the animal world had recovered its wits. It grew restive. The jackals began to shriek. Full moonlight turned the tired stone of the temple into silver plate. After so much darkness, the light was almost embarrassing, and Horemheb felt ashamed of himself. It was after all only a ruined temple and nothing more. These fears were foolish. He led the way back to the boat, and they retired.

Dawn woke him early. He was the first one to rise. The sky was pale green, the cliffs the colour of dead rose petals. Seen by daylight, the temple was much smaller, rather pathetic, and certainly nothing to inspire awe. An ibis stalked gravely through the water. No doubt these trips were only a search for novelty. There was an interest in the past these days, for people in their desperate search for that commodity are doomed from the start by their accompanying hostility towards anything new. Even Pharaoh, now he could no longer hunt, took a mild interest in the antique. The prince's interest was of that sort, and nothing more.

23

Amidships someone had lit a cook-fire. Horemheb stood up and stretched. His body badly needed exercise. Perhaps today, while Ay and the prince grubbed about some temple precinct, he could go into the rushes with a bow and arrow and a cat and flush game. This high up, the Nile was well stocked with game.

But that was not to be. The curtains of the royal compartment parted and Ay appeared, stepping fastidiously over the still sleeping attendants, rather like that ibis through the reeds. He made his way towards Horemheb. They were to turn back for Thebes, he said. He said nothing about the scene the night before. Horemheb did.

Ay shrugged. "It is nothing to be taken seriously. He is only a boy."

"He is twenty-three."

"Age has nothing to do with the matter, and besides, among princes trusted advisors are an excellent substitute for intelligence," said Ay, and thus betrayed his only ambition, before he had the time to turn away.

Horemheb gave the orders. By the time the prince was up, they were already in midstream, with the current taking over from the oars and sail. The temple and its peristaltic gorge vanished behind them, and Horemheb could not say he was sorry.

The voyage back would be faster. They might even be able to stop from time to time, to hunt. But they did not stop to hunt. As though he had been to consult an oracle about pressing affairs and had received a favourable answer, the prince was anxious to get home.

Nor was he friendly or talkative, as people with Horemheb usually were.

Horemheb was puzzled by that. The prince did not make friends. They were the same age, and had been flung together for years. Yet the prince was evasive. The prince kept very much to himself. It was almost as though he felt a slight contempt for what previously he had admired, such as the skill with which Horemheb could shoot a duck, as though he had at last found some way to prove himself superior that now made Horemheb the child, not him.

It was worse than infuriating. It was mysterious.

On the morning they were to reach Thebes he saw Ay, as usual clean-shaven, fastidious, and very far away, coming to speak to him again. His thin loincloth flapped at his waist, and it had to be admitted that for a man of sixty, Ay had a tight, wiry body fit to endure anything. He was the opposite of soft, and therefore Horemheb treated him with respect. Together they scanned the shore.

"What will you say to the Queen?" asked Ay. "About the prince, I mean."

"That Royal Father Ay has interested him in archaeology. I suppose it is better for him to be interested in something."

Ay smiled wryly. "So I thought. Unfortunately it hasn't turned out quite that way. That was a temple to Ra, where we stopped. The prince has discovered he is descended from Ra. The priests of Amon are not apt to like it. Of course he is quite right, Ra is the older god, but since Amon is the stronger, we can only hope he does not insist." He hesitated. "In other words, he has taken to theology. A rather wilful, self-centred theology, but still, theology. It could be an advantage."

Horemheb stared at him. And then he saw that, of course, it could be. The army and the priests of Thebes were always in competition with each other, and in that game Pharaoh was the chief taw.

"It could also be dangerous," he said.

"Oh, I don't think so. He is only playing, you know. It is only a game to him. But it is a game one might conceivably win." And again Ay gave Horemheb a look of tacit intelligence.

25

Abruptly the current carried them round a bend and Thebes lay before them, the whole vast complex of buildings on either side of the river, with Karnak and Luxor too, the great, cancerous, palpitating mass of the Amon temples, the enormous city of the dead, backing up to the cliffs, all gleaming, shining, rich, and powerful, almost hiding the sprawling white mass of the palace, in an endless hive of sacerdotal power. And there, beyond, rising out of the plain, backed by the huge bulk of their silver and lapis-lazuli temple, stood the colossi of Memnon, the twin statues of Amenophis III and his wife Tiiy, gazing blandly at nothing, from a great height.

"I do not like it either," said Ay. It was an innuendo, but not a harmless one. Ay was for once in earnest. "And the boy is only a boy. Let him have his head. He should not be difficult to get under control. One has only to like him a little."

He smiled again and went to put on clothes more suitable to an entry into the city. For already the air was full of the restless clamour of the crowds. They would pull up to the jetty very soon.

Horemheb was surprised. It was unlike Ay ever to make a definite statement about anything, much less than to hint at a possible conspiracy. But he had not the time to think about it. They were landing and there was much to do.

He had thought they would go straight to the palace, but instead they docked on the eastern shore, for the prince wished to make an oblation.

It took some time to assemble the necessary retinue. The priest would have to be warned they were coming and the streets, in so far as that was possible, cleared.

A trip through the city was never a pleasant experience. If the necropolis workers were not rioting on the western shore, then the temple workers were rioting on the eastern. A vast horde of office seekers, sycophants, unemployed workers, hangers-on at half a dozen separate courts, 40,000 useless priests, and the inmates of the theological and military colleges made disorder permanent. There was always mischief there, and if there was none, the army invented it, out of sheer boredom with having nothing else to do. For an army needs something to fight. It should not stay cooped up in the capital, while the Empire slips away.

Life! Prosperity! Health! shouted the crowd, sometimes in irony, or sometimes out of goodwill. But it would stone you one minute and rob you the next, all the same, and then where would your life, prosperity, and health be?

Nor did it help matters that out of all character the prince was a reckless charioteer who always took the reins himself. He had that passion for speed at any cost which is the delight of the impotent, and since he could always pay the cost, the passion never went unassuaged. He did not even know how to sit a horse, but he did know how to drive one. Even as a child, his wet hand had closed round his first whip with the intent fury of someone whose physical passion has at last found the one outlet its body makes possible. And the crowds loved it, of course. Crowds always love to see someone else do something dangerous. He would always be loved by the crowds. It was another aspect of his character that Tiiy and Ay had been so foolish as to overlook.

They at last drew up before a temple, but not the Amon temple, to Horemheb's surprise. Years ago Amenophis III had built within the Amon compound a small temple to his own private ecclesiastical hobby, the royal household god, Aton. It was a tiny white building dwarfed by the huge stone walls of the Amon temple which surrounded it, and was usually seedy and run down, for Pharaoh had forgotten about it years ago, as the priests of Amon had known he would. They could afford to humour him in these small things, since he humoured them in all important ones.

Now it had apparently been furbished up. At any rate its whitewash was new. The prince disappeared inside. Ay and Horemheb, with some reluctance, followed, chiefly to avoid the crowd. Neither one of them went to any temple unless he had to.

As a temple it was not much. Some indifferent reliefs ran along the walls of the inner court. The sanctuary was small and not in the least concealed from public view, as it would have been elsewhere. The prince had already vanished within it. Horemheb and Ay waited in the shadow of the surrounding colonnade.

"By whose orders was this done?" asked Horemheb, looking at the fresh colouring.

"The prince, I suppose." Ay frowned. "I had not known it had been done."

It was not comforting to see Ay disturbed. Ay was never disturbed.

At last the prince reappeared, talking to the priest of the temple, a fat, unctious fool called Meryra. He had a list and a roll and a squeaky voice, and his skin was the colour of lard. They could not hear what he was saying, but the prince was smiling back and answering eagerly.

Ay shifted from one foot to the other. "I do not like that man," he said.

Neither did Horemheb, but the visit was soon over, and none of his concern.

Half an hour later and they were crossing the river, towards the palace on the western side. He looked towards it eagerly. Ay and the prince were too much for him, but Pharaoh and the Queen he understood. Whatever happened, he always knew he would be welcome there.

The palace, at some distance back from the shore, was only in its second generation. Tutmose IV had invented it. Now Amenophis III had extended it until it encroached upon the necropolis. It was built of wood and whitewashed brick, and though it still had the power to dazzle, already, nowadays, large areas of it were walled up and boarded off. It was possible to come across rooms in which no one had sat for years, and courtyards where the water plants had grown top-heavy in the ponds and reached the level of the roofs above. A colony of half-starved greyhounds lived, and nobody knew what they ate, in an abandoned garden of persea trees, even though, south of the deserted harem, the plane trees were clipped as tidily as ever along the borders of the private lake.

Yet in that vast rambling palace the courtiers still circled in and out as aimlessly as flies, though, like the motions of flies in a summer room, their movements betrayed a certain mathematical periodicity. These seemingly irrational motions could be plotted against the lust for sugar and the fear of being hit, the two constants which controlled, however remotely, and it was never too remotely, their actions. It was beautiful to watch, in a way, as beautiful as any other mathematical certainty, for even flies are controlled by necessity.

Horemheb went at once in search of the Queen.

Tiiy, they said, was on the Royal Lake. He might go to her, for who, so long as she preferred him, would gainsay Horemheb, since it was the Queen, not Pharaoh, who ruled here. Only his attendants saw Pharaoh, who was a legend in his lifetime, and therefore kept properly remote.

Pharaoh had had the lake dug years ago. It was a mile and a half long and two-thirds of a mile wide, surrounded by a wall, its shores trimmed with plane trees, pavilions, flowers, water plants, lotuses, reeds, water-stairs, and sometimes an audience. Nowhere was it more than five feet deep, in order to prevent drowning, should anyone fall into it drunk. When he was younger,

Pharaoh had even used it for hunting, shooting on one occasion three out of the four pink baby hippopotami provided. But that was long ago.

He stood on the shore, by a flight of water-stairs, and waved. Someone must have told the Queen, for her barge was already skimming across the water towards him. It was perhaps a quarter of a mile away. Of ebony and gold, it gleamed agreeably on the water. Horemheb removed his sandals and his wig, went down the water-stairs, slipped smoothly into the water, let it hold him voluptuously for a moment, and then stroked towards the boat. The water inshore was flaccid and warm, but farther out it was cooler and fresher. The foam of his movements caught at his high, muscled shoulders and rilled there as though around rocks, before subsiding out behind him.

As he was beginning to tire, he came abreast of the boat and the boat abreast of him. He stood up in the water, which was shallower here and lapped at his nipples, and blinked in the sun. The boat was the *Gleams of Aton*, the barge Pharaoh had built for the Queen when the lake was first flooded.

Tiiy was sitting in a chair, watching him and laughing. 'Get him aboard,' she called, clapping her hands. Her voice was not beautiful. If anything it was a little harsh. But it was full of warmth and amusement, and was always at least politely lively. It was her voice, more than anything else, that he missed when he was away, for now they had been friends so long, who had once only been lovers.

Two of her attendants hauled him aboard. He could feel the resilient hardness of their breasts, as their dresses rubbed against him. They also pinched the skin under his armpits as they hauled. He stood on the deck and shook himself like a dog, innocently proud of the way his wet body must look, but much more concerned with Tiiy.

She was not a beautiful woman, any more than she had a beautiful voice, but she managed to give the impression of beauty. It was difficult to believe she was over forty, for she was too much herself to be dependent upon the uncertainties of time. She had looked thirty since she was fifteen, and ten years from now, she might at last look her age. But not now.

Sometimes, it was true, at dusk, she might become uneasy. Then she would have a dim memory of somebody she had once been, as though she were gazing down at herself through sixty feet of water. The object moved. It was hard to tell whether it was alive or dead. But it was unmistakeably one's self. Then, just as she was trying to catch a closer glimpse of that drowned self, something would divert her attention, and she would take up the performance once again. For after all, was not the performance life? The only way we can survive is to become imitations of ourselves, otherwise the wear and tear of experience touches us, and we change and become dull. And so she made a practice of being always cheerful, for the phoenix kindles its own fire. With immortality at stake, it is not so foolish as to depend upon the rest of the world for fuel.

For the rest she was small-boned, tight-skinned, a little lustful, a little not, a little vengeful, absolutely impossible to pin down, enormously clever, and at the moment, obviously and sincerely glad to see him, as he had known she would be, and as he was to see her.

The boat put back into the middle of the lake. She began eagerly to question him, and he began to answer with Ay.

"Oh, Ay. If the rest of the world did nothing, he would do very well, for he does nothing better than the rest of us. But since we all do something, he will never be anybody to be afraid of. What are these trips about?"

He told her what the trips were about, and also of what Ay had said about them.

She took that more seriously. "He might be right."
She was not laughing now. She was thinking. It put
her in no mood for love-making. She was abstemious.
She ate only when she was hungry, and it was the same
with her affections. That was an attitude to life which,
since he had learned it from her, he thoroughly
approved of. As a result he had lasted five years, where
someone else would only have lasted a week. He was
very fond of her.

"We had better go to see Pharaoh," she said. "I
wonder how Ay manages to know everything? But
since he does, one may just as well relax." She gave the
order and the boat put about.

It was really a whimsical existence they lived on that
lake, if it had not also been a little sad. It was no secret
that Pharaoh, who had once romped up and down
Egypt, was now an invalid. And so the lake was now
his Egypt. When he was well, he rowed about, while
Tiiy ran the government, or a hunt was staged for him,
though seldom these days, since now he preferred to
watch acrobats or tumblers instead. When he was not
well he spent most of his time in a pavilion attached to
the palace, with steps to the water, from which he
could both watch and get the best sun. It was towards
this pavilion that the boat now turned.

"About Ay," said Tiiy unexpectedly. "He is the
wisest of all of us. If you ever need someone to trust,
trust him."

Horemheb did not know what to make of that. But
apparently he was not expected to make anything of it.
They had reached the pavilion.

Though Pharaoh was ill, he still kept up the splendour of a healthy, venal man, and ran from one extreme
of pleasure to another, in search of what diversion he
could get. If anything he was now more interested in
the refinements of such pursuits than he had been when
able to pursue them. For now, since he could only

watch, it was more difficult for him to lose interest through sheer exhaustion. And after all, he was Pharaoh. If someone reported a curious position he had never seen or practised, he could have it demonstrated when he wished. Indeed, it had been necessary to invent a few, in order to keep up with his curiosity, and if they did not work, they looked as though they did, and that, now, was the main thing.

Boys, girls, men, women, nubians, hunchbacks, dwarfs suffering from gigantism and giants suffering from the opposite complaint, in all their various combinations and variations, animals, talking birds, snakes accomplished at divination, and an Indian mystic with an extremely supple spine, had all been paraded before him, and to tell the truth, had bored him extremely. But once he had started, he could not stop. A certain prurient interest was expected of him. He would much have preferred to talk to Ay or Tiiy or sometimes Horemheb. He was very fond of Horemheb, where another man would only have been jealous, and this for reasons of his own.

It is possible to be a narcissist without being in the least vain. In Horemheb he saw himself when young. That was why he had made the boy his favourite. And now that the boy was a man, and Tiiy's lover, he saw the flattery envolved, and was rather touched, that at last she should settle down into some sort of permanent liaison with someone so exactly like himself. As for himself, had he been well enough or had he had the inclination to take any regular mistress, he supposed, she would have resembled Tiiy, if anyone could have resembled Tiiy. For they were a couple. They always had been. They could not have existed without each other, really.

Besides, he liked Horemheb, and was only sorry the man was not his son, instead of the sickly brood he had. Nor had he ever doubted Tiiy's loyalty or affection to himself. In a life full of uncertainty, that much at least was sure; and as for the rest, let her amuse herself how she would. In addition to which it was a delicious joke on the courtiers, who instead of battening on the intrigues they had hoped to promote, strengthened the very situation they had sought to divide.

Thus Amenophis III, Pharaoh of Egypt, who was more astute than one might think, if sometimes capricious, while he watched the tumblers and the acrobats.

But Horemheb, who had not seen him for some time, and who could remember shooting lions with him, up on the desert, only five years ago, was shocked by his appearance. No one knew precisely what was wrong with him, unless he were falling apart from within. He had for one thing grown fat and flabby, for another, feeble and nervous. Pain had drained him rapidly. He suffered from abscessed gums, for which there was no cure. His mouth stank, and he washed it constantly with an infusion of cinnamon and clove, which he spat out into an endless succession of white alabaster cups. These endless cups were disgusting even to him. He tried to ignore them, but all the same, they were there.

Music these days was provided for him only by blind harpers. He found it convenient that they could not see. A blind drummer had been harder to get, and in desperation the household steward had been forced to create one. No doubt the man had screamed, but Amenophis was cruel only at second hand. He knew nothing of such things. The drummer sat huddled wretched, without that strange gentle arrogance of the habitually blind, but rather the inhabitant of an unfamiliar country, tapping away an accompaniment to the dancers. These were not Egyptians, but black creatures from somewhere south of Nubia, handsomely built, sweaty men, who spoke only gibberish, and took tremendous, acrobatic leaps while white plumes waved wildly on their kinky heads.

34

Horemheb and Amenophis watched. The Queen had slipped away. Then, when the dancers had been taken off, the two men were at last alone.

"Tell me about the prince," said Amenophis, and when Horemheb had done, merely smiled. It was disturbing. Resignation did not suit that ardent face.

"I am making you Commander-in-Chief of the Armies," he said.

Horemheb was shocked. To direct armies was something he had always expected to do, and virtually did already. But to hold that title was another matter. The title belonged to Pharaoh and to Pharaoh alone.

Amenophis made a wry face. "Yes," he said. "I know. But you can hold the armies. I may die. It is time to make the prince co-regent. And he could never hold them."

It was true, so there was nothing to say about it. Amenophis closed his eyes. He was tired, Horemheb took his departure and went to report to the Queen.

She could talk to him only for a minute. But she could see how serious his face was.

"So he has told you," she said.

Horemheb was concerned with how the prince would take the news, for princes are jealous of their prerogatives.

He need not have worried. The prince turned out to have no interest in the army. He was at the moment interested only in religion. He had not enough political knowledge to be afraid of the power of armies, and for the rest, he was glad to have the burden off his own shoulders. He merely gave an indifferent smile and hurried off to his temple.

When told how he had taken the news, Tiiy shrugged. For, of course, they saw no danger in his little hobby. He was not fit to rule, and therefore the more seriously he took his hobbies the better. Tiiy and Horemheb and Ay could rule for him. There was no problem there.

To them religion was no more than a public duty and a death-bed necessity. If the prince had gone to the Amon priests, now that would have been a different matter. The Amon priests had quite enough power already. But an interest in Aton worship was harmless. It was no more than the family cult, something they had brought with them when they became a dynasty, which Amenophis had revived out of boredom and ancestral piety. It would soon pass. And meanwhile, if the prince amused himself in these ways, they would be able to transfer the machinery of government from one generation to the next without his inference. Later, they could perhaps educate him to his role and his responsibilities.

They overlooked two things. First of all, Amenophis was not going to die just yet. And second, how could they know that the prince was morbidly afraid of the dark and an hysteric into the bargain. They could not be blamed. It had never occurred to them to ask what he was afraid of, since a prince was supposed to be fearless, and they had never considered him as a person at all, except in so far as he constituted an embarrassment. And then, a level-headed lot, they simply did not know what an hysteric was. In all that city perhaps only two people knew, and unfortunately one of these was Meryra, the Aton priest, and the other Nefertiti, Pharaoh's daughter, to whom Meryra owed his preferment, and whom the prince would have to marry, since though Pharaoh ruled Egypt, it was through his sister that his right to rule descended.

Meanwhile, in that still palace, when once Pharaoh was sleeping, Horemheb and Tiiy went off to bed, and what they did there was their own affair. Or so they thought, until, in enjoying themselves, they did not bother to think at all.

Others, however, do not have the ability so completely to forget themselves in experience. Others can never forget themselves at all, and so their pleasures are a little sly and never, on any occasion, altogether pleasant, which, in turn, leaves them time to think. And among these was Nefertiti, who knew perfectly well what her mother and Horemheb did together, who often spied on them, and who liked neither of them.

Her reasons were simple. She was both vain and neglected, and also afraid, with reason, of her mother. Indeed, were you not so strong as she was, Tiiy could be overwhelming, being a woman who was charming only among equals, among whom she did not count the brood she had hatched.

But though she was not strong, Nefertiti was supple. She knew perfectly well she would one day be Queen, and to this end she had spent considerable time in the study of that enigma, her brother. Nor could she be called impotent, for in Meryra she knew, as soon as she had met him, that she had found her proper instrument.

Nefertiti was fifteen. Her beauty would have been remarkable, had there been anybody to see it, but the royal children were not encouraged to show themselves, and were seen mostly by each other, and the prince had no eye for female beauty. Nefertiti had only her mirror, and now Meryra, to show her what she might do, given the opportunity.

People are foolish about beauty. Few of them realize how dangerous it can be. For beautiful people know they are works of art, and are so busy being the custodians of themselves that they have neither the time nor the inclination for anything else. And, like works of art, they are only an appearance. Underneath that sparkling surface the actual material from which it derives its support, the heart and soul and blood and bone, is inert.

But much rarer even than the beautiful, are those of

the beautiful whose vanity in no measure interferes with their intelligence, but is on the contrary a useful means of concealing it. And these people are truly hazardous, for they have lovely, understanding eyes, they can simulate anything, and they have no contact with the human race at all. They sip emotions as a connoisseur would sip a fine wine, only a little, but that greedily; and move unimpeded and undetected through the world, secure that only someone exactly like them will ever find them out. They can never be defeated, and short of murder they can never be stopped, and it takes them a long, long time to run down.

Indeed, they are so different from the rest of us, and so secure, that they would not impinge on our lives at all, were it not for one thing, which is, that though they are impervious even to their own vanity, none the less, they are vain, and vanity, alas, is not impervious to us.

Thus Nefertiti, an observant and calculating woman of fifteen, with a peculiarly memorable smile and an enormous knowledge of her brother based on the entirely false assumption that he was much like herself, but weaker and easier to control.

Surely no dynasty ever built itself a better ruin. But then the dynasty had no say in the matter. It had bred true to its vices. These were its heirs. And though Amenophis had done his best, he had forgotten that loyalty is not always a virtue, and Horemheb was loyal.

Two

It so happened that astute as he was, Ay had developed an affection for the prince. It was not surprising. One must be sentimental about something, and the more hard-headed and judicious one is, the more unlikely the thing on which one's sentiments will light. For, of course, in those days Ay did not exactly regard the prince as a person. Nor was he one. He had been a person when he was a child, which no one had bothered to notice, and he might be one later on, when life was through with him, but at the moment he was a personage of some importance, and that is not the same as being a person at all.

However of this indulgent attitude Ay showed nothing, for he had early learned that it was wiser to keep one's affection for others to one's self, since they are not apt to understand it, nor is there any reason why they should.

It was Ay's duty to inform the prince of those ceremonies which a personage of importance would be expected to endure during the next few weeks, for a personage of importance is not the same as a nonentity. He cannot be expected to find things out for himself.

Amenophis, needless to say, had not bothered to see his son, for he found him too distressing, and neither, for that matter, had the prince shown the least interest in seeing his father. They would meet on the day of the coronation, three months from now, but in the meantime the great deal that had to be done would be done by Ay.

The apartments set aside for the prince, which Ay had never seen before, were at the north end of the palace. He found what he saw surprising but on the whole informative.

He had always assumed, since that was what the court thought of him, that the prince was a weakling and a booby. Now he saw that this was not so. It was merely that the prince was physically weak, had a strong mother, no interest in sports, and the wrong kind of intelligence. He clearly had a stubborn, feral mind. To talk to him was to talk to some decadent animal, a lemur say, with its great liquid giddy eyes. The impression was bewildering and somehow frightening.

But then the full mouth under those eyes would twitch shyly at the corners, not without irony, and Ay would feel that the world had righted itself again. There was nothing wrong with the prince. It was only that he was ignorant of the right things and entirely too knowledgeable about the wrong ones.

For instance: "If I am Pharaoh, why then must I take directions from the High Priest?"

A difficult question to answer, requiring more knowledge of history than it would be wise to display before the vanity of a ruling prince, and a devout one at that.

Or was he devout? At times it was hard to be sure. For example: "Then if this idol is only a device for delivering the opinions of the High Priest, why is not Amon also a device for maintaining their power?"

They were talking about that scene, at the end of the coronation, when Pharaoh must enter the Holy of Holies and commune with the god alone. They had been talking about it, to be precise, for the past five days.

Which was how Ay discovered that the prince was afraid of the dark, though he did not say so, and afraid too of death, almost as though the fear of death were a form of claustrophobia. He was too young to be afraid of death. There would be plenty of time for that later, when he was old enough, should he live so long. For really he was very frail. His toughness was not of a physical sort.

All of which made him more human, somehow; and looking around his apartments, Ay could see the reason for such fears. On this neglected shambles the prince had somehow imposed a curiously fastidious order, that had about it something rather sad. For example, when Ay shifted a curved wood stool from its aligned place, the prince would put it back again; which in turn led Ay to notice that the furniture was all arranged just so, into a pattern. The Royal Nurse, Ay's second wife, had told him, when he asked her about the prince, that even as a child he had not been able to sleep without a night-light, or until the furniture had been arranged just so.

Which, Ay supposed, was because there had been no one to comfort him. Now there would be many to do so, and Ay saw no reason why he should not be the first. Therefore, if the prince chose to prattle of the Aton and the descent of kings, then Ay would prattle of them too, though that did not mean that the formalities of the coronation could be ignored. Instead, they the more had to be insisted upon.

"And it is dark in there?"

"I have never been there. It cannot be pitch dark, no."

"And the image touches me?"

"Yes, I believe so."

"And then what happens?" asked the prince. His face was taut. Unfortunately Ay did not know what happened then. But each day, once the prince was co-regent, he would have to go to the temple and anoint the god in that dark room. Not literally each day, of course, but whenever the god had a message to deliver.

"My father does not do that." The voice was curt and sharp.

"Your father is ill."

"None the less, the priests come to him, not he to them."

"Even he had to go to them once," said Ay, anxious to get on to other matters. When he left, the prince was playing blind-man's-buff with his younger brother Smenkara.

Really, that was ridiculous. It touched Ay to see how lonely the boy was in his quarters, to be reduced to playing with a child.

The prince saw the matter differently. As far as he was concerned, he was about to become a god, and the prospect pleased him. His father was a god, he was going to be a god, and his children, if any, would be gods. On the whole he felt that that made life much simpler, restored his own, at any rate, to a proper perspective.

For it is not so difficult to be a god. All one needs is a mother, no father (none of the saviour gods ever have a demonstrable father, no matter what the Amon priests might say. He was the child of the sun god, Ra, not of Amenophis III), and the recommendation of at least one politically astute high priest. Of course certain conditions have to be met. A god goes away. He is either admired and not loved, or loved and not admired, but then few men manage to be both. A god is never what his worshippers worship, which, if he be both god and worshipper, is apt to make him difficult to deal with. Also, there comes a time when he finds it all rather ridiculous, for whether he be mortal or immortal, still, he must die.

So ultimately a god fails, for a god is the person we see in the mirror who never sees us. In other words, it is not so pleasant to be a god. They would deserve our sympathy, had we any to give them. No, it is not difficult to be a god. But it is hard to be worshipped. It is even harder to be loved. That destroys us all.

We want to stand naked in the rain. The patter is reassuring. It is like silver finger-tips in the middle of the night. We want to say: I am. But those who need us will not let us be.

And so we say: farewell. I am never now. I was.

And this, alas, is true of all of us.

But then, again, the prince did not see it that way. For despite his interest in the family cult, he had as yet no inkling of the particular god he was destined to become. Godhead, in the sense he meant it, was only the old dynastic game the family played so well, which was only to be taken seriously in public. So he merely saw the amusing side, and tried not to think of the dark.

For to someone with a love of beautiful things, and a sense of self-importance that had been starved for years, the amusing side was certainly very amusing.

First, he could send for people and they actually came.

He could commission works of art, and it is always pleasant to have one's portrait done. His face had suddenly become extremely important. The Queen supplied her personal sculptor, a man called Bek, who modelled his face in plaster. The sessions were stormy.

Bek turned out the standard portrait of a pharaoh, heavy-faced, fine-planed, slightly amused, and utterly impersonal. Though careful not to touch the now royal person, he took exact measurements. That was another of the amusements. As a child, he had been at the mercy of anybody's fingers. Now he was to become Pharaoh, nobody dared to touch him, and that was restful, for he hated to be touched.

"No. No," he said. "Not like that. More truth, more ma'at."

Bek looked hurt. He was a good sculptor and he had

43

been turning out that face now for twenty years. Nobody had ever complained before. He submitted that pharaohs were supposed to look like that.

"I am I. Not my father. People should worship me," shouted the prince, seized the modelling stand, and went to work. What he achieved was lop-sided and shapeless, but it undoubtedly looked different. Bek took the hint.

Thus entered into the history of the period a new meaning for that treacherous word, truth. It was an illustrious word. It meant justice, proportion, harmony, symmetry. It was a way of looking at the world with which no one had ever quarrelled. Now for the first time it acquired in addition its modern meaning: truth is the way I look at things: truth looks like me.

Above all, truth was asymmetrical and always bathed in light. This meant that Bek had to alter his modelling, so that his faces should never reveal deep shadows. And this he did, for he had a job to keep.

When Tiiy saw these new portraits she made no comment. She was not an aesthetician, and art as a branch of propaganda deals only in expensive images of oneself for other people to look at. Out of good taste one never looks oneself. She had a flair for spotting good cabinet work, and that was that.

She had other concerns. It was time to arrange the prince's marriage. And in view of his previous marriage, it might be necessary to explain to him the exact process by which it was possible to produce heirs.

When she appeared with the princess Nefertiti, the prince was in the midst of what could only be called a wardrobe conference. This startled her. But then it was only to be expected, so she smiled indulgently. Her smile had improved in the last few days, and was now a perfect expression of that withering tact by means of which she intended to go on running the government.

The princess Nefertiti had seen her brother seldom,

44

and his apartments never. Boyish, slim, with a narrow pelvis, which might or might not make childbearing difficult, she looked around her, and was very glad her mother was there. For now, without saying anything, or even altering her expression, she could indicate to the prince that they were both in league against their mother, and so, however tentatively, manage to establish an initial bond with him, as a spider casts out one thread, from which to depend the net that is already latent in its body.

For Nefertiti did not underestimate her body. To be childlike, and yet maternal, would, she thought, do best.

Tiiy did not like her daughter, either. She thought the two of them well matched, which they were, much more than she could have imagined possible.

For as well as being shy, saw Nefertiti, the prince was a little absurd. Not only was he physically embryonic, but his body seemed to have been made by somebody with no creative imagination and a shortage of raw material. Physically he would have to be cajoled on the one hand, and dominated on the other. No doubt he would feel as inadequate as he looked, but at least he would be physically undemanding, and that, in turn, she might find somewhat dull. Such things were not necessary to her, as they were to her mother, but though Nefertiti had a strong stomach, she saw there would be times when she would have to think of other things.

Involuntarily she found herself looking at Horemheb's calves, for he, too, had made himself a part of this visit. He was totally unconscious of them, and this for some reason made them the more appealing. They were large, taut calves that swelled from the lower leg, as she preferred, rather than sticking out like wooden balls, and they were covered with black down whose tips had a golden sparkle whenever he shifted about in the sun;

whereas the prince had the white underbelly of a stranded ray and no calves at all. Despite herself, these brown egregious calves drew her attention. Perhaps they were another reason why she loathed her mother so.

While she watched the calves, the prince was watching Horemheb's navel, as he stood on a dais, listening idly to his mother, who was a short woman and was a step below him. He had not meant to watch it, but it was easier to look at than was Tiiy. It held him hypnotized.

He liked Horemheb precisely because Horemheb was his mother's lover. This was a form of hero worship not unknown to the cerebral, a mixture of wistfulness and vicarious self-indulgence. If I were not what I am, which of course I like best, but which is a tremendous responsibility, the argument goes, it would be delightfully relaxing to be a simple, unspoiled animal like that. And besides, he is fond of me, and that is flattering. To the prince, Horemheb was a large loyal dog of his own age, and he had an immense desire to dig his fingers into that fur and grip hard, when he was sad and wanted to cry.

Meanwhile he was hypnotized by that navel. Thebes was the navel of the world, and that was understandable, for since the dominant god lived there, then all acts and decisions came from there. The navel of a man, however, was somewhat different.

Instinctively he looked down at his own navel, which was little more than a crease, or structural flaw, as though he had been snapped off his placental cord like a seedpod rather than a child. Horemheb on the other hand had a flat stomach, and in it his navel was like a concave nipple. It was dark; it was warm; it was deep; and no doubt it had a very special smell. Really, in the womb people must ripen like fruit, detach themselves, and fall uneaten.

The prince very much wanted to stick his finger in it.

46

When he was a child, his nurse had said, if you stick your finger in your navel, it will suck your whole body in, and you won't exist any more. It was a gesture he still made nervously, whenever he wanted to hide. Looking at Horemheb, he did it now. He scarcely heard what Tiiy was saying. With an effort he shifted his glance and caught Nefertiti's eye. She smiled.

He could not say that he cared for that smile. It knew too much. But he found himself smiling back at her. With a thrill it occurred to him that they had read each other's minds. He looked at her closely. She looked different from the others, as he did himself. She was supple, where Horemheb and Tiiy were a little simple and inconvenient.

Still, they were to be married, and he did not altogether like that.

He liked it still less when a few days later Nefertiti came to see him alone. But he need not have worried. She came for a purpose, equipped with a good deal of thoughtfully gathered evidence. It was to his vanity she would appeal.

The prince was already married once, to Tadukhipa, a Mitannian princess, a gibbering hottentot who had arrived at court three years before with three hundred ladies-in-waiting, an indifference to daily bathing, and an entirely new way of applying kohl. She was sequestered somewhere in the ramshackle harem, and nobody ever saw her, but as the application of kohl was as exacting as it was difficult, she was far from bored, and cost no more than would have a permanent ambassador. The marriage had been a matter of diplomacy. The prince had not been expected to go to bed with her. Still, the matter had caused gossip, for he had not shown the slightest interest in the three hundred ladies-in-waiting, either, nor, indeed, so far as anyone knew, in anyone, of any sex. He was rumoured im-

47

potent. She had heard innumerable rhymes on the subject, all specific and none polite. Perhaps he had heard them, too. Courtiers, having nothing else to do, are often cruel.

Nefertiti therefore judged that the prince would be more concerned with appearances than with facts, and it was the appearance she intended to give him, even if occasionally they would have to produce a child. She did not mind. Her interest in venery was slight and practical. For the rest, they would play out a game together, in return for which she expected him to grow grateful and fond. Public display they could manage very well. And really people were naïve in these matters. If it was something they wanted to believe, they would always take the appearance for the fact.

In these circumstances, their first nuptial interview was undoubtedly odd. She knew even then that promiscuity has nothing to do with the emotions. One reaches out in the night for a body as one would reach for a glass of water. It is a thirst or a habit, but in itself quite meaningless, as meaningless as abstention is in those who feel no thirst. In the prince she saw a new, a charming, a diverting, an altogether surprising, and perhaps a generous toy.

When he came to her apartments it was very late. He came not with excuses, but with arguments. That, too, she had expected.

The bedrooms of the palace were distressingly small. They had one door to the corridor, covered by a curtain, a lower level and an upper level. The bed was on the upper level. It was a large sway-backed wooden litter which both rustled and creaked. The room had no window but one high up in the wall. It was almost certain the attendants would be listening in the corridor. It was therefore necessary to whisper.

The attendant showed the prince into the room, left him there with one or two castor-oil lamps, and withdrew. He stood in the middle of the room like a forlorn moth, and then fluttered towards the dais. There was a silence, followed by a flurry down the corridor.

The prince was rather improbably wearing the short loincloth of classical sculpture. His body, far from being majestic, looked as defenceless as freshly risen bread-dough and had about the same swelling curves.

He began with the arguments. She listened with the liveliest attention, and such is the power of monologue that he soon became persuaded she was agreeable to talk to. In no time they were giggling together as happily as twins.

It is necessary to remember that in those days, before the invention of original sin, venery had none of that air of perpetual novelty which makes it so beguiling to the unimaginative, the bored, or the puritan. One could then love or not love as one wanted to, but whereas a discreet matter-of-factness made the business easier to accomplish, at the same time the absence of guilt robbed it of half its charm, for it either had to be done well or not at all. Without a sense of sin to rein-force his pride, your bumbling amateur felt more at a loss then than now.

However, there is such a thing as shrewd beauty, and this Nefertiti had possessed from birth. It was time to rescue the prince from his own arguments.

He explained to her, first of all, how remarkable it was that the privilege of physical contact with Pharaoh should be extended to queens, and she agreed, quite readily, that it was indeed remarkable. He then allowed her to touch him. By massaging the muscles at the back of his neck she reduced him to the warm stupor of a newborn kitten, and though he shuddered when she began, when she had finished he asked her to go on. Her wrists ached, but she went on.

Apparently grateful, he then told her that to be a queen also meant that she would be a god after death,

49

which was clearly to her advantage. She agreed that it was an advantage, but her wrists were becoming tired. There was a prolonged silence. She broke it by suggesting that since the attendants were undoubtedly listening, it would be an excellent idea if they creaked and rocked the bed. This co-operative suggestion won her a quick smile, and after they had creaked and rocked the bed with some vigour, he had almost completely relaxed and decided that they were having a wonderful time. He had accepted her as fellow conspirator.

When she blew out the lamps, however, which meant that she had to leave him for a moment, he grew nervous again, and it was necessary to creak and rock the bed some more. This time, however, it was clearly not so much fun, and somewhere outside in the corridor someone sneezed.

"Make a noise," she suggested, wondering vaguely what to do next. The moment, she knew, was crucial.

He was thinking. She would always be able to tell when he was thinking, because when he was his breath grew more shallow. She could also tell that he was frightened.

"What's wrong?" she asked.

"I don't like the dark."

"I'm here," she said, without thinking of the matter, because she had often been afraid of the dark herself, and so won dominion over him quite by accident, despite all her careful planning. She could feel the difference at once. When he began to talk again, it was as one would talk to a very close friend, a little older than oneself, but thoroughly reliable. But he was still nervous about being there, so he had to trot out his little philosophy. She quite understood that.

"But isn't it rather vulgar to be only a man or a woman," he said. "It seems so ordinary."

There was no point in telling him that even the gods must do as we do, and that though the original god

Aton produced his children by auto-insemination, with the passage of time the method had unfortunately been lost. Instead, she told him that his penis had the texture and faint odour of the flesh of a ripe persimmon. High comedy has its own stench, and if we cannot get our way in one way, why then we must use another. She did not really mind, and the matter was soon over with. Further steps could be taken later, and at the end of it all he screamed like a moonstruck rabbit, which she supposed indicated pleasure.

So everything might have been well, really, had the Amon priests not been so insistent upon that ceremony with the coronation doll. It is wry to reflect that they destroyed themselves and the royal house with that same jointed horror whose only purpose was to perpetuate their own power.

Yet in all respects the day of the coronation dawned propitiously.

It began, according to the elaborate schedule, with an early morning exhibition of the royal family to the loyal populace, a carefully rehearsed audience of ten thousand rammed into the esplanade before the palace.

At least one member of that audience found the spectacle extremely diverting, if sobering. This was Tutmose, a sculptor of much ability and little ambition, who wished a royal commission, but having no access to the palace, hoped that he could retain enough of the royal appearance to do a trial piece. He was less interested in Pharaoh than in the prince, for patronage, now, would lie that way.

In front of the palace a pavilion had been set up, from which the royal family would step into their chariots, the floor of the pavilion being on a level with the floor of the chariots. It was an awkward arrangement, but they had to display themselves, and to use the balcony of audience and then go to their chariots would have been more awkward still. The spectacle was certainly fine. The jewels were dazzling, so dazzling that nobody paid much attention to the features they surrounded, except for Tutmose, who had a board before him on which to sketch.

Royal Father Ay was the first to appear. His was a striking face, lean, Oriental, narrow-eyed, benign, and very far away. Nobody paid much attention to him. He was followed by Nebzumut, Nefertiti's sister, a fat, plump, amiable creature with two attendant dwarfs. She blinked as though she were not accustomed to sunlight, as indeed she was not. She was only a girl and carefully kept indoors. She in turn was followed by Horemheb, who as Commander of the Armies was loudly cheered by the guards and totally unknown to anybody else. Still, it was an interesting face, there was no denying that. It was not, however, relevant to Tutmose's purposes.

A ripple ran through the crowd. A cheer went up, and for once it was a warm and honest cheer. Pharaoh and the Queen were emerging on the platform, accompanied by Smenkara, the youngest child, in the arms of Ay's wife, the royal nurse.

About that immense ruin of a man there was something altogether touching. Vast, corpulent, florid, obviously in pain, with a stoic animal nobility of feature still bony and clear in that puzzled matrix of fat, Amenophis was as always Pharaoh, a little foolish, a little absent-minded, without much head for intrigue, but forthright, clean, and obviously a ruling prince. Tiiy, beside him, nervous, assured, worried, perplexed, but very gracious, was as clearly the Great Royal Wife. It was their best role, the one they played every day, and neither they nor the crowds could have got along without it.

Amenophis was half carried to his chariot, but once

in it, and he stood erect, and would remain standing in it for so long as he had to be in public view. Of such things is character made. And only for such things, alas, is character applauded.

Next appeared Nefertiti and the prince, also to be applauded, not for themselves, but as something of Amenophis and Tiiy's making, as one would applaud a favourite chef's latest dish, even before it had been tasted. At these two Tutmose looked more narrowly and with a smile.

They had caught his attention at once. Your artist who has something he can express only through the human face, cannot say anything, unless he find the right face. And these were the faces he had been looking for. He forgot to draw. He did not have to. These faces had lain latent in his mind for years. He recognized them at once. They were so bored, and boredom prolongs beauty, for since it has no expression, so it forms no customary wrinkles. Nefertiti would never age, he could see that. She would only become more and more desperate.

And as for the prince, he had the face of a heretic, and it only remained to see what form that heresy would take. As a problem in aesthetics his body was a fascinating riddle it might take years to solve. It only remained to meet his patron, and Tutmose's future was assured.

He watched with attention. They were so fragile. But it is a mistake to believe that fragile things are easily broken. Instead they are apt to be as resilient as reeds. And then they were so obviously, so very obviously, he thought narrowly, attached to each other, like a parody of their parents. The prince allowed the princess to put her arm around his waist in public. Even Amenophis never allowed Tiiy to do that, and the crowd loved it. It made them just like you and me, if we were just married and were wrapped up in each other, which we never were. They did not applaud. They roared.

Perhaps only Tutmose realized the outrageous nature of that counterfeit. If so, it did not bother him, for in this life, he knew, the counterfeit is just as important as the real, and perhaps more essential to our survival. For he was a sculptor, a maker of faces. He knew perfectly well that, except for those essentials which if neglected turn and destroy us with self-knowledge later on, the keeping up of appearances is the only reality we have.

Meanwhile, followed by a cloud of excited and anonymous royal relatives, the procession swept down to the river and the temples of Karnak and Luxor on the other side. The crossing would be made by barge, and this, too, was a sight that no one in his right senses would have desired to miss.

The river was clogged with the pleasure boats of the nobility, brave with pinions, statues, and musicians. On the other side the priests of Amon, confident in their ascendancy, conducted the royal party up the great sphinx avenue, around the main temple three times, and then within, on the final road to the throne.

There they made the prince co-regent. He saw how pleasant it was to be co-regent of the world, with absolute power over Ay, Horemheb, Nefertiti, even over Amenophis, perhaps, or Tiiy. No one could interfere with him now. He might do as he pleased. He was absolute and inviolable. But what did he please?

Even the high priest was obsequious, as so he should be. Standing there before the entrance to the Holy of Holies, slim, top-heavy with jewels, alone, as he wished to be, the prince found it not so much a triumph, as to know, that being now untouchable and omnipotent, he was at last secure. So, though tired and sweaty in the sun, he was happy. Not even the dank walls around him, or the dark shadows under the colonnades, could

54

oppress him. Was he not now a god? Was he not now immortal?

It was time for him to visit the Holy of Holies.

He motioned Ay to him. "Come with me," he ordered.

Ay shook his head. "No one may go with you there."

Suddenly he panicked. And the high priest was not obsequious now. There was on his face quite a different look. There was nothing for the prince to do but follow, in a vast beetle-backed wave of priests that dragged him, like an aphis, down into the dark cellars of the soul, there to milk him dry.

They had crowned him only in order to put him in one of those few ultimate situations which we have to face alone. And such situations should not exist, for they involve an unavoidable choice, and every time we make an unavoidable choice a little of us dies.

People are dishonest. They tell us we always have a voluntary choice. And then they dump us, defenceless, into some situation where no choice is possible. All this false splendour of the priests was designed to one purpose. No wonder he had always thought the priests unclean. They were spiritual butchers. They did not save souls. They merely fattened them up for their own purposes.

He ran over everything Ay had told him. But Ay had not told him much.

The high priest going ahead, a row of lesser priests on each side of him, chanting and wailing, and with sistrums that rattled like snakes, they plunged him deeper into this stone charnel-house. Not even the walls had the life to echo here.

All light had gone. Here they used naphtha flares.

This part of the building was very old and no better than a tomb. The corridor became narrower. The priests were ahead of and behind him. They were now silent, as he was forced along.

He had expected the priests to be friendly. After all, belief in all this mummery was all very well for the laity, but the royal family was sceptical. Surely that gave them the right to know the truth?

On the contrary, the high priest would say nothing. The prince was sobered. It had never occurred to him before that the aweful might of this dark, vengeful god Amon might exist, that the god might actually be lurking in this holy of holies, waiting to do something horrible to him, the way shadows waited when you could not sleep at night.

Why had no one told him that scepticism was merely a day-time amusement? Why had Ay not told him that this terrible god they all laughed at was not so laughable here?

He turned to the priest.

They had reached a small, square room without windows. In one wall was a door covered with seals. Not even a sistrum rattled now. The room was unpleasantly fetid from the torches. The priest forced him to break the seals. He did so, and the door swung open on absolutely nothing beyond itself at all.

The priest forced him through the door, which then swung shut behind him, smoothly into the stone wall, by what mechanism he could not tell.

He stood stock still. If he did not do as he had been instructed to do, he would not be let out. He found it difficult to keep from shaking.

Somewhere there must be some concealed source of meagre light. Slowly his eyes adjusted to the darkness. At first he could make out nothing, not even the limits of the walls. He had only an impression of disease and damp.

Then, by a faint glimmer that seemed to spring from nowhere, he saw against the deeper darkness the shadowy bulk of a closed shrine. The god had arrived.

It was his duty to break the seals on the shrine doors.

This, with trembling fingers, he did. He could not bring himself to open them, however, nor did he have to. They swung back of their own accord.

In the glow that came from somewhere inside the shrine he could make out the black and brittle outlines of an enormous jointed doll. It was sleek and glistening, but its head and face were hidden. It seemed to stir, and there were odd angry gleams of blue and red from its jewels. Its eyes were white shell, and they stared.

He was supposed to anoint the god from a small unguent pot inside the shrine. It was only a statue, but even so, he could not bring himself to touch it. He dipped his fingers in the slimy, greasy mass, and flecked the unguent over it.

There was a sound as though someone had dropped a stone lid over a cistern in a stone floor, and a bright magnesium flare of light in the glare of which the giant doll became actual. It started forward jerkily, glaring at him, as the light suddenly went out. He stumbled backwards, over a groove in the floor, and heard as much as he felt the thing whirring towards him in the blackness. Something clawed at him. He felt wooden finger-nails, immensely brittle, poking and scratching across his face. He tried to brush them aside, but could not. And that must have been when he screamed.

The statue withdrew.

He found his back against the wall. He stayed there, his body very tight, shivering, looking this way and that, unable to see anything, and that was when the god spoke to him. Its voice was hollow and dead. It told him that the god was mightier than Pharaoh, that the god could destroy Pharaoh, even as it had made Pharaoh a god, and that therefore Pharaoh must follow the advice of his appointed priests, for it was not wise to contradict the oracle of a god. For just as the god had touched him now, so would the god seek him out, wherever he was, should he disobey. And every day he should come to anoint the god, and when he was in doubt how to act, the god would tell him.

There was an absolute silence. The prince could still feel that touch. It was not the touch of life, to make him immortal, but the prurient touch of death, to make him vulnerable for ever. The silence grew longer. He heard the doors of the shrine shut. He was alone again.

He did not know for how long. At last the panel opened in the wall. He was blinded by the glare of torches out there. The high priest stepped forward. No one else dared to approach.

"And has the god spoken?" he asked. By the peculiar smile that hovered on his lips, the prince knew that somehow, even through stone, his scream had been heard, and that the priest knew perfectly well the god had spoken. It was not a smile he would either forget or forgive.

He allowed them to take him back the way they had come. The false door closed smoothly behind them, but he knew the god was still in there, waiting.

Once more he was presented to the crowds. He had been gone over an hour. Having been touched divinely by the god, he was now proclaimed Pharaoh. Life! Prosperity! Health! shouted the priests. Instead he felt like a sacrificial goat, displayed to the people both before and after the sacrifice, and then to be cut up for the priests to eat at leisure.They were only acclaiming their dinner.

When he rejoined the family, he was very quiet, so quiet that even Nefertiti knew something had gone wrong, and wondered what. None of them had seen him so shaken before.

It is by similar methods they break horses. Amenophis saw this and tried to be jovial. His manner was that they were now both initiates, and perhaps he had forgotten how much the rite had frightened him, in his day. As far as he was concerned, these things had to be got through, and once they had been seen through, things went well enough. It was in this way he tried to reassure his son.

Unfortunately the prince had seen through the scene to something quite different on the other side, and was not apt to forget it ever.

That night he spent with Nefertiti, many attendants, and many lights. There could never be enough lights now. And though he was not supposed to speak of what went on in the Holy of Holies, she got him to tell her.

Nefertiti had a mind as direct as her father's, and saw through things much as he did. She knew very well what the priests had been up to. And if the prince was afraid of the dark, the best thing for her to do was to give him light. She was afraid of the dark herself, and could not know that though light may fail, darkness never does.

She had the Aton priest, Meryra, in attendance. Now she would send for him. If the prince did not like the religion he had, then someone would have to provide him with another one. He had an interest in such things. It was necessary only to feed that interest, and her power over him would be assured.

Thus, in the middle of the night, with five hundred lamps hissing in that otherwise silent palace, fell one god and one dynasty. But the birth of the new god was to take a little longer than the downfall of the old one, for gods have to be evoked, with much cunning, out of the hidden mind, and this takes time, skill, and ambition.

Ambition Meryra had, though Nefertiti was mistaken to think him her creature. He was no creature at all, but like most of us, only an ambition on two legs.

It would be a mistake to underestimate this man Meryra. He was not wicked. On the contrary, he was good whenever he was able and always willing to listen to the troubles of those by whom he might rise.

59

He was forty-eight, and so far he had not prospered. That he was attached to Aton worship was no accident. It was the only job he had been able to get, for the Amon priests would have none of him. They had had others to prefer over his head. He had not been unduly ambitious, but he did know that he had certain abilities. He wanted comfort, ease, and the right to spend long hours in meditation. Without being in the least creative, or having a scrap of insight in his nature, except, occasionally, when watching the lotuses in his garden after a good meal, he was yet a man who loved a system for its own sake. He could play with theology by the hour, for diversion, as someone else would play with a particularly promising child. Sincerity was never in question. He could believe in anything for a day, a month, a year, for the sake of the game, as someone else would accept a geometrical assumption, in order to learn how a bridge was built.

Therefore, when he had managed to secure the chief priesthood of the family Aton cult he had been well pleased. It completely freed him from doctrinal disputes with his Amon colleagues, who did not happen to share his sense of humour, and it allowed him to keep an excellent table.

He was altogether flattered by the attentions of the prince. For one thing, they meant more money for the temple, and therefore ultimately for him. The Amon priests, who scorned the Aton and him, would now be jealous. And besides, he found the prince bright, intelligent, remarkably well versed in theology for a layman, and given to the sort of puzzles with which he amused his spare time anyway.

The prince had decided to enlarge the Aton temple, and this meant that they met daily. And really, if anything, the prince talked too much. For instance, he asked: "What is truth?"

Meryra was delighted. It was one of those unanswerable riddles that one could discuss for hours, if the other person did not suddenly begin to shake like a whippet.

One could answer cynically: truth is the prevailing prejudice of the greatest number at any given time, mystically, except that this tended to cut off the discussion: truth is the perception of God; erotically, truth is what we want others to see in us; militarily, truth is on the winning side; politically, truth is whatever justifies our self-interest; philosophically; truth is that invisible, impalpable reality of whose various aspects appearance is the pale momentary reflection; practically and pragmatically: truth is the best butter, and comes salted, plain, with garlic, and sometimes rancid.

"But what is *the* truth?" asked the prince.

"Why, whatever you think it is," said Meryra.

"And what do you think it is?"

Meryra's thoughts did not move in quite that terrifyingly adolescent way. He had never thought that truth was anything in particular. "Truth", he answered blandly, "is illimitable. To define it, therefore, is to make it untrue."

The prince was not quite up to that sort of thing. Meryra was disappointed.

So was the prince. "Is what I believe truth to be, true?" he asked.

"Why, yes, of course, I suppose so," said Meryra. He was watching the workmen set up the new columns which extended the forecourt of the temple. It would look splendid when they were all in place. "What do you believe truth to be?" he asked.

"Honesty and frankness. Showing things as they are."

"In so far as you can never know what they are," said Meryra, "that's being merely literal-minded."

Fortunately the prince did not hear him. "Is Bek a good sculptor?" he asked.

"No," answered Meryra. "I don't think so. That is, the effect is sure to be very fine."

"Is he deficient in Ma'at, in truth?"

"How on earth should I know?" asked Meryra. "Sixteen statues, you say. The effect will be absolutely marvellous."

"Twenty-four," corrected the prince. This matter of truth was important to him. As for example in the matter of his descent from Ra. If he was descended from Ra and not from Amon, he need never go to that Holy of Holies again. He asked Meryra about his descent from Ra.

Meryra had been saving up his grudge against the Amon priests for years. He was delighted to tell the prince that, yes, he was quite right, Ra was the older god. He was descended from him. But in Thebes, he would still have to go to the Amon temple. Now if he was in Heliopolis, matters would be different.

"You mean, if I went away, there would be nothing the Amon priests could do?"

Meryra was not sure.

And then the whole story of the Holy of Holies came tumbling out. Meryra was not impressed. "A painted doll," he said, "moved by strings, with an echo box behind. Nothing more."

"I shall never go there again," said the prince.

Meryra looked guilty. He should not have spoken. It was never wise to give away trade secrets, if only because it meant that one then had to make up tricks of one's own, which was fatiguing.

"Then it was not a god," said the prince.

Reluctantly Meryra shook his head.

"Then where is God?"

"God", said Meryra, hoping to end what had been an uncomfortable and indiscreet five minutes with a benign platitude, "is within you."

"I know," said the prince.

This, if anything, was even more disturbing than what had gone before. How on earth could the prince know anything of the sort? He was, of course, himself a god, but then that was purely a state manner. Meryra waited respectfully, wondering what to say.

They had reached what had been the Holy of Holies. The prince was having it torn down, as part of his improvements. It was an activity Meryra could look upon with some equanimity. The old Holy of Holies had been bad for his arthritis; and it had been boring to duck in there and wait for the correct length of time, without anything to do, while pretending to receive a suitable message from the god. The new shrine, he trusted, would be larger, airier, and drier.

The prince told him there would be no new shrine. "Aton is a god of light. All good comes from light. All bad comes from darkness. I will not have anything shut up. We will have an open altar and offering tables."

Meryra was astonished. And then he saw the possibilities. There would be a new ritual, priests, temples, new formulas, a whole system.

"With flower sacrifices," he said, and the prince nodded eagerly.

Very well, then, thought Meryra, with flowers it will be, a very small and special cult, patronized by Pharaoh, aristocratic, with a limited clientéle and himself at the head of it. It would be a fascinating game. For so long as he could hold the prince's attention, for so long would the Aton cult prosper.

But to Meryra, already dreaming his new dreams, was added Tutmose, the sculptor, dreaming his. For Tutmose, like Meryra, also combined indifference with ambition, and perhaps also liked to play with the game of appearances, though in a slightly different way. Much more than Meryra, Tutmose held the right keys to immortality. Tutmose, or rather his fingers, knew what Ma'at was very well.

It was no accident that he should arrive at the temple on that day when the installation of the new statues was finished and the prince had come to see himself new, shiny, and reproduced twenty-four times.

The day was mercilessly bright. Only the best work, delicately modelled, could stand up to such strong light, and Bek's, as Tutmose knew, was not the best work. The effects of inferior craftsmanship and too much haste showed plainly. Besides, Bek did not know how to make a virtue of abnormality.

For an instant the prince thought that Bek had made fun of him. He had asked for truth. But Bek had given him a literal-minded veracity so thoughtlessly done as to be a cruel caricature. The prince wanted to turn and run.

From twenty-four pedestals twenty-four jeering parodies leered down at him. Bek was not to be blamed. The prince saw his own ugliness from the inside, where it was almost a grace; but no artist can ever give any subject a grace he does not possess himself, and so there was no veil of art between these statues and the prince's ugliness.

From a height of ten feet his own white face looked down at him, stretched taut like a piece of muslin drawn over the skull of a ferret. The eyes were beady, the skull misshapen, and the lower lip flapped down of its own weight. The pose was stiff and hieratic, after an Osiris mummy. The arms were like spindly cucumbers suffering from winter rot.

Show me as I am, he had said, but this was not the same as sculpting him as he looked. The hips were a calamity, like gigantic white sponges six feet high. And there were twenty-four of them. It was his first defeat at the hands of the fine arts, and once the panic of being seen like that was over, he was furious with the artist. But where could he find a better man?

As it happened the better man had come to find

64

him. Tutmose stepped from the column behind which
he had been lingering.

"You should not blame the man," he said. "He did
his best."

"Where did you come from?"

Tutmose shrugged. "I have been here all morning.
But you are quite right. They have no truth. They are
very bad."

The prince had been taken off guard, and taken off
guard, Tutmose thought, he was charming, slightly
spoiled, only a boy, potential of great mischief, but
still charming. With his guard back up, on the other
hand, he was shrill and difficult to put up with. Tutmose, however, wanted a government stipend and an
adequate workshop.

"You were talking about truth. And you are quite
right. It cannot be shown from the outside. If you will
come to my studio, I will show you. Unfortunately
sculpture is not portable."

It was a daring thing to suggest. Pharaoh went to no
one. But as he had been sure he could, he had caught
the prince's attention.

They went.

It was the prince who arrived first. Tutmose found
him in the outer courtyard of the house, a little bewildered. And indeed, to an Egyptian, no doubt the
house *was* bewildering. For one thing the trees in the
garden were not planted in orderly rows, but scattered
in no pattern. Tutmose preferred to find order rather
than to impose it. For another, there were no clamorous
servants. Tutmose did not care for servants. And for a
third, the building was stripped of all ornament, with
nothing but whitewashed walls, so that the rooms were
full of light and the dancing shadows of water plants
from the pool of the courtyard.

When he led the way to the studio, there was no
work in the studio at all. The room was empty, for

65

Tutmose did not like his own works. There was only a chair on a dais and a work-table.

"Sit down," said Tutmose, and began to mix something in a tub. Rather unexpectedly the prince sat and even sent away his guards. For clearly he felt quite safe here. The room was flooded with light.

"What shall I do?" he asked. To pose still made him self-conscious, particularly after having seen the best of which Bek was capable.

"Do nothing. After all, you *are*," said Tutmose, and began to slap wet plaster on an armature. He had prepared for this for weeks. He had made head after head and smashed them all. He had studied these features until he knew how these features wished to look, and until he could reconcile the way they wished to look with the way they did. For in these matters the prince was no fool. No matter how uncertain his taste, still, obviously, he had taste. Therefore the thing must be done just so, and it had to be done quickly. Well, it would be.

Besides, the subject was interesting. There was some vigour in that boyish voice. All he needed was something to believe in, and then, even if it were an error, he would be worth sculpting indeed.

The model grew. It only took three-quarters of an hour. Tutmose revolved its stand. The light came down through a hole in the ceiling. It played and leaped and altered the surface of everything, as Tutmose gently rotated the stand. And there, out of the still wet plaster, shimmered the prince's very heart and voice, changeable, young, quick, eager, never for an instant the same, and always self-renewing. Tutmose had only to watch, to know that he had succeeded.

"Yes," said the prince. "That is truth."

For that was what Tutmose knew about the truth: the truth is always changing and always the same. And besides, it is pleasant to thrill the sitter sometimes. And

66

the sitter is so easily flattered. All he wants to see is his own conception of himself. Tutmose was rewarded on the spot. It remained only for him to flatter Nefertiti, and about that he had no doubts. It would merely be necessary to make her beautiful. Women were like that.

And so the pattern fell into place. First Meryra, and then Tutmose, the man who showed them the truth, flickering, changing, but always the same, and always beautiful, and always what they wanted to see. He would be personal portraitest to all of them.

And what was the secret of that sudden rise, and of that no less sudden truth? Wet plaster, and a trick of modelling porous surfaces, so that they should always catch the light and so always seem to change.

It was ridiculously easy. Yet it was not so easy as all that, for Tutmose, too, had his concept of the truth. Once the prince had gone he set his face aside and did another one, one on which he spent a lot of time and thought, and which utterly held his attention. The first had been a piece of sleight of hand. But this was a little more than that. It was a study of the prince a few months from now, when he was at last at the mercy of what he was really thinking; when his own fears, so badly nourished by other men's ambition, had at last hardened into a system of belief. For after all, we are all other men's means, even Tutmose, who more than any of them, hoped to save something out.

He had this hope, because he knew what he was up to.

Of course there were times, in the middle of the night, when he wondered if he was any good at all. But, since he also knew that it was only people who were good who had such doubts, these night thoughts, though profoundly disturbing, were also reassuring, for he knew that that very quality of badness which one perceives in oneself is nothing more than the sum of one's merits, for only excellence shows us how we have failed. All the world's most admired works are nothing more than a rubbing of the artist's original idea, an uneven replica of something that at the time was quite clear. And, of course, such is the creative process that as soon as the rubbing is taken, we destroy the original.

But only the artist knows this. It is his great trade secret, the secret perhaps of any trade, for only those at the top know how little is the distance they have climbed, how far there is they failed to go, for only at the top can we catch a glimpse of what lies beyond.

Meanwhile, at the palace, there were problems. Tiiy, Amenophis, and Horemheb were in the pavilion by the lake.

It was difficult, these days, to get Amenophis to do anything, for he was completely wrapped up in the astonishing news that after all he was not dying. The light which this had flooded over his whole life had blinded him to everything else. Now his son was co-regent, he proposed, despite his pain, to enjoy himself. Except for the family hobby of building, he left matters of state to Tiiy.

The great jewelled mortuary temple of the Memnonion, which he had erected to both of them was, they said, finished, and he was determined to see it. Beyond that, his responsibilities were over, so far as he was concerned.

So Horemheb and Tiiy, with Ay for company, were forced to discuss political affairs in the Memnonion, a setting that was not exactly conducive to worry, for into this vast pile Amenophis had poured the luxury of a lifetime. Obscure revolutions in Syria and scrubby revolts in the Delta shrank into insignificance here.

They carried him in in a litter, and even he looked lost in that wilderness of burnished marble, silver and gold inlay, prismatic jewels, shrines of lapis lazuli, and formal statues of himself all taller than he was. Even though they whispered, the walls reverberated to their voices. It was as useless to tell him the Empire was falling to pieces, as it was to tell the prince. Commander of the Armies Horemheb might be, but there was nothing he was to be allowed to command them to do.

"After all, the boy is young. He will learn," said Amenophis.

That was exactly what they were afraid of.

Ay asked if either of them had been to the Aton temple.

Tiiy only half listened. Somewhere behind all this was her daughter, she knew that. And Nefertiti was sly. For Nefertiti now also went to the Aton temple. Meryra had tactfully adapted the ritual to fit her.

"Who is this man Meryra?" demanded Tiiy.

"The prince apparently sets great store by him."

"He must be a fanatic. Put a stop to him," snapped Tiiy, and thought no more of the matter.

By then Meryra could not have stopped himself.

Horemheb had a moment of disillusionment. They were not busy, wise, good, and impersonal. They were not all understanding. They were not gods. They were only Amenophis and Tiiy, two intelligent and beautiful toys, who played with their Empire as though it, too, were a toy; and who would protect that Empire only as a rich man would protect his investments, when at long last he came to realize that his income had shrunk.

For the first time in his life he saw that, dwarfed by the dimensions of his own monument, Amenophis looked smaller, and Tiiy, just for an instant, irrelevant. It saddened him. He had always believed that loyalty was an emotional matter. Now he began to realize that it could also be abstract.

And then the magic was back again. She laid her hand on his arm. She needed his help.

Three

In two years one can persuade oneself of almost anything. Familiarity, in that event, breeds confidence.

Nefertiti had persuaded herself that she was happy. Since she had never been happy, this was not too difficult to do. She was now the first, or almost the first, woman in the Empire.

The prince had persuaded himself he was Pharaoh, the ruler of his people, well loved, universally trusted, the eternal well-spring of favour, powerful, gracious and understanding. He had not persuaded Tiiy, and whether Ay believed it, or indeed anything, would have been difficult to judge. He was much too busy to believe in anything, for he virtually ran the government, and Tiiy ran him.

As for Amenophis, nobody ever saw him, so he was able to believe, despite an inability to move about in cold weather and despite, or even because of, the pain, that he was still a remarkably vigorous man.

Horemheb, who had grown less muscular, but not noticeably so, was almost convinced that it was the duty of a Commander of Armies to stay in the capital and amuse the court. He was still Tiiy's lover. He could not help that. But sometimes, in the middle of the night, he wondered why her body made him so sad and so considerate, and why Nefertiti made him so nervous. He drilled the soldiers in the capital rigorously. Some might have called it discipline, others boredom. He called it strategy.

The prince had stopped going to the Amon temple. He had not been there for almost two years. The priests had to come to him, as they had had, though for different reasons, to come to his father. So far he took their their advice, but if he ever wished to revolt against them, the army would be on his side. For as a poacher fears game wardens, so does an army fear the power of the Church. Whatever happened, the army would remain loyal to Pharaoh. It would have to, in order to seize the country for itself.

But the person who had changed most was Meryra. He was fascinated, despite himself. Pharaoh had given him a problem: invent me a theology.

Of course one did not invent it. One needed the support of precedents. It was those one invented, and this was called the rediscovery of truth. It always had been, whenever a new need had arisen. One had simply to follow the rules. And Nefertiti had to be built into the ritual.

So there Meryra had his first postulate. God is the sun. The Sun consists of male and female energy. But Pharaoh must be more important than his consort, Nefertiti or no, therefore, though Pharaoh represents the male and the royal wife the female energy, co-existent, interdependent, and inseparable, still Pharaoh must be male and female both, since all things spring from him. And so forth.

If there was a flaw in this, Meryra could not find it. The prestige of Pharaoh was enormous. They could rely on that.

A ritual was more difficult. But here again there was no real problem. It could be mocked up.

Nefertiti was big with child. It made her fretful. Whenever she was bored she summoned him. They said little to each other, but they understood much, and Meryra knew where his patronage came from. So naturally Nefertiti had to be built into the ritual. He obliged, and Nefertiti, though pregnancy annoyed her very much, as it would any fastidious animal, rewarded him with a faint smile. Whether these matters really interested her would be hard to say. As a rule, women have no taste for metaphysics. But since they took up more and more of the prince's time, then they also had to take up more and more of hers.

The pregnancy created another problem. It left the prince alone much of the day, and since there was no art, except that of Tutmose, with which he would not meddle, he brought Meryra his own hymns to the sun.

They were not without merit, but to criticize their errors required some tact. The grammar was shocking. But fortunately, as chief theologian, Meryra could tactfully shift the grammar on theological grounds. And what is theology, after all, but a solicitude for syntax?

The changes, on the whole, remained minor.

Unfortunately the prince was learning too much theology. It was difficult, at times, to restrain him. The parturition of a god is no easy matter, and the prince was beginning to kick against his womb. Proper syntax in one system is not proper syntax in another.

All of which made Meryra uneasy. He would have been content to confect metaphysics all his life long, well fed in the shadow of Thebes. But the prince was not. Things were becoming too much for him, and he was beginning to form his own plans. Each new annoyance made them a little clearer.

Since Nefertiti did not have much time to amuse him, he saw life become more limited for him rather than more various. Once people had ignored him. Now they wanted to change him. It was as though people in a house wanted to shut off rooms they could not use. And indeed, he had become vastly over-populated. It was amazing how many people took shelter under Pharaoh. The only way to evict them was to ignore them.

As a result people thought he lacked warmth. Smenkara, his younger brother, did not think so, and so he took real pleasure in playing with Smenkara. Smenkara liked him. He took the boy everywhere, and made a friend of him, for all his grown-up friends had suddenly turned into councillors. They advised him, but they obeyed Tiiy. He was beginning to tire of Tiiy.

"Will you put that child down and listen," she snapped. "Aren't you interested in what happens in Nubia?"

"No," he said. "I'm not." It was the first time he had said it, and he found doing so an immense luxury. In a way it was a decision. He looked at Ay. He looked at Horemheb. He looked at Tiiy. No, he did not care what happened in Nubia. He saw that they all looked exactly alike. Why on earth must people confuse personal ambition with public conscience? During office hours they had created a new sex, called the bureaucrat, whose sexual characteristics were a lack of characteristics, and they all belonged to it.

He had an appointment with Tutmose, and they were making him late.

'You like to govern,' he said. 'Then govern.' He saw a way out. 'We are pleased with what you do in our name. Pharaoh cannot do everything. Therefore he delegates his divine authority to his proper instruments, as his father did before him, and when he is pleased with his servants, he rewards them.'

He peered at them blandly, feeling quite pleased with himself. Tiiy had some difficulty in controlling her features. Ay was the first to give in. Over his face there spread one of those slow, warm smiles with which he greeted anything that impressed him as being clever.

The prince was well satisfied. He went off to see Nefertiti before going on to Tutmose.

Nefertiti was in her eighth month, and refused to be seen in public. She would not even let Tutmose see her. This displeased him. She was pregnant by him, and the world should know that. 'Truth is in itself beautiful,' he told her.

In this case she seemed to feel that the truth was an exaggeration. And really, pregnancy had not improved her. It made her snappish and difficult to deal with. He was puzzled. He wanted her back the way she was. But he told her everything.

"Tiiy will plot against you, you know," she said.

"Very well." He was in a good humour. "We will plot against her." Nefertiti was a woman. She should know how the thing was to be done.

He had brought Smenkara with him. Nefertiti looked at Smenkara, who drew back into shadow. "You do well to encourage him," she said. "If it is not a boy, then Smenkara will be your heir."

The prince let go of Smenkara's hand at once. It was something that had never occurred to him.

Thus began a tug-of-war over Smenkara, for Nefertiti produced a girl who was named Meritaten, after the Aton cult, an act of defiance designed to please neither the Amon priests nor the family.

The prince was just as pleased to have a girl. He liked little girls, who were smooth and slippery to the touch as little boys, and yet who had no sex. It made them singularly charming. Besides, he had Nefertiti back again, though not for long. By 1383 she was again with child.

This time, however, she was willing to parade the fact. Perhaps she had learned a lesson. If truth was what the prince wanted, then truth he should have, but have it only from her. Nor did she care for his continued encouragement of Smenkara, since the second child, too, was a girl, to be named Maketaten.

Tiiy made no objection to the titulary. But she allowed herself to smile, she allowed herself to say that Nefertiti seemed able to produce only girls, and she made no secret of the fact that she was giving Smenkara the education proper to a crown prince.

She even consoled with Nefertiti. She offered sympathy; and subtly, she brought forward Tadukhipa, who blinked and giggled and seemed astonished to be rescued from obscurity. As Nefertiti could see, Tadukhipa had been receiving a great deal of attention. She was thinner. She was cleaner. Her Egyptian had improved. And she, too, it seemed, had suddenly become interested in the Aton cult.

Nefertiti sent for Meryra at once. And certainly, though Meryra was not without scruples, he had much to be grateful for. She thought he would see to the matter.

Meanwhile the prince was restive. After all, life was not so pleasant. He might be Pharaoh, but so was his father. Everywhere he looked he saw temples of his father's building. And though the world bowed down to him, he did not altogether like the way the world smiled when it did so. He had the pomp and nothing more. He could do anything, and yet what was there he could do?

Sometimes, it was true, he went to see Tutmose.

But these days Tutmose annoyed him, too. He had never thought life particularly real, but revelation had not come, and he found being a god was much like being a man. When one's illusions turn into illusions, this is called facing up to reality. But really, reality is nothing but a mirror in which we cannot even see ourselves. In those circumstances Tutmose fascinated him to the point of despair.

Like any artist, Tutmose was a magician, for the transmutation of metals and of the emotions are similar studies. Half of one's life is devoted to what one can do; half to an endless search for what one cannot. In addition to this, he was curious, and curiosity has neither morals nor compunction.

When people have everything, life is little more than a search for a further ingredient. Compared to the boredom of that, the painful search for technique is altogether enviable. For at least it can succeed, whereas the endless search for something beyond technique is almost always doomed.

Apparently, Tutmose saw, the prince did not even know he was a religious fanatic. Perhaps he was not yet sufficiently bored to become one, since one turns to religion out of boredom, in so far as if one knows everything, the unknowable suddenly becomes extremely attractive. It was time to hurry the process up. That was Meryra's duty, not his, but he had no objection to taking a hand in things. The trouble with Meryra was that he had no creative imagination and scholars rouse nobody.

It never even crossed Tutmose's mind that to play with people is sometimes dangerous, for he knew very little about them, except as subject matter. To him they were only scale models of what he was about to do next. He was tired of doing studies in disillusionment. What he wanted now was a man in the grips of faith.

Yet the prince admired these facile masks. "Why can I not do that?" he demanded. "I tell my artists what to make. I have even used a brush to show them. But it is they who do it. Why is that?"

It was a question best left unanswered. "It is not your medium. A king fights wars and founds cities," said Tutmose absent-mindedly. He would rather the prince talk about religion. When he talked about religion his eyes lit up. Besides, it was extremely unwise to tell Pharaoh anything. At the most, one could suggest.

The prince went away thoughtful and entranced. Of course. Thebes was not his city. It was not even his father's city, though it was full of his father's works. It was Amon's city. Pharaoh's city would be different. Pharaoh's city would be Aton's city. No one would be able to interfere with Pharaoh there. He brought the matter up with Meryra.

They were discussing the doctrine of effective per-

76

sonality. It helped to pass the time. The doctrine of effective personality was that once one was dead, one's soul might become anything one wished.

It was the only side of death that had ever appealed to him. You saw some sweetmeats you would like to taste. You became a bird, flew in the window, took them, ate them, and then became yourself again. Why could one not do that when one was still alive? Why could even Pharaoh only do that after he was dead?

Merya seemed abstracted. His face was pale. "And is that what you would like to do?" he asked.

"Oh, no. I would like to be a pink lily, floating open on a lake for a little while. And then, before it shut, I would have tired of it."

Meryra tried to concentrate. Tadukhipa had died that morning. It was against all his principles. Intrigue was not safe. But it had been that or lose Nefertiti's influence, and he knew very well that the Aton cult owed everything to her. It was she who directed Pharaoh. But when he had told her what had been done, she had sent him away at once. She had looked frightened. The responsibility of the secret was then to be his. He knew she would not protect him. Therefore he must turn for protection to Pharaoh.

He caught at that last remark. Did it mean that Pharaoh was becoming bored with the cult? Pharaoh must not become bored, for Meryra needed his attention. He must ingratiate himself.

He had not himself, thank God, ordered her death. He had only hinted. But the people he had hinted to would have to be rewarded, and he had many enemies. Every time Pharaoh gave a new endowment to the Aton temple, another enemy was born among the priests of Amon.

"My divine father, the Aton, has commanded I build him a city," said Pharaoh uncertainly, and looked at Meryra out of distant eyes, his body trembling like that of a stalking cat. "And there I shall build him a temple, for Meryra, his High Priest." It was an out-and-out bribe.

But it was a most convenient one, and who could tell? Meryra had lost his equanimity. Perhaps the Aton did exist. After all, he had not precisely made it up. He had only enlarged upon it a little. Who knew what powers he may have released?

He told himself it was not panic he felt, but inspiration. He told Pharaoh he would spend the night in prayer. The site would be revealed.

And he spent the night in prayer. The courtyard was deserted, the guards restive, the altar empty, and the floral offerings wilted. Meryra was in despair. For of course where was no Aton. There never had been.

Yet there was something here. Something did move in these corridors, and there was something wrong with the night. If one has arthritis, one tires of waiting for revelation. It is easier to improvise.

In short, he was terrified, and inspiration came.

The rustling resolved itself into those gentlemen to whom he had been so unwise as to hint much on the strength of the very little that Nefertiti had said. And they arrived with an ultimate irony, for it appeared that they had come too late. Tadukhipa had died a natural death. Forcible dieting had ruined a heart already strained to the breaking point by obesity.

But no one would believe that. Tiiy would not believe it. Nefertiti would not believe it. The Amon priests would not believe it. And besides, Nefertiti was pregnant for the third time. She was a virtual prisoner in the palace, because of that, and so she could not help him.

Under the circumstances it seemed better to leave. Meryra told Pharaoh the Aton had indeed spoken.

Five days later, under heavy guard, they were sailing northward down the Nile, no one knew why or where.

78

Thus was founded the city of Aketaten, the city of the Horizon of the Sun Disk, which was to endure for ever and ever. It endured, all told, for exactly seventeen years, which was a year or two longer than that glorious god, the Sun, its founder.

But how were they to know that then?

Four

The city was waiting to be founded. Cities do. For cities are like the demons of darkness: they can do their worst only after someone has evoked them. They sit waiting invisible for the right tribe to cross the watershed or ford beside which they are latent.

In the beginning they are charming, and pampered, and a little spoiled, for they are always the favourite child of someone. Their founders dote on them. And then, when they are strong enough, they develop a life of their own and devour those who created them. Then their servants they keep in fattening pens, called slums. They swallow down whole generations. Their founder lies forgotten. The purpose which brought them into being has long been lost sight of. But if they survive their adolescence, they are enormously long lived. Thebes was like that. One did not say Amenophis or the prince lived at Thebes. One said that Thebes was where Pharaoh lived.

But even cities die at last. The world is littered with their exoskeletons. Some cities die young, and they have the pathos of the grave of a talented child. If you have ever wandered through a city at three in the morning, you realize very quickly how well they get along without their inhabitants. But wander through Fatehpur Sikri, and you realize the sadness of a city nobody ever believed in. Cities of this sort never escaped the mind of their creator, and so died when he did. Such cities, in that case, are like casts taken from the brain. The brain decayed centuries ago. But here these streets faithfully reproduce its convolutions. Such a city, you see, has had no time to develop illusions of its own.

But at the moment the city had not yet come into view, and the prince was becoming impatient. In actuality the Nile is by no means a fascinating river, and all the best sites seemed to have been taken already.

The party consisted of ten boats, for the prince, whose organizing abilities were remarkable, had provided stonemasons, architects, priests, sacred utensils, a squad of designers, three chariots, six horses, Meryra, and Tutmose. Tutmose was, as usual, calm and interested. He had never been present at the fulfilment of a prophecy, and he waited upon the event with the liveliest expectation.

Meryra was nervous. He knew nothing of geography, to sail down had seemed easier than to sail up, and he hoped for the best. There would, he assured the prince, be a sign. But so far, on the fifth day out, there had been no sign.

The prince rose early each morning, scanned the river ahead, and by afternoon had become fretful. But now, on this morning, the little birds' flight of barges, rounding a curve of the Nile where the cliffs rose steep from the river, came suddenly to an open place. The oars dipped in the water, lifted, scattered slimy drops, and paused. Caught in a gust of wind, the sails hooped out. And with the vast chattering of a plague of anguished mice, shore birds large and small flowed in a smooth sheet off the water, flapped for an instant, turned with a shriek, hovered, and then scattered once more into constituent birds, as though someone had smashed a curtain and it fell tinkling down again like glass. Swooping and rising over the plain, the black loose-piled carpet of birds curved and arced into the distance. The boats were ordered to halt. The sign had been made known to the prince. Aketaten had been founded.

One can have ghosts before their birth as well as afterwards. Before them rose the shimmering white city that was to be. Meryra, who by this time had grown desperate, said yes indeed, he recognized it, it was indeed the place.

Tutmose only smiled. If Meryra had recognized the spot, it was from the dangerously impatient gleam in the prince's eye. But that was recognition enough. This was the place.

That people moved him so little did not mean that he was incapable of feeling. On the prince's face he had at last recaptured the look of boyish delight he had first seen there. Truly, the site was sublime, and Tutmose was moved.

No doubt the prince saw it much as he, Tutmose, would have looked at a heap of clay, for its potentialities, not for itself. For the more clearly you see what you have to do, the less interest you have in the means whereby one does it. It is for this reason that one develops an increasingly smooth technique, or employs assistants to do the roughing out, for really, one cannot be bothered about details once one has thought out the idea, one wants to be on to the next thing.

And later, when one is older and much wiser, one no longer even wants to do anything so childish as to set down what one has seen. One realizes then that to give insight a concrete shape is only a form of vanity, a desire to show others that one has indeed seen. One comes to realize that the true artist is the one who does nothing at all, for by the making of vulgar images he has come into contact with something beyond images, something more satisfying, that makes the making of images unnecessary. He may occasionally make one to amuse himself or others, but once he has reached that point, his true function is to sit and watch, until he loses all consciousness of self and becomes the function of seeing itself. This, Tutmose believed, was called mysticism, and he was interested to see whether or not the prince would go that far. He rather thought not. For though it is easy to give up everything else, to give over one's identity it is first necessary to give over the fear of falling, and this was something religious maniacs seldom did, for it would not be necessary for them to rise, if they were not afraid of falling.

At any rate the process would be interesting to watch.

It was interesting now.

They encamped there for ten days. The entourage resembled from a distance one of those hunting expeditions in which Amenophis had once taken such delight. Indeed, that was exactly what it was, though with a different beast in view.

The first thing the prince had taken ashore was his light chariot. Once it was assembled and the horses harnessed, he stepped into it with Meryra and whirled across the plain.

Tutmose began to feel some anxiety for Meryra, for between metaphysics and too much exercise, it was a question whether terror or exhaustion would kill him first. He was the victim of a man who has taken to visions.

Yet even Tutmose had to admit that the vision was superb. Now the prince had found his bearings, he sailed into theology and city planning with the same victorious gusto and serene contempt for human limitations as his grandfather had applied to the conquest of Syria; and it had to be confessed that his strategy was ruthlessly as good. It was not his fault if victory in these fields was a hazardous accomplishment. Chats on theology were no longer in order. They were replaced by orders, directives, proclamations, communiqués, and, if all these failed, a temper tantrum was sure to work.

The effect on his face was remarkable. It had suddenly developed the glow of rotten, phosphorescent wood. This made him more interesting to depict. So far Tutmose had been simple image maker to the prince. Now he foresaw that he would be called upon to be iconographer to a myth. It was certainly a challenge to his skill. It absorbed him. A chance remark had given him a whole new subject to explore.

For on the prince's part this was no longer dilletantism. It was mania. Tutmose had always been attracted towards those suffering from dementia, for they had one expression each, and so made perfect sitters, for like apples, pears, and the inanimate world, they decayed slowly. But mania is subtler than dementia, for mania grows bigger every day, until it embraces the whole world of experience and so becomes a mirror to all of it. While it lasts, it is inexhaustible, whereas dementia merely shrinks.

He foresaw now that he would soon be called upon to sculpt Nefertiti, and this made him thoughtful. Well, he had all day to think. The margins of the river were cluttered with a polychromed green mass of lotuses, papyrus, bulrushes, and aquatic plants. They were doomed. They would soon be replaced by buildings. But right now they were a pleasant place in which to spend an idle hour.

The prince was not idle. Every day he rattled up and down the plain, in a cloud of dust that rumbled after him like a burning fuse. Once he had driven past, the surveyors closed in behind him. They charted roads, streets, avenues, palace sites, temples, shrines. Masons built cairns wherever he imposed a building. It must all be done with enormous haste. Here would be the Great Temple. Here the Official House of the prince, here the private residence. Between them, spanning the road, would be the balcony of audience. He absolutely insisted on a balcony of audience. It was from it that the god would dispense favour, so he designed it himself.

And who was the God?

He was the God.

This had been revealed to him so suddenly, that he did not have the time to doubt it. Yet he was not without humility. He was not, it was quite true, literally the God. But he was the physical embodiment of the God, who was of course invisible, and in the absence of the actual deity, he was prepared to represent Him to the best of his ability.

No more was Meryra expected to deliver oracles. Yet the poor man began to lose weight and add to his wrinkles, since if anything, to receive oracles was even worse than to have to make them up, for now he was expected to fulfill them. He was given a corps of labourers and told to build the Great Temple at once. The prince paced out the dimensions himself, stalking over the rough rubble of the site, while surveyors and stonemasons followed immediately behind him. Everything was to be white. Everything was to be sumptuous. And it was to be built in a great hurry.

Then it was Tutmose's turn. He was to direct the sculptors, all of them. And it was necessary to have images of the Queen. Tutmose must do Nefertiti as soon as they returned to Thebes.

It was the last thing in the world Tutmose wanted to do. He did not want to direct the works. He wished to be private. Let Bek or Auta supervise. They were both good men in their own fashion. Eventually he got his way. He would provide only the prototypes, from which the other men would work.

Tutmose sighed. Very well, then. He would do Nefertiti. In a way it would be a challenge to his powers. Being a woman, she would be more difficult to flatter than the prince had been.

They returned to Thebes, leaving Meryra and the workers stranded in the middle of nothing. He had two years to build.

Tutmose could only await developments. The prince had left Thebes an impotent fool. He returned a fanatic of genius, and a fanatic can neither stop himself nor be stopped. He moves too rapidly to be stopped. Willy-nilly, he goes on to the end of the night, and if he be a demagogue as well, then he will draw the world after him.

Unfortunately the prince was no demagogue. He had nothing on his side but absolute power.

Five

While they were away, Nefertiti had given birth to her third child, another girl, to be called Ankesenpa'aten. Tiiy pretended to dote on it, and was delighted, and Smenkara found himself a person of new importance. She was planning the throne to the second generation. She had only to be patient to get her own way. Nor did she think the prince would impede her. She had only to reach around him to grasp the reins of government again, a gesture perhaps awkward, but which would do nothing to imperil her grip.

All this she would do, she was convinced, for the good of the country. She had always ruled for the good of the country, even when Amenophis had been well enough to rule for himself. She believed firmly in the altruism of her own acts, and she took it for granted that Horemheb would believe in it too. Ay, of course, was different. Ay believed in nothing. Nefertiti was also different. But then Nefertiti had no power and so did not have to be reckoned with.

Tiiy made two mistakes in all this: Nefertiti was not in the least interested in the good of the country, she was interested in herself, and so anything done for the good of the country left her totally unmoved, particularly if Tiiy happened to be doing it. And Ay, though he might not believe in anything, really was concerned about the good of the country.

Nor was Tiiy any longer dealing with the prince, but none of them could know that, so the mistake was understandable. She was dealing with somebody nobody had ever heard of before, named Ikhnaton, who though outwardly still the prince, was inwardly the earthly representative of a minor cult figure who had unexpectedly seized absolute theological power. In other words, the god of the family had been turned against them all.

Not knowing this, Tiiy was trying to persuade Horemheb to bring the army back into some sort of alignment with the Amon priests. The prince had caused a rupture there, and if the breach was not healed, the political consequences would be serious.

Horemheb refused.

She gazed at him open-mouthed. She simply could not believe it. She had long ago seen the decay of any sexual passion between them. But she had taken his loyalty to herself for granted. He had never swerved before.

There she was reasoning, for once, as a woman. Loyalty had nothing to do with it. Horemheb was as fond of her as ever. But he was also Commander of the Armies, and if the army could diminish the power of the Amon, that would be to the advantage of the army. In this matter, whatever he might think of anything else, he was on the prince's side.

She complained to Amenophis. Amenophis merely chuckled. She sent for Ay. Ay in turn pointed out that there was so much unrest in the Empire that the army was essential to the collection of taxes, and that though the breach between the prince and the priests of Amon was certainly serious, a little skill and tact might heal it. Nefertiti had great influence over the prince. He would speak to her about the matter. He then took courteous leave and went to pay his court to Nefertiti, who, to tell the truth, bored him.

Tiiy shook from head to foot with rage. She sent Horemheb away, when he tried to see her, and told Amenophis that the army was disloyal. Amenophis said blandly that of course it was, for the army was a professional group, and professional groups are always disloyal to everything but themselves. And there the matter ended.

Rather than have Horemheb fall into Nefertiti's circle, Tiiy felt it her duty to call him back into her favour. Besides, she was lonely. Inevitably her own court had begun to shrink, and she needed the reassuring presence of someone who was fond of her. However, she made it clear that they would never be on the same footing again. Horemheb scarcely noticed. He thought she looked old and made a special effort to be agreeable. Besides, Nefertiti frightened him, whereas Tiiy might almost have been his mother.

As for the nature of that footing, unwittingly Horemheb made it as clear as she had. For they spent the night together, and he was very tired. He was young and vigorous and she was getting older. He tried to cover up his lack of enthusiasm as well as he could, but alas, though we may lie, our bodies cannot. When he left they both knew they would never lie together again.

When he had gone, Tiiy had all the lamps in her apartment lit and did not stir out of her quarters for five days. Nor did Horemheb care for the way Nefertiti now smiled at him, as though she knew something about him that he did not. He avoided her as much as possible.

It was at this moment that the prince returned.

He was much too busy to see Tiiy. He refused to see her. He was even too busy to see Nefertiti. He had disappeared into a flurry of architects, builders, engineers, and experts of all kinds.

Nefertiti was not in the least discomposed. Meryra had sent a courier to tell her what had happened, and in this she saw the chance she had been waiting for. If he was now a god, then she would be a goddess. But that meant work. There would be no more children until she had the situation well in hand. She must be with him night and day. And she was not without her sources of knowledge. Infusions of male fern, rue, sabina, and ergot of rye would keep her barren. As for the rest, Ay, whose duty it was to provide all these experts, and Horemheb, who was as quickly called upon to round up journeymen labourers, were in a position to tell her what was going on, though they did not know why. But having Meryra at her command, of course she knew why.

For it turned out that the prince needed someone with whom to discuss his plans, his gorgeous plans. Ay would not do. Horemheb would not do. Tutmose was merely a commoner. Besides they no longer had the time. But Nefertiti could discuss the plans of a temple all day long.

She not only could, but did, and so strengthened her hold over him. In return he gave her titles. By the time Tutmose came to take her portrait, she was Great Royal Wife, Divine Spouse, The One Who Walks in Beauty, the Divinely Favoured by the Sun Disk, and all the rest of it. Being both humourless and witty, she did not find it difficult to persuade herself that she was all these things. It put her in a position to dispense favour, and she believed that by favouring those whom the prince favoured, but a little more, she would win them to her side. Therefore she would favour Tutmose.

All in all, two people less inclined to like each other it would have been difficult to imagine. Their meeting was a distinct shock to each of them. For they had only to meet to know they saw through each other instantly. They had no choice but to get along, and to avoid each other as much as they could.

Perhaps one has been unfair to Nefertiti; for at bottom one feels very tender towards these people who have no tenderness, in the same way that someone who loathes cats may still be deeply moved by kittens.

With nothing to sustain them but their ambitions,

and unable to relax for a moment, they are the most pitiable when they are the least tired. They have to get on with each other, for there is absolutely no one else in the world they can talk to. There are even times when they would like to be nice. But on the whole, that is when one should trust them least. Then, at last, just when they feel most secure, they wear themselves out and are abruptly defenceless human beings again, with no one left to turn to, since they have turned away from all those who would have been their friends years ago.

It was better on the whole to be Tiiy, and be warm while one could, than always to go through life in this state of cold self-defence. The prince had no warmth either. They were together two over-bred cats, so highly refined that they could not breed with anyone but each other.

Tutmose thought that she must be very lonely. But she was also a woman. He knew better than to present her with an image of herself as she really was. Whatever she thought she was, she would rather be pretty.

Therefore he would make her pretty.

To tell the truth, he was angry. He did not like the way she looked at him. It threw him off his stride. It made him savage. He would rather have talked to her than to the prince. She was more subtle. But precisely because she was more subtle, they could never talk.

Tutmose had never been in love. He had never found anyone complicated enough to evoke the emotion. For the more complicated we are the more difficult it is to find anyone capable of holding our attention, for people of an equivalent complementary complexity are rare. For simple people, love is a physical necessity. But for complex people, a physical necessity is no more than a symbolic act. As they must have the most pungent sauces, so must they have the most esoteric charm in order to be charmed, for they do not really eat the sauce. They savour it, and get their nourishment from it almost accidentally. Your gourmet is always a trifle underfed. It is only your glutton who bloats. Your true hedonist is an ascetic. For such people, the necessity comes afterwards rather than before, and for that matter may never come at all.

Yet something was happening under Tutmose's fingers, something he detested. Perhaps he worked better than he knew.

No more sittings were necessary, he said. He found he did not want to see her again, just now.

If anything, she looked disappointed.

He smiled. That she should do so, was a point in his favour. But he was mixed up with these people, and he did not wish to be. He had only wanted to watch them.

That night he sat alone in his courtyard. She had reminded him of certain things. It is all very well to say we are artists. It is a form of self-delusion not far removed from that of the religious hysteric. We know that, too. But if we are artists, a good deal of our lives is spent at a window, looking out over the moonlight city, alone, wishing someone were with us, yet knowing we could not tolerate anyone with us.

For of course what we do and believe is quite silly. It is only what we could do and could believe that is not. And so we glimpse it alone, at the window, looking over the sleeping city, because we know that what we call understanding in this world of men and women is not understanding at all. At best it is merely concupiscence compassionately disguised as the will to oblige.

It is for such reasons that one makes images and is an artist at all. For though other people have all sorts of reasons for living, the maker of images has only one, his images.

He must have sat there until well on towards dawn, when the sky began to shimmer with the quick, convulsive, metallic glitter of the throat of a humming-bird.

At dawn he went back to work, and a week later, when he was adding the polychrome, Nefertiti came unexpectedly to the studio. She looked at what he had done.

"How do you know I have to smile like that, without moving my lips?" she asked.

It was the detail no artist can ever resist the impulse to include, the one that ruins his pretty images.

"What smile?" he asked.

"You know what smile. I think perhaps your statues never look the same twice."

When he looked, she was right, and he thought he had been so clever, to secure his own position with a pretty image. With that smile he had ruined everything.

"It is only a trick of the light," he said uneasily.

She shrugged. "No. It is a trick of time." She looked at the statue. Long, slim-necked, and a little impossible, it was still a queen.

"Is this the way he wants to see me?" she asked at last.

"Yes."

"And doesn't he see what it is?"

"No."

"So that is what he means by truth," she said.

He looked at her with some interest. "Truth is anything. Truth is only a lie we want to believe in."

"Why?"

He did not want to answer. "You are not satisfied with it?" he asked.

She looked at him oddly. "What do you want, Tutmose?"

"I am a sculptor. I like to sculpt. And sculptors must eat."

"Oh, you will eat," she said. "You will do me again."

She tapped the bust. "But on one condition. Keep this. Put it high on the studio wall, on a shelf, so it can look down on you. You see too much. Let it see you for a change. You please the prince, but you are only a sculptor. I think you sometimes forget that. I shall not."

She did not seem exactly angry, but at the door to the studio she paused. "Do I really look like that?"

"It was the way I saw you."

For a moment there was the ghost of a warm smile on that face. "I think we understand each other," she told him. "It is a pity. We could have been friends."

Then she left. After she had gone, he did as she had told him. He put the statue high in a niche in the wall, and knew it would travel with him everywhere. For she had caught him out. He had only wanted to flatter her. Instead he had caught the serene bitterness of that curious smile. For that she wanted to punish him, and he saw no reason why she should not be allowed to do so. He even found it agreeable to be punished in such a fashion.

Yet perhaps she was glad he had caught it, for that smile was what she had become. It was the one thing that made life worth living, the almost invisible smile of that ultimate defeat, success. And it was as a loss that he had shown it, though perhaps even he scarcely realized that.

Meanwhile the smile went off to play with the prince. After all, this serious game with God was to last for ever. He even had intimations of immortality. And in that case, everything had to be well planned.

Unfortunately, though we may be immortal, our bodies are not. Another member was therefore added to the intimate circle, Pentu, a physician, a dull, odious, cringing, raven of a man, but one who did keep the prince well. He was someone else for Nefertiti to deal with, until she saw there was neither good nor harm in him. He was interested only in medicine.

94

Meanwhile, even a mystery play requires an audience, and for this, too, the prince had made his preparations. He saw more of Horemheb these days.

Nefertiti did not altogether care for that. Since he was as complex as she was, she knew she had nothing to fear from Tutmose, except knowledge. But Horemheb was a relatively simple man, and simple men are dangerous. Besides, she found him physically too attractive. She was not without curiosity. He was her mother's lover. He must know a great many things about Tiiy that could only be repeated in bed. Yet he was so uneasy in her presence that his demeanour was an unconscious form of flattery. She was younger than he was. She found it very pleasant to treat him like a child.

He was in truth a scrawny bear with puzzled eyes. But honesty is always treacherous, she thought, since it refuses to obey either its owner or us.

As for Horemheb, his respect for the prince had risen. He had only to look at that precocious face, the full, moist, eager, unweaned mouth, the sad and dangerously sparkling eyes, and something androgynous and shockingly naked about the features, to see that here was no man and no Pharaoh. But on the other hand, he had only to listen to that hypnotic and elaborate voice, to be aware of something that was the more powerful for not being quite human. It was very easy now to believe that the prince knew something the rest of the world did not.

Nor was it correct to say, as Tiiy said, that he had no grasp upon reality. He was, on the contrary, quite clever. He merely held reality from the opposite end to the rest of the world. Now he proposed nothing less than to hand the country over to the army and Horemheb. It was a dazzling offer and Horemheb took it.

It was not necessary to tell Horemheb everything. It was sufficient to make him believe that together they were making an effort to free the throne from the domination of the priests, by means of the army. If Horemheb wished to assume that the throne would then be dominated by the army, that was his own concern. We all need our illusions. The prince recognized that.

With Horemheb so easily won over, it was only necessary to suborn Ay. That was even easier. For without the army there would be no taxes and revenue, and without taxes and revenue, there would have been no Ay. Besides, Ay had gently opposed the Amon priests for years.

There remained the courtiers. Ay said they would be difficult to win over. The prince merely looked at him out of that distant face and smiled. He proposed to enjoy himself immensely. He had put up with the shrugs and smirks of the palace cabals for too long. Now he proposed to break them by the simplest of all possible means. He had watched them for years, and if a god be also a little cynical, it does give him a certain advantage over the devout. For in looking over the heads of the worshippers, he knows what they really believe in. One then knows how to make them more seemingly devoted.

First he summoned Meryra back from Aketaten.

Then he held a public audience.

A joke in good weather is certainly much better than a joke in foul, and the day was excellent. Horemheb had provided a well-behaved crowd, and the natural cupidity of the Thebans could be relied on to do the rest. It seemed to him the cream of the jest that Tiiy should also attend, with Smenkara. This idea had actually come from Nefertiti, but then Nefertiti often did have entrancingly amusing ideas.

It was his first appearance as the new god, but this he had carefully kept to himself. The balcony of audience was at the front of the palace. It was not so fine as the one that must by now be almost ready at Aketaten, but it would serve. Tiiy was already there when, in a cloud of fan-bearers, guards, and musicians, he and Nefertiti appeared at the end of the tall, narrow corridor that led to the balcony stairs. Trumpets blown in that constricted space were deafening and Tiiy was given to migraine. Silhouetted before them, she quite perceptibly winced.

Hand in hand he and Nefertiti came down the corridor. He was very happy. He was smiling. Nefertiti gave his hand a conspiratorial squeeze. They looked like enchanted children.

With a particularly shattering blast the trumpeters swept by Tiiy and out on to the balcony, followed by cymbal clangers, sistrum shakers, and six particularly high-pitched harps. Tiiy looked pale, but her face was commendably expressionless. Nefertiti tugged at her skirt, gave her mother a bland, distant smile, and walked up the stairs and out into the dazzling, theatrical light of heaven. The first item on the programme, as it almost always was, was a well-rehearsed cheer.

The prince looked down with considerable pleasure. It had been given out that he was to reward his loyal followers, and as a result the courtiers were assembled directly below him, somewhat puzzled, no doubt, by a small knot of nobodies with whom, quite clearly, they had no desire to mingle.

They would not be nobodies much longer.

Horemheb and Ay were also in that expectant crowd. Tiiy looked surprised, and the prince decided to improve her expression. They were rewarded with gold collars for loyal service to the Aton.

It was a type of service of which she and the crowd had never heard, but of which they were to hear much more. The collars were handed down from the balcony. The prince caught in Ay's eye a distinctly speculative look, and the man's lips twitched with amusement. It

97

never did to underestimate Ay. In his own way he had a sense of humour, which certainly improved his posture. Horemheb's ramrod posture was utterly humourless.

There was a brief pause.

Below him he could see the round, sweaty, complacently expectant face of Ramose, Tiiy's court chamberlain, a sixty-year-old place-seeker who was always rewarded at these occasions, as a matter of course, and who had in consequence grown quite rich by doing absolutely nothing. This enviable condition he owed entirely to the fact that his uncle was not only High Priest of Amon, but highly respected for the regularity with which he emitted, decade after decade, a thin diaretic stream of harmless moral apothegms. At his age Ramose must find the duties of court chamberlain a burden, and out of compassion if nothing else, it was a burden the prince proposed to lighten.

It was time to call forward the nobodies.

To Pa-wah, the son of a petty scribe in the foreign office, of whom nobody had ever heard, two hereditary titles, the office of Superintendent of the Royal Harem, one-tenth of the Theban taxes on barley, and a tomb at Aketaten at Pharaoh's expense. For services to the Aton.

To Meryra, a nobody everybody had forgotten about, High Priest of the family cult, one hereditary title, eight honorifics, High Priesthood of the Aton in Aketaten, with Pa-wah as his assistant, a tomb at Pharaoh's expense, for though the prince did not find the building of tombs a happy subject, still, everyone wanted one, High Priesthood of Aton for all Egypt, the estates and their revenues of eight villages in the Delta, a palace in Aketaten, and forty bars of gold. For services to the Aton.

To Pentu, Royal Physician, the lucrative post of Superintendent of the Granary and of the Cattle of the

Aton. A particularly humiliating rise to power, since he was the son of a keeper of the Theban necropolis. Chancellor, also, of Northern Egypt. For services to the Aton.

To Huya, Harem Superintendent to Tiiy, and inseparable from her, out of sheer mischief, a tomb at Aketaten, to which his body was to be carried after his death, forcibly if need be. For services to the Aton.

To Hiatay, a building contractor, the extremely high dignity, reserved for nobles of the first rank, of Fan-Bearer on the Right Hand of Pharaoh. For services to the Aton.

To May, an obscure priest at Heliopolis, a cousin of Nefertiti's chief hairdresser, the titles of Prince, Royal Chancellor, Overseer of the Soldiery, and Bearer of the Fan on Pharaoh's Right Hand. For particular services to the Aton. Behind the scenes, he had brought the priests of Ra at Heliopolis into line. Temple rents and benefits would follow.

And last, but most delightful, to a minor official under Ramose, Nakhtpa'aten, who had been so good as to change his name to something cognate with the new god, all Ramose's offices, the gift of a large house in the South City of Aketaten, and a tomb at the royal expense. Ramose's burden was at last lightened. For splendid services to the Aton.

To the nobles loyal to Tiiy, nothing.

He looked down at them delightedly. Already these nobodies were somebodies. It vastly improved their appearance. It gave them an assurance they had lacked before. And to underscore the lesson still more firmly he was now ready to issue his proclamation.

No longer was he to be known as Amenophis, son of Amon. Now he was Ikhnaton, the glorious son of the Aton. A glorious sun which in this case would set on Amon utterly. He had not forgotten that dark Holy of Holies. He never would. And Nefertiti, too, was to have a new throne name. From now on she should be Nefer-neferu-Aton, co-existent with the god, the female aspect of the Divine Principle.

Even Tiiy has never climbed so high. Nefertiti's smile was if anything more gracious than ever, and her slim arms writhed gracefully in benediction from the balcony.

Against all protocol Tiiy left the balcony at once.

It was further stated that in four days the birth of the new god would be celebrated at the Aton temple. Four days should be enough. When men are confronted with decisions affecting their self-interest, they are apt to act rapidly. He was quite sure the nobles would turn out in force.

The next day news was brought to him that Tiiy was closeted with the Amon priests. It angered him, but she could do nothing, so long as the army was loyal to him, and he had seen to it that it would be.

The day after a riot broke out in the stonemasons' quarter, Horemheb squelched it at once. Perhaps it even had value as an object lesson.

The day after that a gang of Amon priests pelted Meryra with mud, as he drove through the city.

That was a different matter. That was an act against Ikhnaton's appointed prophet. The Amon priests would have to be taught a lesson. And he knew what that lesson would be. But first it was necessary that the service at the Aton temple should take place, and take place, moreover, in an immense display of military pomp.

That cautionary ceremony did not proceed without a certain sense of strain. Only within the white walls of the temple, open to the sky and bathed in blinding light, was it possible really to relax. And though Meryra had been given a heavy guard, he could scarcely stumble through the service for cowardice. However, it did not greatly matter. They would not be in Thebes much longer, and in Aketaten they would all be quite safe.

Surrounded by his new court, Ikhnaton paced through the ceremony with pleasure, with Nefertiti beside him. He was delighted to see that more than half the court was there. No doubt there were a few diehards, who would prefer to live in error. Tiiy was welcome to them. As for belief, belief is very like marriage. One undertakes it for the most practical of reasons, and then, if one is not utterly incompatible, one grows fond of it after a while, He quite understood that.

The ceremony over, the party retired to the palace. For a month now they would pack. And packing unnerves courtiers as much as it does any other kind of household pet. They do not want to be left behind. Their sense of security destroyed, and therefore too anguished to plot, they do everything they can to please, and do not breathe easily until they are safely installed in the new quarters.

Even Tutmose packed, but more calmly. He had been careful to accept neither dignities nor titles. He was going only because he had to follow his subject matter, placidly eager to see what would become of it. He was an indispensable part of this new world, for it was he who had given it a face. Nevertheless the expression of that face would be its own, and to find out what that expression would be, he would have to take its death-mask, too.

Tiiy was stranded. For Ikhnaton had an advantage. He was portable. Whereas all the wealth and splendour of Thebes, its temples, tombs, and the vast responsibility of its necropolis, was rooted down. It would become provincial, as soon as he sailed away from it.

He was not ready to sail away from it just yet. There was still one last thing to do, before he could rest easily. Even a god of light is not secure until he has destroyed the powers of darkness. The army would not support him in this. So he did not bother to ask the army to do so. He went instead to the grave robbers of the necropolis. They were the suitable men for what he had in mind.

And when they told him that what he had ordered to be done had been done, he believed them. For it never occurred to him that what he ordered to be done might not be done. Not only was he god. He was also Pharaoh. For two thousand years Pharaoh had been obeyed. Absolute power so long maintained naturally assumes that to give an order is the same as to see it carried out.

Besides, had he not heard the sounds of rioting by night, and a vast wail over the buildings, a lament for the destroyed god? That at least was convincing.

He forgot that priests are the best of actors, having but one role to perfect. He had ordered these grave robbers to penetrate to the Holy of Holies and smash that horrible black, brittle god into a thousand pieces. It had been done.

But the priests were wilier than that. Distributing an ample bribe to the assassins, they had merely rolled the god away and given out that it had been destroyed. For though gods die, the priesthood goes on for ever. It always survives the god it pretends to worship and it always will. Priests are of necessity cynics. Unlike divinely inspired persons, they know that men are mortal, and with a little care can be made even more mortal yet. So they could afford to wait. The new god was physically frail and limited to one mortal body. When he had died they had only to roll the old god out again, to regain their power.

When Tiiy heard the news of this supposed destruction, it sobered her. She had thought Ikhnaton had merely been playing. She was resigned to ruling Thebes in his absence, until he or somebody else came back.

But now she was nonplussed. "My God," she said, "he believes it."

She was quite right. He did. It was now too late to stop him. Alone, she could only patrol the shore, in an empty palace, with a dying king.

The court was sailing away.

In its own way that was an unique and a glorious event. It was something that had never happened before in history. Dawn rose like a glass curtain on that scene. An orchestra was absent, but does not dawn have its own sound? True, the music of the spheres is something we no longer believe in. If stars make a noise, we feel it must only be like the whirling of a gyroscope. But the harmony of the world is something to which we always return, after each period of experiment, the ground base of our existence, on which we improvise.

For listen to silence for a while, and you soon discover that mere sound is nothing but a vulgar substitute for what music ought to be. With what ultimate capacity does silence give meaning to the small and furtive, as well as to the loud, sounds the world can make. Restive, the boats squeak down at their berths in the harbour. In a rusted ring a rope lifts against the echoes of all dead voyages. A stone expands. A chorus of frogs provides the ornament.

Almost unnoticed, the vast arpeggiatura of light flies out from the sun until it fills the sky. Then, slowly, as it dies away into every nook and cranny of the sky, from here, from there, from everywhere, a vast chorus of reflections states the theme of day, and vanishes in its development, only to reappear, inverted, at evening, when the work is done, and the world gives way to the stately choral movements of the night.

It is an enormous work, this harmony of the world. It can get along without us very well. Wherever one enters it, one is always at the beginning. One did not hear it five minutes ago. One cannot remember, though one has heard it all one's life, what it will do next, for it has not done it yet. Always the same, it is yet always new. Concerted, it is yet diverse. It has a beginning and an end we think. And yet, like music, it occupies not time, but space. It is always simultaneous. It is always now.

It is as though a vast net were cast out into eternity, of which, at each instant of its falling, each knot, and yet the whole seeming pattern of the knots, were now. That net is not only music, not only silence, not only light, but also history.

So all history is one unique event, while in the sky over Thebes, that three thousand two hundred years ago, the voice of silence, which after all must issue from some image in our minds, raises a compassionate and warning finger to the lips, as a warning, as a friendly sign, or as an order to be still, it would be hard to say. Yet we are used to that sad face with the finger to the lips. It is always there, to tell us where we are, and we are always grateful for the advice. But few of us would wish to repeat the name of that place, even were we able.

At dawn Thebes was an empty shell. From a great height the temple of Amon, that vast and overpowering complex of irrational damp symmetry, looked small and pathetic. The colossi of Memnon were a pair of startled rabbits, flushed, at the instant before they turned and fled.

But down by the quays along the river, sails billowed out, voices shouted, and in an enviable disorder of departure, a hundred and fifty boats put out into the main stream, caught at the current to pick up speed, and with the instinct of rotifers, ciliated the water all one way. To the music of harps, the shouts of strokers, the clamour of hoisted sail, the fleet got under way. It was as though the guests at a party should, with the entertainers, migrate on impulse to a house they had never seen.

Gold, gilt, and ebony, staring statues on the tillers, of himself and Nefertiti, silk sail and jewels, flowers, perfume, and incense, that vainglorious flotilla moved off. If some looked back, in a moment there was nothing for them to see. With an almost audible sigh, as the oars dipped through the flaccid water, Thebes seemed to fall behind, and there was only one way left to look.

"My God," Tiiy had said, "he believes it."

He did, and the god was going home, to a home as new as he was, which he had never seen, but from which he had vowed never to stir, and where he would live for ever and ever.

Meanwhile, it was pleasant to have this vast concourse on the water, with a hymn to the Aton, which in a way was himself, sung every dawn and evening, and Nefertiti beside him more amusing than she had ever been. Truly, there is nothing so delightful as eternal youth, particularly when one is twenty-eight, and so knows how difficult a thing to keep is youth, and with what care one's youth must not be contradicted.

In Aketaten there would be no one to contradict.

Part Two

Six

This matter of age is as important in a city as in a man. If one feels young, one is young. The rest is merely a matter of keeping up appearances. When people angrily ask you to act your age, what they usually mean is that you should act theirs. Here at Aketaten there would be no more of that.

The fleet had been on the river for ten days, and Ikhnaton was eager to catch the first glimpse of his new capital. He did not expect it to be finished, but he did expect a rough sketch, much as Tutmose never blocked out the figure himself, but let apprentices do that to his design, so that he might improve the details at his leisure.

And a rough sketch was exactly what he got. Aketaten was an imposing fraud, designed chiefly to be seen from the water. He wanted to arrive there at dawn, so he and the sun would both animate it at the same time. Therefore the night before arriving the flotilla anchored around a bend in the river. Now it was under way again. He did so hope he would not be disappointed.

Nor was he, for appearances, to him, were reality. As the boats rounded the bend the courtiers looked west, and saw only a barren desert, planted here and there to garden vegetables. They should have looked in the opposite direction.

For there, sleek, white, and smooth, lay Aketaten. It was exactly as he had imagined it, but a little smaller. From the quick intake of her breath, he could sense that Nefertiti was impressed. He smiled knowingly. It was agreeable to show them what he could do. He almost wished Tutmose were beside him; for it was all very well for Tutmose to pride himself on his ridiculous little faces. They were of merit. But he, Ikhnaton, had made a world. That was what the sun could do.

Indeed, given gypsum and whitewash to reflect from, the sun could do a great deal. Seen from this distance, and newly faced, the city did not look jerry-built. It looked poised and self-contained. Seen from the water, the jetties seemed hungry for boats. Behind them rose the blue and green gardens of the palaces, with here and there a white shrub. Beyond the palaces themselves rose the roofless white bulk of the chief Aton temple, its pinions snapping briskly at tall golden poles, against the angry rose of the cliffs.

A crowd had been assembled to welcome them. As the royal barge floated into the royal jetty, there was Meryra, backed by a corps of priests, the army, and the police, waiting to receive him.

He and Nefertiti, together with Ay and Horemheb, went at once through the gardens and into the cool white and polychrome high-ceilinged rooms of the palace. Here they would rest, before crossing the balcony of audience, in actuality a bridge, to the official palace where the nobles would receive their first audience in the new capital.

Meryra had become officious in his new security. And how would a god look at a priest? Much as a judge would look upon the attentions of an overly zealous recorder. Ikhnaton sent him away with an indulgent smile. There are times when even a god wants to relax.

Aketaten was really delightful. Even the servants were new. Except for Ay and Horemheb, there wasn't a person there to remind him of the past. He had finally found a solution to the awful boredom of rank, or so he thought. One made the rank higher still. He was not the first nor would he be the last monarch to become a god out of ennui. For the gods must have some amusements. It is only necessary to find out what they are.

To its rulers, the world is an occupation. Inevitably one's small talk becomes overly professional and therefore dull. But to its gods, the world is an avocation, and any hobby is in itself entertaining. To a god, the world has all the intricate joys of a scale model. One is always installing new improvements here and there.

He looked at the city with animated eyes. It was simply wonderful to have so much to do. What Horemheb and Ay thought of it all was another matter. They did not say. Probably Horemheb saw that the workmanship was poor and Ay that the surface was rich. The only thing to break the silence was their own voices and the roaring hunger of the animals in the well-stocked private palace zoo.

The zoo had been Nefertiti's idea. She could not move about without a zoo. Ikhnaton found large wading birds restful, and was not unresponsive to the leap and plonk of fish. Nor were monkeys to be despised. He esteemed especially the cynocephali. Now nothing must do but that they look at the menagerie.

Horemheb found it disturbing. Amenophis and Tiiy had also had their raree show, but theirs had been a matter of keeping wild animals in confinement to listen to them roar. Here the principle was somewhat different. This generation was more subtle. It had learned that though one cannot clip the tiger's claws, one can give it a manicure.

No one had seen Nefertiti so animated before, except possibly Ikhnaton. That face she carried before her like a shield, was now burnished by a genuine admiration. At long last Horemheb had found out what interested her.

For Nefertiti collected the greater cats. Ten or twelve

feet below them, among the persea trees and the syca-mores, they roamed sulkily at their leisure. One had only to release a deer among them, or, if one felt capricious, an ostrich, to see them race. Alone, disdainful, bored, but sleek, resourceful, and quite dangerous, there were the lion, the lioness, the lynx, panther, and ocelot, and that was what she liked, the way they moved and the way they did not move. She used them for purposes of study. How to move, how to be beautiful, and more than those, how and when to think, and how to re-arrange oneself with great care, at the exact moment when it was time to strike.

She turned to Horemheb, her lips drawn back from her teeth, and said something, he did not exactly hear what. But for once her eyes were unveiled.

The expression in them made him thoughtful. He had always regarded her as a silent, unreliable, and selfish girl. She was nothing of the sort. She was an enormous force, quietly waiting in the wrong body, which none the less she turned to her own purposes with fantastic guile. The smooth muscles under her lovely neck moved with the same involuntary purpose as those of a cat who has patience and so can wait for hours for the one particular sparrow that, out of its vast boredom, it has decided to find edible.

Beside such skill, Ikhnaton was merely ingenuous. It made Horemheb feel both anxious and tender for the man.

The time had come for the first ceremony at the Aton temple. Proceeded by sistrums, they passed down a long corridor which made a right-angled turn and opened into a small square room gorgeous with animal frescoes, from which a ramp led upward towards day-light.

The atmosphere had changed. The zoo was for her. This was for Ikhnaton. And watching her also alter, Ay, in his turn, could see that, yes, this was exactly the religion a cat would like, clear, bare, ceremonial, and centred squarely on itself.

They passed up the ramp. At the top was a large room painted to resemble a grape arbour, floored with lapis lazuli, and with three windows on each side, the centre ones large and with low sills.

It was the balcony of audience, curiously like a Holy of Holies turned inside out. It was from this elevation that the new god wished to be seen: Ay looked out the window, wondering how the god would look from the street. Ikhnaton also paused.

But the city was still so new, that there were not enough people to see him from the balcony and from the outer enclosure of the temple at the same time. The street was deserted. For a little way, in either direction, it swept smoothly by the palaces and temples, and then petered out into a confused mass of vacant lots, stone cairns, and naked scaffolding. So much crouched silence was somehow mocking.

They went down the ramp on the other side and into the temple.

The nobles were assembled on either side of a long ramp leading through the outer court to the pylon at the farther end. To them these ceremonies were a novelty, and a courtier without a protocol looks lost indeed. They were waiting to see what Pharaoh would do.

Unfortunately they were doomed to disappointment. For Pharaoh's nature as a god was threefold. He was the incarnation of the God, and thus holy and to be worshipped. He was the image of the God, and thus symbolic. But he was also the God himself. And what the Father has to say to the Son, when they are both the same person, is entirely a family matter. The gods themselves worship before a mirror, *en famille*.

The priests chanted laudatory hymns, which the nobles echoed with a nimble mumble. Floral offerings were laid on each noble's assigned offering table. Then a trance state descended with luminous immobility upon the royal faces, which it had to be confessed Ikhnaton did very well, and Nefertiti even better. They were now inhabited by the Father. There was a judicious, even a shocked, silence. Then, to the rhythmic sussuration of the sistrums, followed by one sonorous beat on a shoulder drum, the royal party moved forward.

It was undeniably impressive. Even Ay had to admit that something did happen. Quite visibly the royal pair had changed, and quite visibly they did look like two aspects of the same thing, whatever the thing was. But who could say what the thing was, for to catch a fluid you must first have a cup. It was decidedly unnerving to see the same person before you in two bodies.

Because of the nature of the god, the construction of the temple at the second pylon was something never before seen. At the entrance, he must have appeared after the drum, stood Meryra. There was nothing godlike about that face. It was affable, human, and safe.

Perhaps Meryra had never seen the double god before either. As Nefertiti and Ikhnaton swept forward, his face underwent a rapid alteration, in which confusion and fear gave way rapidly to unctuous gravity. No longer was he the host of the house: he became the previous owner, allowed to stay on in the servants' wing.

It was, thought Ay, a remarkable performance. Even he felt slightly unnerved by it.

In most temples the avenue of progress led straight and without impediment to the inner shrine, the Holy of Holies alone being concealed from view. But here, since Ikhnaton was in his third person, a large wall of masonry made an L-shaped baffle which concealed the inner temple from the outer world. Pride does not like to be watched licking its face.

None the less, pride needs an audience. Horemheb and Ay were allowed to follow. They descended a right-angle stair and came out on a loggia. Here they were to stop. Indeed, they were so blinded by the sudden light they could not have moved anyway.

The inner shrine was smaller than the outer, but being an enclosed space, seemed larger. Thirty-foot walls stood open to the sky. A ramp ran between more offering tables to an open altar against the far wall. Niches around the walls had yet to receive their statues. The courtyard was apparently deserted, and every inch of its exposed surface was whitewashed and unadorned; but flecks of metal had been ground into the whitewash. The surface of the far altar was of silver. The effect was that of a glaring crucible, hot enough to melt the eyeballs, and in this white fire, for even the flowers on the offering tables were white, the top of the altar was an incandescent core. From the blue-green sky overhead the rays of the sun poured down like invisible hands.

As a study in aesthetics it was overwhelming. Ay, who had played with mathematics all his life, was deeply moved. But physically it was unendurable. The idea that Pharaoh could go where no one else dared to venture was amply underlined, and was even, in some unintelligible way that not even mathematics could demonstrate, convincing. Physically it was incredible. But as a glimpse into the unsuspected vastness of a singularly ingenuous mind it was absolutely staggering. For mathematicians are apt to underestimate the non-figurative abilities of those without mathematical training. If Pharaoh could show even this much, what on earth was it, beyond the farthest limits of his mind, that he saw? It was as though one leaned on a balcony at the end of being, to watch something that stirred beyond. It was so far away that even there few people could so much as catch a glimpse of it.

It was all very well, in one's capacity as family advisor, to deplore Pharaoh's childish approach to practical affairs. It was equally possible to take his religion with a grain of salt, and to make use of it, as Horemheb did, politically. But this was a concept and an ability far beyond the limitations of religion. To affectionate loyalty, Ay now added something close to awe.

The trouble was Ikhnaton did not even know he had such power. Given the proper mental tools, he could have changed the world. But for that kind of thought there were no tools, and so all that power was frittered away on an unconscious religious mania. That made Ay angry.

Beside him Horemheb grew restive. To Horemheb, no doubt, this was only a light that hurt his eyes. At the altar Nefertiti and Ikhnaton took large white blossoms from a covered tray and cast them on the silver altar. They shrivelled brown almost at once.

The royal pair returned. It was amazing. They did not even sweat. As they started back down the ramp, a chorus concealed beneath the loggia floor burst into the hymn to the Aton. Nefertiti and Ikhnaton swept by, and Horemheb and Ay fell in behind.

This was the best of which Ikhnaton was capable. The worst of which he was capable was equally embarrassing, if in a different way.

For no one minded Pharaoh's building his city. But what would be left when at last the scaffolding was taken down?

This insight was not the result of reason. It was the result of a fear so strong that it had driven him right beyond the limitations of his own mind and out at the top.

He was afraid of growing old. He was afraid of darkness. He was afraid of anything strait. He was afraid of dying. When you captured a grave robber, as often they did at the necropolis of Thebes, his punishment was terrible. He was wrapped with mummy wrappings, sometimes with his head exposed, sometimes only his nose. The wrappings were very tight. He could not move. He could only writhe. His body was smeared with naptha, which burned and ate and corroded his flesh while he squirmed and screamed. A death like that took a long time.

That was what Ikhnaton was afraid of. That was what death meant to him. Death meant being unable to move.

Thus no one was to be buried at Aketaten. No one was to die there.

It was Meryra, poor foolish Meryra, who so wanted to be wise, who brought this subject up. It was not his fault that Pharaoh had been ill and locked up with Pentu, the physician.

Pentu had been forced to tell Ikhnaton that though of course Pharaoh was glorious, immortal, beautiful, and eternally young, still there were degrees of youth, and that though the epileptoid seizures to which he was subject were in fact the means whereby his body was eternally renewed, a statement in which there was some truth, at the same time there was not much even a god could do about chronic bronchitis. He would have to rest a good deal more from now on.

So now Pharaoh slept in an immense pavilion in the garden, with lamps, attendants, and Nefertiti always within call.

As far as ritual went, as Nefertiti suggested, his burden could be lightened if she took over the dawn and evening worship. At those hours the Aton is weak, yielding, compassionate, and feminine. Pharaoh could thus gather his strength to carry on the worship from ten until five in the afternoon, during which hours the sun is strong, vigorous, powerful, and masculine. The suggestion was adopted, and gave her much power.

But it was as Pentu left that Meryra entered to bring up the matter of the royal tombs. It was untactful of him.

The courtiers had by this time settled down. Those Ikhnaton had ennobled already had their houses at Aketaten. The others, with their palaces as yet unbuilt, lived in light tents or on the hospitality of the parvenus. There was nothing else for them to do, for they were courtiers. What else would they do, where else could they go, but at court? Therefore, willy-nilly, they had been forced to build, if only to get free of those parvenus whose hospitality they found so galling. The city was full of palaces now.

But as a courtier has no choice other than to attend upon Pharaoh in this life, so must he crowd for place in the world hereafter. It was true, Pharaoh had promised them tombs out of the royal bounty. But could they rest comfortably in their tombs, if Pharaoh's was not there near them?

It was a very serious matter.

Ikhnaton refused even to consider it. Nefertiti had to take the argument in hand. She explained to Pharaoh that since, as the Sun, he was the source of all life and renewed himself every day, he was also the source of the life hereafter. It would be necessary only to change the formula of mortuary inscriptions. Instead of a prayer to Osiris, a humble petition to Pharaoh asking for that eternal life he alone was capable of giving would solve the problem. Seen in this light, the tombs were not tombs at all, but only personal temples to the god himself. Ikhnaton agreed, but only on the condition that nobody should ever be buried in them.

Being a woman, Nefertiti was content to let the matter coast, but took care to choose the chief courtiers from among those who were reasonably young, healthy, and vigorous.

The matter of the royal tomb was somewhat more

difficult, but she managed it in the same way. It was to be excavated up a far gully, and Pharaoh wished to hear nothing more about it.

Therefore, since Pharaoh was absolute, he heard no more about it. But now the matter had been brought to his attention, he solved it in his own way. The priests of Amon, of Osiris, of Ptah, and of Isis, even of Ra, made an immense revenue out of death. It was their chief industry. He forbade it. If there was no more death, why build tombs? In Thebes alone thirty thousand mortuary workers, embalmers, guards, architects, painters, sculptors, priests, attendants, day labourers, and officials were cast out of work. The following riots were inevitable. So were the plots, the counter-plots, the intrigues. In Thebes a rabble of five thousand pulled his statues down, while Tiiy stayed in the palace and said nothing. Horemheb and Ay urged caution. Revelation, said Ay, must come by degrees. Order, suggested Horemheb, demanded that more troops be shifted from the capital.

Ikhnaton refused to listen. Aketaten was not restive. The people had no choice but to obey. He had only to stand on the balcony of audience, to see how loyal the people were. Besides, they were going to have their portraits done, and Horemheb and Ay must come along.

Horemheb and Ay did.

These drives through the city were Ikhnaton's principal recreation. The chariots stood ready in the courtyard. Nefertiti and Ikhnaton stepped into the first one, Horemheb and Ay into the others. The royal couple was almost naked. It was the new impertinence. But it was entirely logical. If god stands revealed, then he can scarcely wear clothes. Nefertiti shimmered beneath the most transparent of muslins. Ikhnaton wore an opaque kilt beneath which his genitals had the colour and confusion of the nest of a trapdoor spider. Was he not the generator of all things? There should be only a thin veil over this mystery. Nevertheless, they both wore the pschent, for majesty, god or not, never gives up its crown.

Tutmose's house and studio were large, for not only is asceticism prudent, but it knows how to make itself comfortable.

Ay looked around curiously. As far as he could tell, the man had no private life, and yet the house was full of presences, and of an odd, peaceful, yet obscure vitality.

Tutmose had not changed, yet somehow he had managed to become imposing. It was something about his face. It had very little expression, yet somehow it had become the total of all his works. It resembled anything he looked at, and also something else. It was that something else that was unnerving. It had the look people have when they are watching us and unaware that we are watching them watch, a look as though somehow they weren't in their own bodies any more, but ours.

It was as though he, Ikhnaton, and Nefertiti, without liking each other in the least, shared some secret, or perhaps only different parts of a secret, that no one else knew. Individually you might have understood it, but when the three of them were together, the whole thing became an enigma.

But there was a clue. In some way, Ay saw, in some very disturbing way, they all had the same smile.

Perhaps that was not so surprising.

For every artist, even the most depressing, or, as the case may be, what is even less attractive, the profound, for when will people learn that profundity is no more than a cleverly concealed set of false bottoms designed to return one to one's initial superficiality, has a never-never land of his own. And his popularity depends not upon the depth of his message, the skill of his fingers, or the resemblance of his works to whatever need may be crying on that particular day, but quite simply, upon whether or not his never-never land happens to be a superior version of one's own.

So the appeal of the profound artist only shows us how superbly we should suffer, if we wanted to, and could at the same time remain untouched. For the most touching image is the one that leaves us essentially untouched. That is the ultimate flattery. It was also the secret of Tutmose's grip upon their emotions.

He knew how to show them as they thought they looked. He had, quite unconsciously, even though he made use of the skill, the ability to show them beautiful in the midst of the most dolorous distress.

Since they did not see the significance of what they did themselves, they could scarcely be expected to see it as he reflected it back to them, and this was his margin of safety. That was because they still saw his portraits as portraits. It never occurred to them that they were in themselves little more than animated symbols of their own beliefs, and if it occurred to him, it was a knowledge he deemed it wiser to share only with posterity. Let them have their little now. It was all they were up to.

But he found them charming. He had amused himself by doing all of them.

There they stood in the studio, heads without bodies, in a precise row along one wall, Ikhnaton, Nefertiti, and the three children. The effect was not altogether agreeable. It was as though someone had made the same thing over and over again out of less and less material. The head of the youngest princess, Ankesenpa'aten, was little larger than a persimmon.

Ay wondered why he thought of a persimmon, when this little head was of green stone. He glanced up at the opposite wall, feeling that someone was staring at him.

It was that bust Nefertiti had insisted that Tutmose

keep. It was set high on a shelf. It could not possibly see anything. Yet Ay did not like the look of it, nor the way Tutmose and the Queen exchanged what looked like, and yet was not, a smile.

With a shrug Tutmose turned their attention to the new work in the centre of the studio, under the light that poured down from an opening in the roof. The statue thus seemed to be in the act of rising into a column of light. It was an uncanny effect.

It was a statue of Ikhnaton, kneeling, or rather, caught in the instant before rising straight up. His head was raised. His arms were also raised, as though the light were helping him to his feet. The belly and thighs were full, the back covered with fatty tissue, like the back of a middle-aged woman. The expression of the head was precocious. The statue showed that moment at which the light was about to revive him.

Ikhnaton inspected it with the same look with which Nefertiti studied the great cats in the garden. So then, as Nefertiti drew some sort of knowledge from animals, Ikhnaton came to Tutmose to be fitted with gestures, as though with artificial limbs.

Ay glanced at Nefertiti. Remove only the breasts, and the two of them had the same body.

Quite suddenly he understood something, which was the secret both of their charm and power. It was sexual, in so far as real sexuality is beyond either sex. It sips at both, but partakes of the nature of neither. That overwhelming directive force which in most of us pushes each sex on towards the confluence of both in middle age, was to them something they rode on, a cart on a double track. Thus they could use a man's weapon against women, a woman's weapons against men, and goodness only knew what they did to each other. But seeing the world in their own amorphous image, of course they could not possibly know what the world was like, since the world is divided and can only be one sex at a time. It explained a great deal about many things.

This curious androgynous power had one serious limitation. It could not reproduce itself. They could only make sexless, infertile copies of themselves, such as the royal princesses. No wonder they had to stay young, for they would never have heirs. They could only die. The knowledge of that must make them a little desperate.

Ay glanced quickly at Tutmose, and saw that, yes, this was indeed their secret, and that this was what Tutmose knew. But knowing someone else's secret is not the same as having to live with one's own. Ay felt oddly compassionate. At least Tutmose could make images.

Ay also looked at Horemheb. As far as he was concerned, Horemheb now had an importance he had not had before.

When the royal party left, Ay stayed behind. There was a flicker in Tutmose's eyes at that, but he said nothing. He busied himself around the studio.

"I want you to take my face," said Ay.

Tutmose hesitated and then nodded. "I have always wanted to."

"But you would not do Horemheb, would you?"

"No one has asked me." Tutmose stared at him gravely. "But you are right. I would rather not."

It was what Ay had wanted to know. Nor did he expect any answer to his next question, not, at any rate, in words.

"Why are you doing it?" he asked.

He could see that Tutmose knew perfectly well what he meant. "It is my subject."

"Yet you are only a man."

Tutmose took up a pat of clay. "An artist seldom finds his subject matter. I am very lucky. For an artist can have nothing else, you know. There is nothing else he can have. For he is always a little more than himself, and a little less than a human being." He began to build up the clay.

"And I am a little more than a human being and a little less than myself, I suppose." Ay looked round the studio at the overwhelming sadness of those faces. "Don't they ever frighten you?"

"When I am frightened I sit in the garden. What else can a man do?"

"Then you admit you are merely a man."

"Oh, we were all men once," said Tutmose. "But who can remember when?"

To that Ay had no answer. For it was true. He could not remember when. And like Tutmose, no doubt, perhaps he was no longer sure that he wanted to. It was quieting. For it meant he could only be added to the gallery, as the last of them, and that made him what he was already, a very old man.

"So I am the last," he said.

This made Tutmose angry. "Everybody is the last of something," he snapped.

And there they let the matter rest.

Seven

As a result of this visit, Ay sent Horemheb back to Thebes, on a trumped-up errand to the royal estates.

It was five years since he had been Tiiy's lover and swam so delightedly across the royal lake. That self was gone, even though he had not had the leisure to notice when. Tiiy was now a woman of almost fifty, and a woman of fifty, moreover, without a lover. She had aged.

Yet her skin had only tightened round the bone, and was if anything firmer than ever. It was something inside her that had aged, not something external.

Thebes, half-deserted of favour, was an unwieldly place. It had fallen into a series of armed camps, the priests of Amon undergoing one kind of siege, and those in the royal palace another. In the palace they were barricaded against time.

Amenophis, though approaching the business as slowly as possible, was none the less dying, and that, as far as those in Thebes were concerned, made Smenkara the heir.

The plight of that royal child was not enviable. Tiiy made the same mistakes with him as she had made with the other one, the criminal of Aketaten. Smenkara was growing up in a world of eunuchs, women, and one old man.

Yet Tiiy was clearly pleased with him. He was febrile. He was amusing. He hunted ducks in the gardens with a toy bow and arrow. He had respect for ritual. He accepted the Amon priests as a matter of course. And though he could not help developing a certain sense of his own graceful self-importance, he was extremely good at his lessons. It was perhaps a pity that he was too frail to attend the royal military academy, but then that could not be helped.

However, his frailty was a source of worry, so Tiiy was determined, despite her age, to make one last attempt to produce a male heir before she reached menopuase.

Amenophis had given her this idea. He had sudden spurts of energy, like the twitchings of a dying rabbit, and she had humoured him so long, she saw no reason not to humour him in this.

It did not seem to her ungainly. Not only did she love him, but that love had become a habit. But she could not be sure she would become gravid, for he was very weak. It might be best to make sure, so under these circumstances she was eager enough to receive Horemheb.

He found the palace disturbing. It was cracked and dusty, and much of it had been allowed to fall into ruin. The sedges had grown thicker in the lake. He was not so difficult as she had imagined. He was now a man of some consequence in the Empire. He had been fond of her once, and their quarrels were behind them. If this was what she wanted, he was quite willing to do her the favour. He only wished she would not try to cast a romantic glow over the proceedings.

"What is lost?" she asked. "Only our ability to love each other. Apart from that we are totally unchanged. We can still relive old times."

He found that horrible.

"We shall have no new ones, so we may as well make do with those," she added lightly, and saw she had appalled him. She had forgotten. He was still young. "It is such a pity", she said, "that our bodies grow older than we do. You have no idea how that feels."

It satisfied neither of them, but at least it was done.

She even told him why it had been done. That shocked him, but he said nothing. Instead he made much of Smenkara.

He did not altogether like Smenkara. The boy was too girlish and too soft. But he played with him out of duty, hoping his own presence would be a good influence. He even took the boy hunting and to military reviews.

Unfortunately Smenkara was reserved and shy. There was no way of getting at him, and Horemheb could only do his best.

As a matter of fact, or so it seemed, he had already done his best. Nine months later the child was born, a male, named Tutankaten, at Ikhnaton's request, but that could be changed later.

Amenophis was delighted. His almost toothless mouth broadened into a grin. The child was a testimony to his vigour. "Now I shall be remembered," he said. "That's something." He poked at the tiny curled hands, like fern fronds, and looked at Horemheb and Tiiy with relief. To him the child was a sign that he would not die for a long time.

It would have been difficult to say why such a ruin of a man should be so intent upon living. Perhaps it was because he was a realist, and had seen too many men die to want to repeat the process himself. True, there was the promise of eternal life, but he was Pharaoh. He knew that promises are often broken.

Looking down at Tutankaten, Horemheb knew that it was not his child. He was relieved. For of course it would take after Tiiy, as all the royal children did. There was something in her too dominating for any man.

Of this even she seemed uneasily aware. As she watched the child she looked frightened. "I don't like the way they look at you," she said. "As though they would remember you later, when they were big enough to strike back."

She also could see it was not Horemheb's child, and she had been trying at the last moment to break the pattern of a dynasty. So of the three of them, only Amenophis was pleased, and perhaps Smenkara, flitting unnoticed through the garden. Smenkara was by no means averse to having a younger brother over whom to tyrannize, and had his own ideas of power.

"If the son accepts what his father says, no plan of his miscarries," say the instructions of Ptah Hotep. Unfortunately Amenophis III had never said anything to his sons. They were thus cast adrift.

Of this Horemheb was aware when he returned to Aketaten. He found the atmosphere there subtly changed, he could not quite say how.

The truth of the matter was that Ikhnaton was having one of his occasional fits of boredom, that temporal vertigo with which the spiritual so often have to contend. The building of cities was beginning to pall. Of this Nefertiti knew nothing, so she was unprepared for it, with the result that he was left most unwisely alone. They had all become so clever at managing his illusions, that they forgot that he sometimes had real thoughts as well, and these he confided to no one. And there are moments when even our illusions turn into illusions, and we are left indecisive, with nothing more substantial on our hands than reality.

It was in this mood that he took to wandering at night about the gardens, and would often come to one of the piers out into the Nile and stand there for a long time, looking up at the stars. For something was missing. Being a god was too easy. There must be something beyond godhead, then, which could somehow be reached. But what?

Whatever it was, it sounded rather like a distant music.

For there are some sad little melodies which do not exist in time. Instead they throb in space. They come from nowhere, and one never realizes they existed until after they have gone. They glitter like sudden stars, but they are tender for all that, and they make us want to cry.

So we go to the terrace, lean our cheeks against the furry whitewash of a column, and wish that things were otherwise. Where is that missing thing?

Look, there it is now, and it falls like a star. And stars are an omen. They presage great events. Yet when the awaited event comes it fails to satisfy. And, like the comet, it may not return again until long after we are dead, so we have missed our only opportunity to see it. Or perhaps we fall asleep. Dawn comes. The sun flows gently over our closed eyes. We smile in our sleep, for there it is again: the little melody. It was not after all so sad. It was the only happiness we ever knew, the one we knew we knew only afterwards.

So one looks at the stars and wonders what to call them. For since nothing has a name, what then shall we call it? Whatever we call it, it is difficult to suppress the impression that there is something up there rearranging all the pieces, so that one comes back to play the same game on a constantly shifting board that looks, but is never quite, the same. But that something is certainly not a god. It is only something that does not happen to share Man's opinion of Man, and teases him the way we would tease a snail, merely to pass the time.

It is better, realizing that, to ignore the stars. Better far to love the sun, for the sun makes us feel ourselves again, if those *are* our selves.

Unfortunately the sun does not shine twenty-four hours a day and in particular it does not shine on loneliness.

But the moon, shining down on the pools in the garden, showed him, at last, the approaching figure of the Queen.

Eight

By this time she thought herself invincible.

And why should she not? As the second most important person in the Empire, she was the source of power and favour. She had her court. She had made herself indispensable to Pharaoh while at the same time keeping her thoughts apart from him. She knew every nook and cranny of his mind, he of hers only what she wanted him to know. Therefore she could afford to be gracious.

She overlooked one thing, which was, that though women, like cats, enjoy boredom and derive great strength from it, men do not. So she did not try to feed his interest. She merely tried to provide diversion. It was a fatal error.

None the less, for a little while diversion worked quite well. For a little while, and a little while only, it usually does.

She knew he was annoyed that Tiiy had had another son. Equally she knew he did not want a son. Yet she knew she must try. He was not so strong as she. Immortality was all very well, but he could not live for ever. So there, in the garden, she seduced him. It was not very difficult to do.

But there were too many distractions. The boats creaked at the jetty. The stars seemed to have a frictional smell. The shrubs and bushes rattled. When he was nervous, sounds were louder to him, she knew, and more full of danger. It would not do there in the garden. She persuaded him to go to the new palace, at the southern end of the town, where he had built a pleasure lake in miniature, much like that at Thebes.

Here they would spend the day and the night on the water.

She was mistaken to attempt to hold him by sexual attraction. She soon saw that. For physically they got along so well that they bored each other.

Their sexual relations, indeed all their relations, were a form of vampirism. They sucked each other dry. But from being exchanged so often, that energy had weakened and run down. Even when she was attempting to excite him most, and with success, she could feel boredom underneath her finger-nails.

And watching her, from that infinite distance which prevented him from ever forgetting himself with anyone, he saw her bald head, for she had removed her wig, and wanted to giggle. He had at last discovered the terrible joys of having mental reservations about things about which we seem to have none. But he did not realize yet that she was as bored with pleasing him as he was with being pleased. Really, the royal masseurs were as efficient and moved him as little. And the very fact that she could arouse him, against his will, made him the angrier with her, since he hated to do anything involuntarily.

Still, in a way she succeeded. She was with child again. She was to be with child three times more, and they were all girls. By her he could have nothing but girls, and meanwhile in Thebes Smenkara and now Tutankaten were patiently waiting.

It did no good that after each birth she explained that they did not need sons, being as they were invincible and eternal. It was all nonsense. Of course he was eternal. But that would not prevent him from dying. He could not very well be eternal without a son. He began to watch her. It was something he had never done before. He had only looked at her, as one would look in a mirror, to admire.

When she sat with him on that double throne, to

receive the court, she had a special way of running her pink tongue around her gums, and her small, regular teeth were intensely white. It was a gesture he had watched on those cats she kept in the garden. And when they appeared at the balcony of audience, almost naked, to accept the plaudits of whatever nobles were to be rewarded for nothing in particular that day, he could not help but feel now, as she put her arm so casually around his waist, with what extreme care she arranged her hand and fingers, always to look her best. And having cleaner, sharper features, being physically more in focus than he, even when she hovered in the background, it was she who dominated the scene. In a sheet of highly polished marble, the sheathe of a column, he had noticed that one day. It was not amusing. Also she saw too much of Meryra.

She saw all this, or sensed it, it disturbed her highly, and after the birth of each catastrophic girl, she tried to amuse him. But what could she amuse him with? The only thing that amused him, apart from chariot driving, was the fine arts. They went off to see the glass-works.

But there, again, they always had to come back from seeing the glass-works, and there were times now when he would not see her. That worried her. He said he wished to be alone with his god. But that was sheer impertinence. She knew there was no god. It was almost as though he were becoming tired of her, and at the thought of that she panicked.

In this way another two years went by. One speaks of them as though they were alone. On the contrary, they lived in the midst of great pomp, saw three hundred people every day, and were under the constant vigilance of their domestics, any one of whom might be a spy and probably was. For that matter, even the servants had their own spies. The butler bribed the tiring woman to learn what her mistress would eat that day, because the chief cook bribed him.

And really, now she was beginning to feel trapped in it, this panoply was inexorable. She was tired of these eternal trumpets and processions. The sistrums now sounded like a thousand scorpions angrily sliding down a greased chute. And it was quite dreadful to have only one hymn to the Aton. It could not be cut, it could not be speeded up, and it was endlessly long. She had not listened to it now for three years. She stood there, graciously sweating in the furnace of the inner temple courtyards, where one did not even have the distraction of an audience, and recognized only certain phrases, by which one knew the ceremony was one-eighth, one-third, one-half, two-thirds, three-fourths, seven-eighths, and so on over. The last section in particular was virtually unendurable. The fraction counting then became very fine. In the morning worship, which was hers alone, she at least introduced the mercy of a sunshade. This was stored for her at the entrance to the inner shrine, and of all the secrets kept from Ikhnaton, it perhaps was the best kept.

She sensed that he should not be left to himself, and yet ceremonial swept her away from him. Someone should be with him in the morning, for in the morning he brooded. But as the Great Royal Wife she had to undertake the sunrise oblations. By the time she returned to the palace, he was already preparing for the noon service; and after the noon service they both had to appear in audience, at which nothing could be said of a private nature, after which they separated to change for the evening service. And after the evening service came the evening entertainment.

And since he had set up the convention that in public they must always appear fanatically devoted to each other, even now when they seemed to loathe each other, they still had to keep up the pantomime of being devoted, gracious, inseparable, fondling, and always smiling, with the added irritation that the father of his country must always be surrounded by his six daughters, who were playful as rabbits, and if they did not scream, squeaked, which was equally unsettling to the nerves.

She would beam at their flat sexless little bodies and hate the sight of them. She induced them to be acrobatic. It was just possible that under some severe physical strain, a pallid set of male organs might unexpectedly plop down to save both her and the dynasty.

It never happened.

Nor did they like her, and she knew how vengeful royal children could be. Maketaten was Ikhnaton's favourite. She preferred Ankesenpa'aten, as being more tractable. Meritaten, the eldest, hated her, and the other three were too small to bother with.

So she went on smiling and waited for some chance to speak privately. Nowadays she had headaches and her eyeballs hurt. Never mind, she must go on smiling. The evening entertainments were apt to go on far into the morning, since Ikhnaton did not like to be alone at night. Sometimes it was three or four before they were over.

Once they were over he would lock himself up with Pentu. For Meryra had faded into the background. A god can dispense with a high priest, but with his doctor, never. Even Osiris, after all, had had to be picked up and sewn back together again. Pentu held the keys of life and death. Sometimes he was closeted with Pharaoh for hours, and at those times no one else was admitted.

The god might be ageless, but Ikhnaton was now thirty-four. It was becoming increasingly difficult to keep him young. His chest was weak and his bowels uncertain. He was much given to flatulence and to falling down. A fit, being little more than divine inspiration, was harmless. But a persistent hacking cough was another matter.

These days he lived chiefly on meat and fruit and an emulsion of water, cinnamon, and honey. He simply gorged on meat, of which he was fond, in particular on that coarse-grained joint cut from the thigh of calves, cooked with the bone exposed at each end, as a sort of double handle. Unfortunately fowl, the approved food of invalids, merely made him vomit. The thigh cut he could keep down, if he swilled enough honey and water, but he did not chew properly, so the meat increased his flatulence. Also so much meat eating gave his breath a dreadful stench.

She could not help averting her face, sometimes.

And more than anything else he made her angry. He had almost ruined her body with six daughters, and now he would lie with her no more. Her touch seemed to revolt him.

Had no one ever told him how revolting his own body was? He was like a slug with legs. The face, it was true, being like her own, though disturbing, and given at times to a slight dribble from the mouth, which he could not control, and which embarrassed him horribly, was beautiful. She was twenty-eight. She was much younger than he. She took good care to be. When her cosmeticians had worked all day, and she was in a good humour, she might still have been fifteen.

Alas, the dawn service of the Aton was too early for the application of cosmetics. And the sun in that inner courtyard was mercilessly bright. Without make-up her skin, she could not help but notice, looked coarse. As she lifted her wrist, to cast flowers upon the altar, she could see how wrinkled the skin had become at the wrist and knuckles. It was not much, but she had only to look at her children to know that it was not youth, either. And the bright glare from the walls made her squint. The Aton was giving her crow's-feet. Her maid said not, but alone at her mirror she counted five. Her breasts, too, needed more massage than formerly. They felt lighter, and yet the skin was loose. And though she had managed her pregnancies capably, the striae along her belly were unmistakable.

It was appalling. It was also unfair. She was still beautiful. Was it her fault that she was no longer a child? Did Ikhnaton actually believe he was still twenty? Did he no longer look in any mirror? In need of reassurance, she turned towards Horemheb.

Now that Ay had taken him up and the two men were friends, Horemheb had become a better courtier. He went through his paces with the bored finesse of a favourite pupil, but only when his presence was required, for he still took his army duties seriously. She let it be known that she was worried about disorders in the northern part of the city, the quarter over which she presided. True, two in the morning was perhaps an odd time to become worried about such concerns, but it was the only time she could be certain that their meeting would not be spied upon.

Reached by a long frescoed hall stretching north from the palace was a compound of buildings used only for larger public entertainments. It had not been occupied for a month, and was now safely deserted.

Preceded only by one serving girl, a deaf mute with a lamp, she threaded her way through the darkness, and came at last to the great hall, a room perhaps eighty feet long and forty wide, supported every six feet by a wooden column. On each side aisle a row of raised fishponds supported water-plants, now in flower, and these brushed against the marsh life murals.

Here she found Horemheb sitting on a dining couch with his legs spraddled, gazing down at the pavement by the light of four or five gently hissing lamps.

No doubt it was a pavement of absorbing interest. Indeed it was a masterpiece. Along its edges dogs and cats hunted fish and game through an endless series of sedges. Down the central path alternate rows of painted Asiatic and African captives waited to be walked on. In the deceptive light of the lamps their rolling white eyeballs rolled more than ever. But masterpiece or not, he should not have gone on looking at it rather than her.

At first she thought he was stupid, since that was always her first thought about anybody not obviously clever. Nor could she very well throw herself at his head. As a matter of fact, she could not even see his head, for he kept it lowered. She sat down, but it was she who had to do the talking.

So she ploughed ahead, discussing what she wanted done in the northern suburb. She called for wine. She even became a little rattled. For she was strongly attracted to him. She caught herself trembling. He had a by no means disagreeable smell, and he was certainly healthy. She saw his biceps, where the light from the lamps caught them. They were not so developed as those of a professional wrestler, but they were very fine. She wondered how it would feel to be held by them. Besides, to have Horemheb attached to herself would make her position at court much stronger.

Having been given a problem to solve, he went on talking in that even, deliberate, slightly puzzled voice of his.

"Must we go on talking about that," she demanded at last.

"I thought that was what you wanted to see me about," he said, and gave her a quick glance, before looking down again. "I wonder if a painted captive is the best an army can do any more."

It was ridiculous. She caught the undertone of quiet amusement in that voice, and for some reason it made her blush.

"Don't you know why I asked you to come here?"

"I know the reason you gave," he said. His hand paused for an instant, holding its wine cup.

Irritably she swept the wine cup to the ground. The lamps flickered in the unexpected draught and then were still. The dark-brown wine spread over the faces of the captives, but here and there the floor must be oily. Over those places the fluid parted and the eye of a captive showed through.

"Men would sometimes like to make love to me," she said, to her own surprise.

"I can quite believe it," he said easily. "And were you an ordinary woman, no doubt they would do so. May I go?"

It was almost as though he had slapped her. And yet instead of making her angry, it made her sad.

"Yes, go," she said, and watched his retreating back. The hall was empty. She sat there until the lamps began to splutter, and then made her way to the garden. She would cross it to her own apartments, and the night air might restore her calm.

The question was, would he speak of it? She was sure he would. He had always hated her, and not everybody can refuse a queen. It would make a good anecdote in barracks.

Seeing a figure slip out of the Harem wing, she went forward to challenge it.

It was Ikhnaton. He would not speak to her. He brushed right by. In her own apartments she soon found out the reason. He had been making his own experiments in the harem. He had got farther than she, only to be humiliated the more. Without those special skills she had developed to rouse him he was impotent. It was quite certain. He could never have heirs.

She had the girl sent away. In the morning, however, when she would have talked to her further, the girl was missing. No one was ever to hear of her again.

In the same week, without comment, he gave orders that the painted banqueting hall was to be shut off from the rest of the palace and boarded up. That really disturbed her. No doubt Horemheb had talked.

Yet it was a pity to shut off that hall. It was the first step down, the first sign that the glorious and eternal reign was shrinking.

Two days later he sent for her. It was unexpected. He wished her to participate in a ceremony at one of the public altars, in the desert between the cliffs and the town. She could scarcely believe she was taken back into favour, and yet she seemed to be. Perhaps he was lonely. After all, he had to talk to someone. His voice even became a little animated, as they paced down the double line of courtiers on either side of the carpeting which led to the altar.

She watched his intent face and it made her thoughtful. She had made a mistake. After all, they had been married for almost ten years. She could not be girlishly attractive for ever. Therefore maybe theology was the better way to hold his attention. Certainly nothing else ever had.

It happened she was right. Ikhnaton had turned back to the only fascination he had ever known, the one that made his isolation not only excusable, but valid. Theology filled up the cracks.

In one form or another the worship of the Aton now took up every moment of the day. It had to, if Ikhnaton was to be kept from thinking. Every moment must have its ritual purpose, to conceal the fact that it had none of its own.

The household rose at dawn. No household in the city but had its obligatory altar. Pharaoh worshipped standing up, and sat down on his throne only in order to be worshipped. He went to the temple early, for he took some amusement from arranging the flowers. He did not do so himself, of course, but he liked to stand near by and tell others where to put them and how.

There were now four fixed religious ceremonies a day, each of which took two hours, not counting the morning and sunset services, at which Nefertiti presided alone.

It made life very difficult. True, one could talk to Pharaoh along the route, but just as it seemed he might give some definite answer, the pylon was reached and he vanished alone into the inner shrine.

In such circumstances those with private petitions were forced to make use of Meryra or Nefertiti. It enhanced both their followings. Meryra had as a consequence grown quite rich, and therefore now had many enemies. He had also been foolish enough to deputize too many of his offices to his chief assistant, a man called Pa-wah, with the result that Pa-wah also had a petty court around him, and was only waiting for the chance to make it a larger one.

If anyone wished to speak to Pharaoh directly, as Ay and Horemheb did, the only way they could do so was to become as devout as he was. Up and down the avenues, the approaches, the ramps they would ceaselessly move, while secretaries came and went with despatches that somehow never did get delivered, for at the moment when they were to be delivered Pharaoh would always dodge into the inner shrine. Nor did he give an answer when he returned, for his worship was a form of sunbathing, and who can give a clever answer when his head is addled by the sun?

They were waiting now, Horemheb and Ay, for Pharaoh to leave his inner shrine. The religion was no doubt sublime, but it was not without its embarrassments. Ay believed in making unavoidable burdens as light as possible. For this purpose a sceptical curiosity made an excellent fulcrum. But the effect on Horemheb was less pleasant. He had no scepticism. He could only remove doubt by pushing against it with his full weight, which was tiring.

Ay did not wish to see him tired. He had great plans for him. He wished him to conserve his strength. Therefore, as he had to all the others, he became adviser to this man, too. For though his real career seemed to be to outlive the dynasty, this man would almost certainly outlive him.

It was a pleasure, given those circumstances, to be congenial and kind. Besides, Horemheb sometimes surprised him by the possession of quite a different kind of nimbleness, the kind that would be needed very soon, the practical.

But right now Horemheb was grumbling and restive. "I am surprised," said Ay. "For can't you see, that the Aton is intensely practical?"

Horemheb could not see it.

"But you must at least grant it is all very innocent and charming."

Horemheb saw nothing of the sort.

"But it gives him something to believe in, and that in turn gives the court something to believe in. So in a sense it prevents anarchy. And since they do not understand it, they cannot be sure what would happen if they ignored it, so they believe it, and so keep out of mischief."

"But it's ruining the country."

Ay shrugged. "The country is ruined already. This makes it easier to pick up the pieces when the time comes, that's all. And since he would not do anything about the country in any case, perhaps it is as well that he does this. Besides, he does believe it. He is quite sincere."

Horemheb gave him a suspicious look. "And I suppose you believe it, too?"

Ay smiled slowly. So much hard-headed honesty was inconvenient. He did not want Horemheb to say an incautious word and so fall from favour. "It is as easy to believe in one thing as in another. As for what one really believes in, who knows? Who would believe in it, if it were not a mystery?"

To his surprise Horemheb seemed to find this entirely intelligible. It was for much these reasons that one believed in the army. But still, he did not trust Ay. "What are you trying to tell me?" he asked.

"To have patience, for your own good. Believe in it while it is still here, for you will never be able to believe in it once it is over. And besides, in its own way it is rather grand and beautiful. Allow yourself to admire beauty for a little while."

"Beauty threw thirty thousand rioters from the cemeteries into the streets of Thebes."

"Undoubtedly it is a powerful force," said Ay amiably. "But then its reign is comparatively brief. And a commander of the armies out of office is as helpless as an adviser with no one to advise."

They looked at each other for a while.

"Yes," said Ay, and glanced towards Pharaoh, who was leaving the inner shrine. In his eyes, as he watched that fluttering white figure, there was a remote but loving pity. For Pharoah was alone with his god, and no man should ever be wholly alone with himself, for of all things, the self alone is undeviatingly pitiless.

However, it is also remarkably clever. Its immediate duty was to cure Pharaoh of doubt, and Ay could see that there was no doubt that it would succeed in doing so. Observing which, and also the way in which Horemheb and Nefertiti avoided each other, he even found it possible to feel sorry for the Queen, though not much.

For really did the Queen not know what was wrong with her?

Apparently not. But Ay, whose medical knowledge

was if anything better than Pentu's, and whose admiration of beauty was none the less sincere for being tacit, felt profoundly sad for her.

So, in his own apartments, did Pharaoh. For Ikhnaton, though he might be blind when it came to himself, saw the rest of the world all too clearly. He never underestimated a motive, or a fleeting expression in a courtier's face, and so, though one deplored his stupidities, it would have been a mistake to under-rate his grip upon those whom he saw every day. Who knows, had the rebellious Syrian provinces been under his nose, he might have been able to do something about them, too, with that amazing instinct he had for playing one kind of greed off against another.

A great statesman had been lost to theology, and Ay, for one, found that good cause for relief, for unlike competent bureaucrats, great statesmen are a perpetual source of endless harm, since their greatness depends upon the degree to which they change the *status quo*.

Pharaoh had saved himself from disillusionment at the last moment, and in a quite remarkably severe way. It was a pity no one could have known how, for Ay, at least, who had had some insight into the gymnastics of which that mind was capable, would have admired the process for the contrivance it was.

The tensions of Ikhnaton's life were too much for him. He fell down in a fit. Fortunately only Pentu was with him. The fit sobered him. He called for his chariot and sent Pentu away. He knew he had to escape the palace for a while. It was about four in the morning when he left.

The sky had the pre-dawn darkness of a man who allows himself to frown before breaking into a smile. The city was populous now, but there were still many vacant places. Grandiose buildings alternated with short sand grass, and slums with unfinished avenues. The flags of the Aton temples hung limp on their rods.

The streets were empty, except that here and there a cat or a dog yowled. Under the silence ran the steady disturbing hunger of the Nile.

Beneath the late stars, the cliffs shimmered and were still. He intended to ride to the top of them, He had not bothered to dress, and the night was cool. He whipped up the horses and raced through the city like a neglected ghost or a criminal fleeing his crime. And was that not true? Was he not called that criminal of Aketaten? And for him these fits of his were a crime, since he was helpless during them. To lose consciousness, to him, was the only crime there was.

The wind woke him up. While the chariot was moving, he was always gay. He swept through the northern suburb, past the clumsy state palace Nefertiti maintained there as High Priestess of the dawn, and took the cliff road to the ancient quarries. Above him in the rock face the doorways of the unfinished tombs gaped like the blood-clotted sockets of extracted teeth.

He knew very well where he was going. He whipped the horses at a dangerous corner, the horses whinneyed, the wheels jounced at the rim of the cliff, and he laughed. Half an hour later he was on the plateau above, bouncing along the meagre patrol road from which sentries guarded the city. He could see Aketaten below him as he drove, and really, it did not seem much.

An altar had been built up here, perhaps ten feet high and approached by ramps. He stopped the chariot, threw the reins over the horses' heads, and ran up the ramp. The sky was already beginning to grow green, the stars indistinct. They went out like lamps that had used up their oil, though where, in this world, would you find an oil so pure?

On top of the altar the wind was almost a gale. The flapping of his wig and loincloth bothered him. He took them off. The wind stirred a little that incompetent thing, his penis and its hair, but he did not find that unpleasant. His power, if he had any power, was not there.

The city lay six hundred feet below him, somehow pushed up by the desert sand against the green band along the river. He could see, from here, very clearly, that those triumphal avenues led nowhere. Even the altars looked like transient bedouin tents. It was inert and lifeless down there. It was not impressive and it bored him. He turned the other way, shivering slightly, to that point on the eastern horizon from which the daylight was certain to spread. Down in the plain even the light made shadows. But here it would make none. Here they were high above the shadows, "they" being himself and his god, that merciless, abstract, dangerously dazzling, and truthful disembodiment. Yet, as the sky lightened, he knew he had to believe, and so he managed to. It was not so difficult. The mind, finally cornered, in order to survive exerts itself, and from nowhere finds the strength to leap over its ultimate boundaries. Then the chase is on again. From insanity to the water wheel, all great discoveries have been made that way. As it enriches itself, the mind moves through larger and larger rooms, and confronted at last with a wall without a door, it breaks through and makes a new addition.

For even when one has seen through good and evil, there is still a moral responsibility, that which in the world of events we call keeping up appearances, a much higher one than mere good and evil. For good and evil are only toys, invented because in order to play any game it is necessary to have two sets of pieces. To tell them apart, we colour them differently, but they are made of the same stuff and have the same shapes. Good we use for evil purposes, and evil for good, and this makes no difference, for the board will be swept clean in any case. It is the board which allows us to play our little game of good and evil. It is this which keeps up our appearances.

For such is the limitation of our minds, that a belief in nothing is, after all, and on the contrary, a belief in something. So the act of belief itself sustains us, even when we call it disbelief. For then we believe in our disbelief. So even though we have long ago seen through those vices and virtues with which others play the game over us, we are still there keeping up appearances, since without our appearances our moral critics would have nothing to play their game on. Belief and disbelief in that sense are the same thing. It is merely a matter of where one happens to be standing in relation to the board at any given moment. And since in actuality one keeps hopping about all the time, the two alternate so rapidly that to our somewhat limited vision they seem to be quite stable and solid.

Therefore, no matter how much we may be given to doubt, our belief is for that very reason quite unshakeable, since in alternating between the two we perceive they are about the same. So in darkness he was indeed the glorious child of the Aton. And besides, he did like the sun.

But at the same time, having seen the board, it made him a little weary that he still had to go on pretending to believe in the relative moral permanence of the highly impermanent pieces. For instance, such pieces as himself, truth, Egypt, and the Queen.

For since truth also was merely a matter of keeping up appearances, it too must be equally true and untrue. So like everything else in this world, its very nature consisted in its having no nature whatsoever. Like all stable contraries, truth was only a matter of keeping up appearances.

It was strange that he, who so wanted to believe in things, could do so only in this way; whereas Ay, who believed in nothing, would have been shocked to the very bottom of his tidy mathematical soul by such a system of essential sophistries.

There was only one piece he could not fit into this admirable system, whose firmness came from the fact it was so shaky, and that was death. For unlike good, evil, belief, disbelief, truth, and untruth, death, he was uneasily aware, could touch him. True, if one could believe there was life after death, then life and death became a like system of stable alternates, but he could not believe so. He had consulted the best spiritualists, but one could never be certain that what they said was true, for the best charlatans were the most convincing, the most truthful people were always lying.

Perhaps the matter was better ignored. For it was dawn, and under that soothing light, death seemed very far away, though not, perhaps, quite so far away as he assumed.

Nevertheless, while he had been so reasoning, the dawn had come. And really, dawn made reason unnecessary. The wind, by cooling his body's surface temperature, had made a change in his thoughts possible. When we are asleep this produces nightmares, but when we are awake, geometry, philosophy, and other systems to prove that the actual is not there. However, though it is not there, still we have to move about in it, and for that we must needs keep up appearances.

Now the sky was full of light. As he turned, suddenly cold, to pick up his clothes, he saw that the light had kindled against the metal disc set in the centre of the altar, and glowed there like a great blob of incandescent silver. Instinctively he shoved his hands into that reflection, as though it had been some kind of celestial *hibachi*.

Meanwhile, one of the sentries who patrolled that cliff had seen him. "Halt, who goes there?" he demanded.

Ikhnaton picked up his loincloth and wig and

stepped back into his chariot, once more holding the reins firmly in his hand, or at least, as firmly as he was able. He, too, believed in keeping up appearances. "Pharaoh," he said, and whirled back to the palace the way he had come.

So much for truth, and at breakfast it might be pleasant to play with the children, or even, in a slightly different way, with the Queen, though these days it was impertinent of her to appear in public at all. He loathed disease. Surely she must know that.

If she knew, she certainly refused to believe it. She had so many worries of vanity, that this real one had almost slipped by her notice. So she was not at breakfast. She had gone to Tutmose to be flattered. He had always flattered them. He, at least, knew she was still beautiful.

Alas, she had never realized that Tutmose's theory of beauty was not at the mercy of any single flaw, but was rather enhanced by one, since the artist knows better than to expect a perfect beauty. Only a woman would demand that.

None the less she did demand it.

He was surprised to see her so early. He was sitting on the rim of a pool in his garden, with one leg extended, eating a honey cake, while the soft green and yellow light turned blue among the leaves of the sycamores. He looked a little tired, a little old; but he stood up, smiled, and came forward to greet her, with his usual amused gravity.

What did she want?

She wanted to see her portrait, the one she had given him so derisively, knowing it was only a pretty image he had made to take her in. Now, it appeared, it was she who wished to be taken in.

If he was shocked by her appearance, he said nothing. He led her into the studio.

148

At this hour of the morning it was a shadowy place. These faces, which were supposed to be bright images of heaven, were children of darkness after all. They had always seemed deceptively alive. That was his skill. But here in the half-gloom one saw what that deception was. The serenity was only a trick of the light. Here in the half-dark one could see they were really images of pain.

The kneeling statue of Pharaoh had been removed.

She must have looked up at her image on its bracket for a very long time, and even she could not control the expression which crossed her face.

"What are you doing now?" she asked at last.

He thought perhaps it would be kinder not to show her what he was doing now. Gently he led her aside and showed her a mask. He had made it five years ago, but there was no need to tell her that. It was her own face staring up at her. She examined it with care.

"Am I no longer beautiful?" she asked.

"You will always be beautiful."

"Then why do you not make me like that," she said, with a glance towards the bust on its bracket. "Why do you have to make me like this?" She tapped the mask of five years ago. "Surely I have not aged so much."

The bitterness in her voice distressed him. But what could he say, except not to say that even as she could not repeat herself, neither could he.

"You have not aged at all," he said, and almost meant it. For in a way it was true. Her mind could not age. It could only grow disillusioned.

"You lie," she told him. "Why do all men always lie?"

It was not his place to tell her that in these matters lies were even more important to women. "Perhaps because it is a way of telling the truth."

She gazed once more at the bust on its bracket. And

149

then, it was incredible, it was the last thing he would
have expected of so dishonest and resourceful a
creature, tears came into her eyes and worked slowly
down her cheeks. She seemed startled herself. She ignored them. And out of politeness, so did he. She
turned away and left the house.

For a long time the studio was quiet.

At last he got up, parted a curtain, and looked at the
new work.

He might finish it or he might not, since it would
never stand anywhere but here, behind its curtain. It
showed her, a little older than she was now, walking
out of the stone, serene, proud, worn, but indomitable.
The eyes had the sadness animals have in their eyes.
How is it animals look so sad, since they do not think
the way we do? Really, they have not our opportuni-
ties to be sad. Yet the look in their eyes, when we come
upon them by surprise, resting, is heartrending. And
he had not lied to her. She was still beautiful. Indeed
she was more beautiful than ever, for this to him was
beauty.

It was a beauty, however, which made him angry.
Later in the day he got up on a stool and knocked her
left eyeball out of the statue on its bracket. By evening
he had a polished pip of moonstone set in the empty
place.

Why he did this he did not know, for the neck and
chin were as proud as on the day he had sculpted them.
Perhaps it was because he no longer wanted to see her
as she had been. For the Queen had glaucoma. She, the
most beautiful, had fallen victim to the most common
disease in Egypt. A fly had laid an egg in her left eye.
In another two or three months it would be as gela-
tinous and as blankly white, as the moonstone he held
in his hand.

Nine

One must understand Ikhnaton. He did have feelings. He had lived with her for ten years. But he could not help it. He loathed deformity.

She still sat with him on the throne. They were still as affectionate in public as ever. But now she must stand and sit on the other side, so that he could not see her eye.

It was one of those evenings when they had public music. There were perhaps forty people there. The hall was gay with tall stands of flowers and fruit, and the drinking had been heavy. Nefertiti seemed reassured. After all, he had not sent her away. This made her almost happy, and as a result her jaw-line was prouder than ever, her smile more austere. That was how she took happiness: as something beyond our self-control, to which we should be wiser not to give way.

The tumblers and dancing boys were replaced by drums and harpers. They came forward, to do the slow dance demanded by the strophe and antistrophe of what they were playing.

Blind harpers were essential to all temple rituals. Indeed the demand so exceeded the supply that it was sometimes necessary to blind them. They were thus, in a way, themselves holy. As with eunuchs, an operation which cut them off from life was their one means of obtaining a sinecure, and some of them had undergone it with as little compunction, and for the same practical reasons, as had the eunuchs. For what man would be whole, if success and security depended upon his disfigurement?

They had elected to sing that part of the hymn to the Aton in which all creatures sleeping and in darkness salute the dawn as the eternally renewed source of sight, warmth, and security. They shuffled in an unpleasant manner, like men edging their way down a cave with a lowering roof. Most had their eyelids shut, but some did not. One could see the empty socket or the gooey colourless mass within. But the ugliest thing about them was the silly satisfied inhuman look on their faces.

Ikhnaton could not stand it, nor would he. He stood up and ordered them out of the hall, while a muscle pulsed in Nefertiti's cheek. "I will not have cripples around me," he shouted. It was certainly shocking. In the following silence it was difficult for the guests to pick up the pieces again. Guards hesitated, and then led the harpers away, while all that silly satisfaction in their faces gave way to panic. While he was at it, he abolished them from the temple services, too. Then, losing control of himself, he went to his own rooms and left her alone there on the throne.

She found it hard to control herself.

Next day he behaved as though the scene had not happened. But since it had happened, she took the harpers under her protection, in the service of her own dawn temple. They scarcely knew what had happened. They fluttered round her like chickens bewildered by a cyclone. Nor did she find their ignorance displeasing, for those who know nothing have much to teach, and at last she had something under her control that he was afraid of.

Nor would she forgive him for that scene. It was the first time that that solid front they presented to the world had cracked in public, and since there was much advantage to be gained by taking sides, everyone at court would be there to drive a wedge.

The court might make profit out of his fear of contamination, but she knew that nothing could save him from it. Contamination is unavoidable. Only two things in life are inevitable, starvation, if we cannot sing for our supper, and death, even though we can. As the most powerful person in the world, he was in no danger of the former. But the latter was now coming much more close and very rapidly.

News came from Thebes that Amenophis was dying.

Ikhnaton kept to his own quarters, but Tutmose was sent to Thebes, no one knew why. He returned in two weeks. Ikhnaton drove to the studio at once. Amenophis was the first of them to die, and he wanted to see how death looked. He was sure there could not possibly be any resemblance between that man dead and himself living.

Here he was wrong. For death returns the features to their primal condition. Amenophis dead *was* Ikhnaton living.

It had clearly not been an errand that Tutmose had cared for. He watched Ikhnaton anxiously. The mask itself lay on a bench in the centre of the room, Ikhnaton circled the bench as one would circle a dangerous animal securely caught, yet was any snare that secure?

So this was death. It was, at any rate, death at fifty-four. It looked startled and angry, but not after all so horrible, locked up in somebody else's face and unable to get at him.

"Hold it up," he ordered.

Tutmose held it up, so that it seemed to float in space. Out of those heavy, pain-raddled features the very shimmer and cast of youth stared leanly out, the eyes stubbornly turned inward, and the mouth set to get what it wanted, yet with some sort of shimmer on the cheek-bones less easy to define, a contradiction, if one liked, of cynicism. It was a face that knew more than it wanted to know, and very beautiful.

153

And also meaningless. For no matter how long it takes to die, it does not take long enough. Death is the worst abstraction we have. What does it refer to? Not to the dead, not to consciousness, not to the process of dying itself. Not to what was, or is, or will be. It does not even have a physiology. Dying does. Decay does. But death does not, for what happens to the body after death is only what happens to a house after its tenants have moved away for good. It doesn't hurt particularly. It is the body that hurts.

The most one can say is that one watches oneself dying with a certain interest, as though one were peering out of an egg just as someone steps on it. One can hear the shell crack before it has cracked. No doubt that is what death is, a part of time that takes place outside time, a split second existent independent of duration. That is a natural death. But a sudden death must be quite different, since we have no time to get ready. Aplomb of necessity must go forewarned.

On the other hand it takes an age. One realizes that everything else in one is dead already. The arms, the legs, the emotions, have all been closed off. There is only the will left to go. So one sits and waits as though one were sitting on a chest, waiting to go off on a journey, with the horses late and the chariot nowhere in view. It is very tedious. One feels very tired. One had so looked forward to the outing. And now, despite oneself, when it is too late to change one's mind, one finds oneself asking if after all one really wants to go. For the journey is a lie. One is not going anywhere. And if one is not going anywhere, why all this fuss about getting ready? Why can't one stay where one is? Simply because one's time is up. One has either paid one's bill at the hotel or not paid it, but at any rate one's room is lost. The condemned cell is needed for another man. If you come on Thursday, people say, I'll arrange to have the coachman meet you at the cross-roads. But this isn't Thursday, and maybe the cross-roads aren't even there. One can't even get in touch with them, to say one is coming. At the last moment one lost their address.

In short, one cannot say anything about it. One simply has to give up and look the other way. Ikhnaton refused to look the other way. He had to prove himself different. He was the son of a god, and so could not die. He was not the son of his father. If his father had died, it was only because he was the son of a false god, Amon.

He did not like the way that mask caught the light. He asked Tutmose how he had taken it. And then he asked Tutmose to take a life mask of him.

Tutmose hesitated. He knew Pharaoh's claustrophobia. He had always wanted to take his life mask, but had not suggested doing so, out of prudence. But now he shrugged his shoulders. To understand a thing, in this case Pharaoh, it is necessary to judge it by its own standards, not by ours. And not being a fanatic, but an urbane man, he did want to understand it, even though, trapped in that plaster, Ikhnaton might panic and so turn against him.

"Lie down," he said. He inserted two straws into Ikhnaton's nostrils, smeared his face with grease, put gauze over his eyelids, and began to apply the plaster. Ikhnaton trembled, but said nothing. Tutmose did not like what he was doing. It was always interesting to see which part of their faces his subjects most clearly identified with themselves. Some took the whole process with equanimity, but most would flinch and grow rigid when the plaster covered their mouth, their nostrils, their eyes, or even, in one case he could remember, their cheek-bones. He would have expected it to be the eyes in Pharaoh's case.

It was not. It was the mouth, the mouth that gave him the voice to command.

The plaster was all applied. He looked at the body, the shapeless thighs, and the big belly. It occurred to him that perhaps Pharaoh was tubercular. His chest was so meagre. It now rose and fell convulsively. The room was still. The only sound was the laboured suck and hiss of air in and out through the straws.

He bent over. "You must keep very still," he said. "The plaster is warm, but later it will grow cool and seem to tighten and grow heavier, as it contracts. Nothing can go wrong. I will wait here. It will take perhaps half an hour. Keep your eyes and mouth firmly shut, and try to breathe shallowly."

He went to his workbench and honed a chisel. Then, aware that something was happening, he turned round to watch.

Pharaoh's body was rigid, as though tensing itself for some ordeal. Tutmose frowned, and put his hand on Pharaoh's belly. It was taut beneath its fat. The head jerked upward and Pharaoh turned on his side. Tutmose flipped him over, but the straws were crushed. He was having a seizure. Inserting his finger-nails hastily under the chin, Tutmose ripped off the mask.

The face glistened with grease and was utterly expressionless. Yet at the same time it seemed to smile. The body contracted again, the mouth gaped, but a sort of animal scream lost in the throat was followed by some kind of inner struggle. It was a body. At the moment there was no one inside it at all. Still holding the mask, Tutmose backed away. Then it was over. The body lay still, and slowly the breathing came back, at first very fast, then very slow, and then, with a final convulsive twitch of the body, more regular. Tutmose looked down at the flattened, faintly mauve and brittle nails of Pharaoh's hand.

Then Ikhnaton opened his eyes. "Send for Pentu," he said.

Pentu was sent for.

"Is the cast safe?"

Tutmose held it up.

"Can you make the mould now?"

Tutmose could and did, moving back and forth across the room, while Pentu came and went. No wonder Pharaoh was afraid of death. As an epileptic, he repeated the experience whenever he had to renew his nerves. But there was no real need for Pentu. Epilepsy was quite harmless, and frightening only to those who had to watch. Still, there was that instant before one became unconscious, when one realized one could no longer control one's body and would so be at the mercy of outsiders for a while. That could not be pleasant.

Tutmose was not frightened, but he was sobered. He had not known. It explained much. No wonder Ikhnaton loved the sun. For when a capillary bursts in one's brain, which happens once or twice in everybody's lifetime, one has the same sensation as an epileptic, of a cool, overwhelming, yet somehow healthy, all-pervasive light that sweeps one instantaneously in and out of an hygienic void. It happens so seldom, and runs so counter to everything we are accustomed to, that most of us forget it. But an epileptic repeats it too often to forget it. Therefore he is often mystic and frequently devout.

The cast had set. He removed it, and at Pharaoh's order set it beside that of Amenophis, propping it against the wall. Despite a difference in feature, the resemblance was exact, which, in turn, told one much about Amenophis. He had been a visionary, too, but one with nothing to look at. No wonder his death mask was so sad.

Ikhnaton saw no similarity at all. As far as he was concerned this difference he saw abolished death. He went away content.

He forgot that his father meant nothing to him. Yet

like an assassin, who closes in on us, by dodging from tree to tree, strangling first the outer sentries, and then the guard before our tent, death was moving closer. A month later, and it had reached his tent.

Since Tutmose did all the rest of them, he had done the princesses too. Their tiny shell-like heads were perfectly suited to small chunks of highly polished stone, and this was work he enjoyed, finishing them with as much care as a man, to relax, would lavish on the pip of an apricot. It was a sort of hobby, and of course we love our hobbies best for being so meaningless.

There were six of them now, and when he finished one he did another. Meritaten was twelve, too large to interest him any more. Maketaten was ten, Ankesenpa'aten, whose facial planes were the most satisfying, eight, and the other three three, two, and one respectively. If he wanted to please Pharaoh, he had only to hand over one of these scrimshaws of Maketaten, who was his favourite, though personally Tutmose found her the most insipid of the lot. He preferred Senpenra, the baby, in green serpentine, which he carried about with him in his pocket, to play with when the day was hot, because the stone was always cool. It was pleasant to twiddle with it when he was thinking.

Nor was the idea irreverent, for Pharaoh himself played with the children as though they were pet mice. And why not? Lonely children keep white mice, lonely men usually have a box of their old toys hidden away somewhere, and one must have something to lavish one's affections on, without fear of reprisals. There is a good deal to be said for white mice.

What the children thought nobody knew. They were secretive children, and since the secrets of children are not ours, we should not understand them even if we knew them.

Then, quite suddenly, Maketaten died.

Tired of being little, she had circled up like a dormouse under a shrub in the garden and gone to sleep, partly because it was so hot, and partly because she didn't want to play hide-and-seek any more.

It was well on towards evening when Ikhnaton found her, for Meritaten, who at twelve insisted on running the others, had said she had gone off to sulk, and please, couldn't they go on playing. She was a little old to play tag, but she enjoyed it, because it gave her a chance to be close to her father, who had a passion, so it seemed, for tag.

There was a light breeze off the river. It was time to go indoors. In the declining sun the stalks of the plants already looked blue. So he pattered up and down the paths, while the others waited, bubbling happily to himself and calling for Maketaten, while Meritaten, who was jealous of her younger sister, watched scornfully from the doorway.

Then he found her, circled up in a ball, in the long untrimmed grasses under a persea tree. He stuck his hand into the warm flesh between her drawn-up knees and belly, and it wasn't warm at all.

"Sleepy," he said. "Wake up. Wake up." He bent down, scooped her up, and jounced her in his arms, the very favourite of all his children.

That high-pitched, febrile scream must have been pent up for thirty-four years. It echoed endlessly across the water, while the rushes danced and waved along the shore. At long last death had reached Aketaten.

He advanced, tears streaming down his cheeks, which tingled as though they had been slapped, while her legs dangled helplessly below his arms. Servants came to the door. Meritaten stared.

"Get out," he shouted. "Get out, all of you."

He must have sat there for hours, on the garden seat, with her body across his lap. For this was not his father. This was different.

He had made the ultimate discovery. Once they are

159

gone, they are irreplaceable. They take away that part of us that loved them. It and they will never be there any more. There is nothing to say. It is as though one had lost all one's teeth.

He would not even see the Queen.

Ten

The embalmers had an unvarying schedule. To reduce
the body to immortality took eighty days. But there
were no embalmers at Aketaten. He had refused to
have them there. He had to send to Thebes. And Thebes
refused to send them. It was unheard of. They would
come only if the princess should be buried after the
traditional ritual.

He blinked, but said nothing. He gave in. The men
came, and an area for them to work in was set up at the
northern end of the palace.

No one knew what he was thinking. No one dared to
ask. Only Meritaten, being most like Maketaten, was
allowed to see him. She was most like, but even she was
not the same. Still, at this time she got what she had not
even wanted, complete dominion over him.

He spared himself none of it. He had to see it all for
himself. But there should be no dancing and feasting, as
was traditional, before this mummy, before it was
settled in its tomb. He could not have borne that. He
would have ripped apart the cases and the wrappings,
to get her alive again, only to find a shrivelled, contracted, bituminous skin, like the shed skin of a snake.
Immortal life, there was no immortal life, unless immortal life could be mortal. What was the use of an
immortality you could not touch?

He had that section of the garden shut off. Like the
banqueting hall, it was a place where no one would
ever again go.

The procession formed before the gates of the palace.
There was no rite in the temple, for no rite had ever

been devised to deal with such a thing. Under the hot sun the party moved up the final gorge to the royal tomb. Carried in a litter, he jounced ahead of the Queen in hers, and bit his lip. It was a distance of five miles. Nor was there any hymn he would have sung, except the eternal hymn to the Aton, which was now a mockery. There was no formula to deal with such an event, except the noble's petition to Pharaoh, as the glorious child of the Aton, to grant them eternal life.

He could not even grant his daughter eternal life.

And lying back, with his eyes half-closed, in that bouncing litter, he could see the sweaty, sanctimonious faces of the court, re-echoing the words of that petition as though they believed in them. How dare they believe in them, when he did not.

The gorge was majestic but its walls were too close. The sun scarcely penetrated here. The air was fetid and dry and there was too much dust. Far ahead he could see, borne aloft, that small gold and lapis lazuli coffin carried feet first towards what these foolish people dared to call eternity.

Nor did he spare himself even the royal tomb.

He had never entered it before, and would never enter it again. The litter was set to earth. He stepped out and glanced angrily at all of them. But they were bowed down. He could not see their faces. That hymn they chanted was only a monstrous jeer.

Meryra would have spoken to him, but he brushed Meryra aside. They entered the tomb.

The builders had done their job too well. It was commodious enough to hold a whole dynasty. Beyond the entrance hall lay his own chambers, looming dark beyond the light of the torches, except for a reflection out of darkness, where a stray gleam caught the edge of his own pink sarcophagus. Maketaten was to be buried in a hall to the left. From all the walls shimmered stucco reliefs full of gaiety. They showed himself, the

162

Queen, the princesses, and the court, rejoicing in the light for ever and ever. He could have smashed them.

It was the Queen who placed upon the coffin case, once it was in the sarcophagus, a tiny circlet of small white and sapphire flowers, such as one gathers in a meadow, nestled gently in green leaves, cornflowers, and some bitter sweet thing shaped like tiny stars. The rope was cut and the lid of the sarcophagus came down with a dusty slam that seemed to shake the walls. The lights retreated. Nefertiti hesitated and then turned towards him, touching his waist with her hand. After all, it was her daughter.

But she had turned the wrong side of her face. Caught in the flickering obscurity, but lit pink by a torch, he saw the white, tear-stained mass of that blind eye, staring at him helplessly, sightlessly. So though her fingers were timid, he shook them off and fell back.

There was nothing to say. She stood rigid, and if anything her chin went higher.

They left the tomb. But he would not leave the outer hall, until the attendants had piled into the room every stick and piece of furniture or personal possession Maketaten had ever owned, until the black hole was a mass of gold and gilt and precious stones, and glitter. He wanted no reminder of her, for if she could no longer be, then it was as though she never had been. He stayed until the masons had bricked up the opening, and it had been secured with plaster seals.

When he left it was already evening. He had the bearers virtually run back down the gorge, having given orders that all work on the royal tomb, and on every other tomb at Aketaten, should cease.

It was a matter, now, of staying awake every night until dawn. From now on it would always be a matter of that.

When he entered his bedroom, alone, with all the lamps lit, he found on a stand beside his bed a small sandalwood box, and when the servants had been dismissed, though only to sleep across his doorway, he opened it.

There was no message. It contained a small quartzite head of Maketaten, four inches high, done years ago, when she was five. He did not acknowledge it, but he fell asleep with it in his hand, and he was always to keep it by him.

Tutmose had not expected him to acknowledge it. Nor did he see any point in admitting that it was one of two, the better of which, with his name on a scrap of papyrus, he had sent to the Queen.

In these matters one is better off without words, but they had had a long tug-of-war, he and she, and somehow he had wanted to send her at least his name, whether they were friends or not.

Maketaten was never referred to again. But two or three days later Horemheb was sent to Thebes, to fetch back Smenkara and Tutankaten, the male heirs. From now on they were to reside in Aketaten.

Eleven

He would have gone in any case, Pharaoh's displeasure or no. He had his virtues, and therefore his responsibilities, and only official business in Memphis had kept him away when Amenophis was dying. For more than anyone else, Amenophis had been his father. They had loved each other in their own fashion.

About Tiiy his feelings were more mixed, for she was now almost fifty, and he in his thirties, and a great deal was over between them. That made it awkward to know what to say.

It would be a mistake to say that Thebes was deserted. It was rather as though its important people were hiding out in the hills, waiting until it was safe to return. Indeed, in view of all those royal tombs in the cliffs of Pharaohs loyal to Amon, was that not literally true?

Tiiy was still a woman of some importance, and she did not hide. Her retirement was not occlusion, but the invisibility of an important official, temporarily out of office, but yet with much to do. Her weakness was not that she was weak, but that she had been too strong for all of them.

She even continued to receive ambassadors and envoys of state. Unable to appeal to Ikhnaton, they appealed to her. She knew all the affairs of the Empire, and even more than Ay, perhaps she was the only person who did know. She still had much to teach. Society might converge like sheep down a slaughter-house runway upon the capital at Aketaten, but the political capital remained at Thebes, if it could be said to be anywhere. In her own person, she was the political capital, what was left of it.

Horemheb found her, rather surprisingly, at the Memnonion. That vainglorious, echoing, and be-jewelled monument to vanity had at last, somewhat unexpectedly, actually become what it set out to be, a shrine. For we are apt to forget that bad taste is by no means incompatible with a noble character, and that a noble character, for the matter of that, has little or nothing to do with being good.

Then, in the heat of a particularly hot summer, the place had the merit of being cool. In a way, too, it was rather as though, now Amenophis was dead, she drew some comfort from sheltering behind the remains of his identity.

An attendant went to fetch her. She came clattering up across the brightly polished floors, from some wing of the building, very assured and tight-skirted, her sandals showing off the taut, brittle ankles of a woman who refuses to grow old. Her face broke into a smile of pleasure when she saw him.

"You came," she said. "I was wondering if you would." And she looked at him shrewdly, from the immense distance of what had once been between them, and showed, in that way, that she was both touched and enormously gratified.

He was touched himself. For he had always felt guilty about her. Or rather, since guilt is not an attri-bute of character, but a substitute for it, wistful and sorry. Still, one of them had had to tire of the other first, and if it had been she, she would not have been so fond of him now, for what she admired best in others was independence of herself, so that she could not help both to despise her children and to reduce them to the very thing that she despised.

Now they were old friends she could accept, rather than resent, the strength of character that had made him fail her. Besides, she was safe on the far side of menopause. Her emotions were therefore less demanding, and sensation could be, and in her case no doubt was, satisfied anywhere. This had the effect of making her somehow more humorous and brisk, as she had been in the days when she had first taken him up.

Now it appeared she proposed to take him up again, though in a different way. She was full of politics. She had an immense desire, as had Ay, who had already taken him up, to pass on what she knew to someone capable of remembering it. So though their pleasure on seeing each other again was mutual, the profit was almost entirely his.

"Ay has told me he finds you promising and only slightly stupid," she said. "What happens down there, in that madhouse?"

He laughed, for it was a little warmth again, without having to be so eternally guarded. He had discovered the relaxed and amiably mocking joys of that old acquaintance which is perhaps the real end of any love affair, though we may not think so at the time. Certainly it makes new love affairs more endurable. For one thing it gives us someone to grumble to about them, a thing scarcely possible to the young.

So he gained some insight into that relationship of hers to Amenophis, which had survived so many lovers, and which had so puzzled and defeated everyone.

About Aketaten she was completely cynical. Honesty, clearly, at least in her case, was a much more physical matter than her son supposed.

This made it easier for Horemheb to tell her the purpose of his errand. He had expected her to take it badly. She did nothing of the sort.

"Yes, he would want them now," she said. She looked up and her face was sad. "Have you seen them yet?"

He shifted uncomfortably.

167

"It doesn't matter. I'm old enough to be honest. I had the wrong womb. Let him have them. They won't do him any good. They're even weaker than he is. Ay will probably outlast us all. They should go very well with all those girls of his."

And indeed, thought Horemheb, a few days later, she was quite right. They would.

He watched the princes from the shelter of the deck-house, on the way back to Aketaten. Tutankaten, who was five, had thrown a scene on having to leave, but only about his pet rabbits. His mother filled him with indifference, but pet rabbits were another matter. For a child so thin, he was surprisingly tough, but those periwinkle eyes, though determined, were not intelligent.

Smenkara, on the other hand, was twenty-one. He looked at you as though wondering how much you cost, and his precocity was frightening. No doubt he meant to be agreeable, but he also meant to keep his place and he had little energy. He knew twenty-five ways to be indolent, all graceful, and if occasionally he left one out, you could be sure he would put it back in again later, out of series. In particular he had an annoying habit of throwing you an impromptu, but none the less well-rehearsed, happy smile over his left shoulder as he left a room. It was impossible not to notice that he presented always his better profile.

The simplest thing to do was to shrug and give him up. It seemed unlikely, somehow, that Egypt would ever be ruled over the left shoulder, smile or not. At least there was no harm in him.

Tutankaten, even at five, was spiteful.

Horemheb was well content to hand them over to the household steward at Aketaten and go to his offices. There he found Ay waiting for him, and with good reason.

For the next few months the Commander of the

Armies would have more than enough to do. Ikhnaton had promulgated some violent and ill-chosen orders, in a spirit of bare-faced revenge. From his own stand-point, he could scarcely be blamed.

After the scene over Maketaten's funeral, he had sworn revenge against the Amon priests. Not Meryra, but Pa-wah, had shrewdly played on that, in his own game for power. Besides, unlike Meryra, who had made it up, Pa-wah was a fanatic where the religion was concerned. Why should he not be, since he wanted the office of high priest for himself?

He had served up the rumour that the Amon priests were praying for Ikhnaton's death. No doubt they were, but privately, and without feeling any need to bring the matter to Pharaoh's attention.

There are some poisons a drop of which will tincture a whole glass. There are also rumours that do the same thing. Pharaoh's health was in a state of collapse. His tuberculosis had advanced. There was nothing Pentu could do but prescribe anti-spasmodics, and it is not pleasant to watch one's body rot while fools get on quite well. They might pray for his death, but it would do them no good. He would abolish them instead.

Whether for Maketaten or himself, he gave orders that everywhere, throughout the double kingdom, the name of Amon was to be destroyed, chiselled out of all monuments, and never mentioned again. A hundred thousand workmen, under protection of the army, were to begin work at once. They were to enter even the tombs, and pull down whole monuments. Workers, sculptors, and vandals were to be remorselessly drilled in what to do, and watched and whipped, if necessary, until they did it.

All the Amon temples were to be disbanded and, if possible, torn down, the priests forcibly secularized, their farms, fields, cattle, chattels, treasure, preroga-tives, and possessions seized for the crown. He had smashed their Holy of Holies and that horrible black doll. Now he would smash them.

It was a war against death, and since he was Pharaoh, it would be fought and won. And why stop there? Ptah, Osiris, even Ra, they all served death, and they should all be destroyed. The Aton alone served life.

Since he was Pharaoh, it was fought, and who was to say whether it was won or not?

It took the entire army to keep the riots down. Never mind disaffections in the Syrian Empire. Troops were withdrawn to serve in Egypt, at his order.

And again, he was wilier than people supposed. In Thebes the army was expected to defect. The army did nothing of the sort, and for a very simple reason, and one, moreover, that he had thought of at once. The wealth of Egypt came from the Nubian gold-mines. Its distribution was a monopoly of the Amon cult. He blandly turned the monopoly over to the army, at no loss to himself, and since the profit of the monopoly was one in four, the army had no difficulty in remaining loyal.

Meanwhile he had the royal princes, his little brothers, firmly under his own thumb, and could bring them up as he pleased. Death or no, the rule of the Aton would go on.

In the resultant confusion everyone overlooked Smenkara and his twenty-five ways to be indolent, all graceful, and one a smile over the left shoulder. It turned out to be a mistake, but then the one thing wisdom does foolishly, is to overlook the power of folly.

Twelve

It was the thirteenth year of the reign, which left them only five to go. But of course they could not know that, for secure as they were at Aketaten, nothing much happened in this year.

True, the temples were closed and the economy of the country was wrecked. The army was growing stronger than Pharaoh, which was dangerous. But nobody in the army had bothered to tell Pharaoh that. In Asia, Egypt lost Mitannia to the Hittites and six cities in Syria; in Africa, Nubia as far as the Fifth Cataract. The coastal trade, however, continued to flourish, since the Phoenicians ran it at a sufficient profit to themselves to keep them loyal, but even so, new waves of piracy hampered the steady flow of goods. The cost of wood went up, the supply of spices down. Pharaoh did not care for spiced food.

Thebes, they said, was orderly, apart from the perpetual strikes, but then there had always been strikes, because the officials in charge of grain allotment were hopelessly venal. When they grew too venal, which was every three or four years, one changed them, and the strikes abated for a while. It was a nuisance, but quite traditional.

All these things had nothing to do with Aketaten, and were in any event scarcely Ikhnaton's concern.

It was in this year that he saw his first pair of gloves. They came from the interior of Arabia, and they were marvellous. They were so impersonal. Anything you did in gloves, you did not do at all. He had a pair made for Smenkara.

If you cut off a man's hand, as was done with prisoners of war, you could not use it for anything at all. But here you had something that could do things you would never dare to do yourself. Inside gloves your own hands felt secret and safe, and could do as they pleased without anybody ever being able to see. If surrogate hands, why not then noses, eyes, a penis, ears? We already have wigs instead of hair. On the same principle, gloves made the dirtiest moral action clean, for one had no responsibility for what one touched. Any dirt that might be involved rubbed off on the gloves.

They said Royal Father Ay was Pharaoh's right hand. Why not give him these surrogate hands, then, a pair of gloves? Then Pharaoh would have no responsibility for anything done in Pharaoh's name. The gloves would bear the responsibility.

They were a marvel. He would distribute them to Ay from the balcony, as soon as the matter could be arranged.

And so we have the scene, on a rock painting done the same year. It was a gala event, and one of the Queen's infrequent recent appearances. The nobles in the street below cheered themselves hoarse. Smenkara had begged for the privilege of being on the balcony, but since Ikhnaton kept him in the background, was not visible.

The irony of the scene made Ikhnaton giggle.

Unfortunately, as far as Ay was concerned, gloves were only gloves.

To tell the truth, Ikhnaton was a little bored, though not unpleasantly so. Mostly that year he played with the children. Their little fists grabbed rapaciously at things, like the tentacles of a stranded octopus, before it dies in the sun. He enjoyed that. It was agreeable to be the father of small girls, even if Meritaten was now too old to play, and had been relegated to the harem, though Smenkara seemed to like her well enough.

They owed one everything. They had sometimes the power to annoy, when their voices piped too loud in very hot weather, but they were charming, and they did not have the power to hurt. It was a little like keeping cats, if cats were not sacred, and always remained kittens.

He played with them as though they were toys, the clay toys one gives to children and which grown-ups play with when they are sure they are not observed, or feel nervous. For this he could not be blamed, for they were not children. They had been brought up to be toys, and that is what they were. They could never be taken over into adulthood, and made to serve some purpose. They could only be forgotten, broken, or discarded. It must be said it gave them a certain gaily painted charm that would only later seem horrible.

Thirteen

Nothing much happened in the next year, either, not that was, at first.

In the State Department, the foreign minister under Ay received his fifth appeal from Rib-Addi of Byblos, against the disloyal manœuvres of Aziru, who had gone over to the Hittites. Byblos was of some importance as a trade centre. But the foreign minister knew better than to bother Pharaoh with such matters, and since the bribe offered by the Hittite ambassador turned out to be surprisingly large, he did not mention it to Ay either.

At court one saw rather more of Smenkara and of Nefertiti rather less. She now appeared only for Aton worship and the distributions of gold collars and other valuable honorifics from the royal balcony. In public the Royal Couple was as affectionate as ever. In private, she could be seen alone by anyone who sought her intervention or interest. The foreign minister was not among her party. She had no interest in politics in Syria, and supported Pharaoh in his disinterest in the matter, as she always had. It was another way she had of holding his attention, which these days was increasingly difficult to hold.

She found it prudent to avoid the court, for Smenkara did not like her. For the most part she stayed in the northern suburb and strengthened her position.

Tutankaten did seem to like her. He was seven now, and quite knowledgeable. Since Pharaoh neglected him, she had virtually adopted him, and thought his affection almost genuine. One does not expect self-interest from a child of seven. Unfortunately for her, he was, like the rest of them, precocious.

Since he showed an aptitude for sport, wiser than her mother, she hired male tutors and bowmen to instruct him. She also paid them well. She did not think much of Smenkara, and a prince with a faction is more useful than a prince without one. She made sure that Tutankaten's servants should be loyal to her.

Smenkara, who collected art objects, had not only reawakened Ikhnaton's interest in them, but had added a new piece to his own collection. In Pharaoh's rooms he had found a small quartzite head and admired it. Ikhnaton had given it to him at once, without the slightest compunction. He had almost forgotten Maketaten. Not only did he have Smenkara to talk to, but he had a new interest now, or at least he tried to persuade himself that he had.

The matter was kept quiet, and in any case was rather pathetic. He had added a male harem to the royal establishment. Nefertiti could scarcely blame him. His tuberculosis had had the usual side effects, and in a way she had taught him the method, years ago. It was only because he could not sleep at night, and she doubted if he enjoyed it; but then again, thinking the matter over, he might.

She grew thoughtful. Purely apart from the desperation it revealed, boys were apt to be more spiteful than girls, and in sexual intrigue, more quarrelsome and adroit.

She need not have worried. Smenkara, though unduly decadent, had no such interests, and besides, it was an entertainment which Pharaoh preferred to keep locked up in one room and never refer to.

However, if he had no interest in the fate of the Empire, Tiiy did. Copies of all official documents were sent to her as a matter of course, not by the Foreign Office, but by their original senders. She sent word down from Thebes that now Amenophis was dead she wished to visit the new capital. She was not so naïve as to believe her visit would produce any particular result, but it might, and besides, she was not without curiosity.

Ikhnaton would have refused her permission to come, but then his eye was caught by the death-mask of Amenophis.

He had forced Tutmose to give it to him. Having it about satisfied his new and restless mood. Having his father's dead face there to watch somehow made life a little livelier. The Queen admired dangerous cats. This dangerous face might serve him equally well. He kept it by him, he supposed, out of defiance. Therefore, why not defy it now?

His mother, no doubt, thought of him as a weakling, incompetent to rule in her stead. If the Foreign Office did not plague him, she did. He was tired of all these petitions. He had begun to tire of the whole panoply, and was by no means averse to a chance to show off, which would make it for a moment new, seen through someone else's eyes. He would let her come.

The preparations took six months. Unexpectedly Nefertiti found herself back in favour. She had built herself into the religion solidly, and now she was needed to show it off. She knew all that and tended Tutankaten with particular care. She had never liked her mother, either.

The preparations rejuvenated all of them.

She brought the blind harpers out of retirement with her. She thought she deserved the gesture. But Ikhnaton did not even notice them. He was too busy, for there was building to be done, and a pageant to be organized.

To Ay and Horemheb that pageant was ironic, for by this time, by force of finding it around him every day, Horemheb had had to master irony himself. Irony, in this case, turned out to be hugely expensive. The treasury was not so full as it had been, but the army coffers were fuller. He had no objection to paying up, if the object lesson provided did any good.

Needless to say, it didn't.

As a national symbol, however, it was effective, in a way that Tiiy may have overlooked. For in coming to Aketaten, Tiiy made it look very much as though the old order had at last been made to bow down before the new. On the other hand, her personal prestige was so great, and the partisan motives for applauding her so complex, that nobody bothered to look at the matter that way. To many she was the glory of the Empire, Pharaoh only what was left of it. Her reception by the army she found especially gratifying.

Nor did she see any reason to remove the figure of Amon from the prow and rudder of her own barge, or his standards from among those of her personal guard.

The shout these raised, when her flotilla approached the jetty of the south custom house, and the size of the crowd that raised it, was no doubt one reason why Pharaoh had caused the flotilla to dock there rather than at the wharves opposite the palaces and the Aton temple. She smiled graciously and was satisfied.

As for Ikhnaton, he relished the impertinence, for here, at Aketaten, he could put it in its place, which is what he had planned to do all along.

Rather than let her proceed to the dwelling built for her, he insisted she join in Aton worship at an altar built along her route for just that purpose. She could scarcely refuse, he thought. She had no intention of refusing. She felt the liveliest interest.

She was a pragmatist. Religion to her was a branch of the government, whereby one handed over spiritual ownership of the state to a series of venal officials, called priests, whose sole function was to maintain metaphysical order in one's name. Like any officials, they sometimes forgot themselves, and had to be brought into line or even stripped of office, but one could not do

177

everything oneself, and by and large the arrangement was satisfactory. The priesthood in other words was a branch of the police, and only slightly more corrupt, but then corruption is the price we have to pay for order, and always has been.

As for the rest, she was superstitious about trifles and needed religion on her death-bed, and that was that.

She thought the white altar with its four staircases very pretty. Flowers she had always been fond of; she had never minded hot sunlight, and the hymn, of course, should not have been written in the vernacular, but the harpers played it very well. Meryra she did not even recognize.

That bright feverish glitter on her son was somewhat more disturbing. She looked round at the rest of them. The princesses did not count, but Meritaten looked as though she could bear children, which would be some help. Smenkara she had given up, but he was at least physically normal. To Nefertiti she was deliberately gracious. Tutankaten was too young to be forced to toddle through such fatiguing ceremonies, at his age so much standing was bound to make him bandy-legged. She made a note to mention it.

Indeed the only people she enjoyed seeing were Ay and Horemheb. They were very close now, those two. They even stood close together. It was always agreeable to see Ay. His cynicism was refreshing and never rude.

She saw what he meant about Horemheb.

Horemheb had turned out well. It was odd and even startling that he should be the perfect popular image of what a Pharaoh should be, manly, supple, direct, and powerful-looking, when they all looked like something else. Or perhaps it was not so odd, for in point of fact his family was older than the dynasty. In the obscurity of poverty they had probably taken the opportunity to renew their blood. Whereas her own brood was clearly the scuttle-butt of inbreeding. It always happened. After two or three generations a family fell in on itself.

Like everyone else, she looked at Horemheb's calves. One forgets at times that it is not always the face that sums up the character. It may as easily be some other part of the body, the finger-nails, the hand, the navel, even the foot. In his case it was the calves. They were so firm and sturdy.

They left the altar and she was escorted through the city.

She was escorted mercilessly through all of it, and exposed to a good deal of aesthetic prattle as well. She thought it was a pity Ikhnaton had no other hobbies. Between architecture and theology she was beginning to find it an unduly hot day.

The temples, she could see, in a light summer pavilion way, were pretty, but she was more interested in the Foreign Office.

It turned out Ikhnaton had never been in the Foreign Office.

She stared when he said that, and beside her, Ay gave a slight shrug. The courtiers, too, were little better than an ennobled rabble. She was relieved when she had been left alone in the temple of reception he had had built for her. The temple was decorated with alternating statues of herself, Amenophis, and Ikhnaton. The workmanship was bad, but it was a graceful touch. She took a nap.

There was something to be said for ritual and cere-monial after all. Moving that way in processions, appearing only at state dinners and other public func-tions, it took her longer to lose her temper, for not being alone with anybody, she had nobody to lose it with.

Private meals were less agreeable. She sat in one chair, and Nefertiti and Ikhnaton sat in another, ten feet opposite her, the space between occupied by food racks, flower arrangements, and wine bottles. The acoustics in the banqueting hall were bad and the orchestra noisy. It was really a relief when the acrobats arrived, and made sustained conversation unnecessary.

Ikhnaton's table manners had not improved. If anything they had become worse. Nor were Nefertiti's much better. Seen thus, gnawing away at a chicken or a roast, their faces had a look of abstracted bliss that seldom came over them in the temples. If they washed their hands frequently, it was only to prevent their slipping on a greasy bone.

She was astonished, sipped wine, and watched. Nefertiti, at least, had always been fastidious. Indeed physically, despite that eye, she was still fastidious, in a curious sick-bed way. But they were gluttons. On the other hand, there was some excuse. The cooking, she had to admit, was superb.

Conversation was boring. Nefertiti, to her surprise, talked about the religion rather more, and Ikhnaton, less. Perhaps, as the fountain-head of inspiration, he preferred to staunch the flow of a well that could not be inexhaustible. Nefertiti on the other hand almost talked as though she believed it, and of course, as she well knew, Nefertiti believed in nothing.

Tiiy saved her conversation for Ay and Horemheb. They acted out their game of domestic affection well, but she was not convinced. She knew what domestic affection was, and it was not this. Even as a performance it seemed a little tired. There was no feeling in those understanding smiles.

Also, Smenkara was rude to her. Not even Nefertiti seemed to control him. No doubt they all wanted to show how independent they were, since they were her children. She could not help but find them saddening.

She found the pageant of foreign tribute even more so.

They viewed it from a reception hall built for the purpose at one side of the Foreign Office.

It came in three parts: a spontaneous demonstration of loyalty on the part of the ambassadors of subject states; a procession of captives, which was an excuse for the army to parade in force; and the presentation of tribute. She settled into place and was not impressed.

For one thing, there had been some difficulty with the ambassadors. The Foreign Office, caught between Pharaoh and the facts, had been forced to improvise. Ambassadors should have presented themselves from the Sea Peoples, Crete, the Mitannians, the Hittites, the Phoenicians, and all the lesser cities of Philistia, Sharon, Acre, Esdraelon, Beth-Shan, Damascus, Kadesh, Aleppo, Lachish, Beth-Shemesh, and Judea. Unfortunately Lachish, Kadesh, and Aleppo were undergoing siege, and could not get their ambassadors out. It had been a task to find natives of those regions in the foreign quarter and dress them up. The Sea Peoples were no longer under control, but one of their petty chieftains, who hoped to defeat his countrymen with Egyptian help, had been pressed into service. The Mitannian kingdom had fallen ten years ago, and so had Crete. None the less a real Cretan had been obtained in the person of a Mycenean merchant, and without his beard he did very well. The Phoenicians were there in full force, but twenty Phoenician ambassadors, though they filled out the procession, might seem excessive. This had been solved by having each one represent a different city.

The Hittites, however, were openly at war with Egypt, though they sent protestations of loyalty, but since they had absorbed the Mitannian state, three of whose daughters had married Pharaohs, including Amenophis III and Ikhnaton himself, these protestations failed to convince. So they had been left out.

All the same, it made a brave show.

The procession of captives had proved more difficult, since the army had not been active for twenty years. It had been necessary to comb the slave gangs in the marble quarries and gold mines, but those who had not died of exhaustion were now in their late forties, and looked more as though they had been defeated by old age and overwork than by Pharaoh. Fortunately, the chieftain of the Sea Peoples had been able to provide two boatloads of pirates. These were unruly, and gave the army something to push against, which looked well. Forty Hittite hostages, most of them craftsmen from the recently founded ironworks, also helped out. The yellow and white peoples accounted for, it was necessary only to fill out the throng with a few Africans.

This proved harder. A forced draft on the court dwarfs added pygmies, but three hundred Nubians in various states of preservation were not many. An extra four hundred men of the right build had been pressed into service and brought down from the Sudan. Unfortunately intermarriage with Egyptians had reduced their racial characteristics to a minimum. But someone had suggested that by pricking their lips and rubbing in tar, the resultant swelling would make them look properly central African, and this had been done.

So the captives did not make such a bad show, particularly as the army made a very good one. Horemheb had done well with the army.

The army was followed by the tribute.

Since the army monopoly of the gold-mines kept the treasury relatively well-to-do, despite the drains of the building programme, the tribute was impressive. The display of logs from Lebanon was particularly fine. Still, the treasury was not that full, and it had been necessary to exhibit the gold bars from the army treasury and to eke the whole thing out with a few ostriches and lions and a raree show from the royal zoos.

All in all, the Foreign Office could congratulate itself on having done a good job, and to Ikhnaton, who had never seen anything like it before, since his father's last campaign had taken place before his birth, it was overwhelming, and he had a sketch artist on the spot, to take it all down.

Tiiy was not impressed. This procession had taken three hours. That after Amenophis's last nominal victory twenty years ago, and it had been a very minor campaign, had taken six.

For the moment she said nothing.

They went back through the Foreign Office, where the dust lay thick on clay despatches and dictionaries stacked on shelves, and out on to the balcony of audience.

Ikhnaton was very proud of his balcony of audience. Here he passed out gold collars and cones of incense to all those responsible for arranging the pageant, amid hearty cheers of congratulation. But Tiiy, who stood between Nefertiti and Pharaoh, looked down on the vacuous faces of the courtiers, and could not help but notice the grass growing up through the paving, or the deserted streets beyond the crowd.

In her own quarters, with Horemheb and Ay, she held a council of war. She was furiously angry.

Ay had nothing to suggest. He sat in the shadows, playing with something, and watching them.

"Will you stop doing that?" she snapped.

He did not stop. "You should look at this," he said. "I bought it in the market last week. All the children have them. They're really very ingenious. And instructive."

She looked. On a tabouret in front of him he had a clay chariot on movable wheels. Standing in the chariot were two little monkeys, driving. The resemblance to Ikhnaton and Nefertiti was unmistakable. Ay felt around on the floor of the chariot and lifted up three more monkeys, smaller, and set them on the tabouret. "The children," he said.

She stared at it. "It's only a toy."

"Of course." He held up one of the drivers. "But you see, detachable. It's very convenient. This one already has a crack. If one breaks, you can replace it." He turned it over in his fingers. "It should break very soon."

"Doesn't he know he's dying?"

Ay shrugged. "We none of us know that until too late. Besides, he's been dying now for fifteen years. There's no reason why he shouldn't go on dying for quite a while yet."

"I'm going to speak to him."

"Don't you think we've tried? Besides, would someone else be any better? Smenkara, say, or Tutankaten?"

She couldn't help staring at the toy. "Put that thing away," she snapped.

"If you wish," he said. "But don't underestimate it. In its way it's a very clever toy indeed."

She went to speak to Ikhnaton, taking Horemheb and Ay along with her. And Ay was quite right. In its own way, it was very clever. It also found the toy, after a brief silent pause, very amusing, and asked why it had never been shown one before.

There was no answer to that. They watched him roll the cart back and forth on a table, while Tiiy lectured him. He looked like a guilty child.

But the guilty child had rather liked the pageant of Foreign Tribute. It was something, after all, to be Pharaoh. He said Nefertiti had persuaded him to neglect such matters. He had perhaps come to lean too much on her advice. Which in a way was quite true, since she had always made a practice of advising him to do what he wanted to do anyway.

From now on, he said, yes, he would act. He would take measures at once. He would save Syria. And meanwhile, would she please go and leave him in peace. She was impertinent. He was Pharaoh, not she.

184

When they left he was still playing with the toy, his face thoughtful.

None the less, when she went back to Thebes, he escorted her to the wharves. Ay and Horemheb had decided to accompany her a little way up the river, on the return journey. Ikhnaton even stood there while the boat pulled out into the current, so that the last thing he saw was the figure of Amon on the rudder of her barge, staring back at him, as the flotilla set sail for Thebes.

He was not sorry to see her go, but true to his promise, he took action at once.

When Horemheb and Ay returned two weeks later, they discovered he had instituted an entirely new service, in the temple attached to the Foreign Office, a hymn to the glorious disc of the Aton, requesting that the light of Ma'at should break over the dark hearts of the rebellious. In addition, he had increased the staff of the Aton temples in both Syria and Nubia. That, he thought, should do. The service was to be held daily, and Nefertiti was to be rigorously excluded from it. After all, though it was convenient to have someone to blame, she had made him look ridiculous before his mother.

It was the beginning of her fall from power.

Meanwhile, the cart was quite fascinating, and he ordered three, with improvements of his own devising, for the children to play with.

Fourteen

Boredom produces its own sense of urgency. Aketaten had become a little feverish. They had three years.

Smenkara had done well. His whole art consisted in sliding neatly but gravely into an empty place, and he blended nicely with the girls. Not being a monotheist, or indeed much concerned with such matters in any way, he even accepted the Aton. In his own way he had summed things up, and he was waiting. He knew perfectly well he would become Pharaoh some day, and so he had nothing to be ambitious about. This made him restful. Still, it could not be denied that a certain sparkle of anticipation came into his eye, when he saw how his opportunity was ripening, though when people gave him things, he was ingenuous enough to receive them with a quite sincere exclamation of, "Oh, is all that for me?" As a result people gave him things for the pleasure of it. In short, he had become the favourite. He had scarcely the volition of a minnow, and was quite content to drift with the current, and to preserve that air of never wanting anything that made everyone but Nefertiti overlook him.

She had only two defences in her new position. No one could dislodge her from the Aton cult, which gave her power; and as virtual guardian of Tutankaten, who would one day be the second man in the Empire, she was in a secure place from which to bargain. Because of this, though she detested the child, she gave him everything he wanted, automatically, out of policy. It was somewhat humiliating to descend from the status of Royal Wife to that of no less Royal Sister as Aunt, but she made the transition unobtrusively. And so to her own adherents were now added his.

All of which went on behind the scenes. To public view she and Ikhnaton were as devoted a couple as ever, though a close observer might have noticed something wrong with their smiles.

In the height of summer, however, he fell dangerously ill, as unexpectedly and almost in the same place as Maketaten had died in the garden. He was thirty-eight now. To look and act like a boy was one thing. But to live like one had ruined his health. He was carried into a pavilion in the garden, and over that white glittering city there fell an intent and almost surgical hush. Everywhere, both in the palaces, and in the temples and hovels, the inhabitants huddled like immigrants, miserable to know where to go next.

Pentu had no easy time. More even than most physicians, he knew his own health depended upon that of his patient. But what could he do? He looked at that bloated and yet wasted body, motionless in its coma, and had no idea of what went on in there. He was the cleverest doctor in the Empire, but all his knowledge amounted to no more than that he knew virtually nothing.

For thirteen days Ikhnaton lay still. He had become the mummy of himself. One could only watch for the slow signs of certain death and hope one would not see them.

As for the court, it had not given way to panic yet, but there were rumours. Horemheb and Ay advised Nefertiti to move back to the palace from her own retreat in the northern suburb. Of all that crowd, she was still the only one who could hold the court.

No doubt many of the nobles made their secret preparations. There were more messengers to Thebes than usual. But hold them she did. She even went to the temple more often, rather than less, and Meryra was instructed to hold the rites more publicly and with a firmer splendour.

In Pharaoh's pavilion there was no sound. She went there at night once, to see him, attended only by Ay.

She did not like what she saw. That garden was the world he loved. And now, through it, off the river, there blew a disturbing wind that ruffled the stagnant water of the tanks and drove the flowers each way. There was even an angry shimmer from the trees, as though black death were playing some game up there, crouching to drop down on their heads, and unable to suppress a giggle. The flowers stood in their precise beds, a little past their prime, washed out of their colour by the moon, their stiff foliage turned a mouldy blue. It was not nice. It had a futile melancholy. And the creaking skiffs at the jetty, invisible beyond the garden wall, made the scene no better. Why is everything we own so anxious to depart?

The pavilion was spotless, its curtains drawn back against their poles. The attendants, who had just washed him, withdrew. Even now his orders were not disobeyed. Courtiers are the first, servants the last, to seek a new master. Fifty lamps must have been burning there, on the floor, on stands, or hanging by chains from the eaves.

It was the twelfth day of his coma. He lay motionless with his eyes closed, slightly propped on cushions, his hands aimlessly at his sides. His breath was not perceptible. Bathed five minutes ago, his forehead was again beaded with sweat. Between slightly parted lips one could see the bone-white glitter of his teeth.

The room smelled of aromatic gums, it all seemed purposeless, and they were both so much older now. Nefertiti stood quite quietly, without so much as stooping, about five feet away. Her face was empty. Ay could not tell what she was thinking. Yet something in it woke up and turned over for the last time, that was obvious. He wondered what.

Then she went away.

The next afternoon Ikhnaton opened his eyes. In the evening he took nourishment, a thin gruel, but moved little. The first thing he saw was that life-mask Tutmose had taken of him, which stood on a stand at the foot of his bed, where it had replaced that other mask of Amenophis. He stared at it for some time.

A week later he was allowed to sit up.

Nefertiti, coming with her personal attendants to pay him a state visit, was stopped and turned back at the entrance to the garden. No explanation of any kind was given.

He would see no one. He came out of the pavilion only at dusk and midnight, for short walks. And so matters went on for the next month. In the circumstances such state business as had to be handled, which was not much, was routed to Nefertiti.

About that lady Horemheb felt a certain curiosity. But she had become evasive. Without either head present to direct them, those in the palace became disorderly and at the same time strangely preoccupied. The banquets went on as usual, but before an empty throne. The consumption of the very good and very old rare wine of Aketaten significantly went up.

Horemheb wandered uneasily about the endless corridors and courts, but perhaps it was no accident that he came upon her at last. Subconsciously that was what he had wanted to do.

She was on the terrace overlooking the enclosure devoted to the great cats. Now she had withdrawn to the north palace, they looked singularly shabby and neglected. But they seemed to know her. In a clearing beneath the terrace they prowled back and forth, and he could hear an occasional snarl.

Nor was the reason for that snarling far to seek. She

had an enormous basketful of joints of meat which, as they began their nervous pacing, she threw down one by one.

He could sense, rather than see, that she was sad. If she knew he was there she gave no sign. But the night was cold and at last he went up to her. She turned her face towards him, and he had a momentary impression of that white, diseased eye. Then, swiftly, she turned her back to the balustrade, so that he was on her good side, and so manœuvred him around, until she could face the garden again. She threw out another piece of meat.

"Pharaoh's favourite roast," she said almost dryly. "Why are you here?"

"I don't know."

Very faintly, in the moonlight, her lips curved into the ghost of a smile. "I think we understand each other perfectly," she said.

He put his hand on her hip and then let it fall. Over the garden the stars were hard. He would have wished them softer. Angrily he took one of the joints and threw it down to the cats.

"If I were younger I should mind," she said.

"And now?"

There was a brief silence. "No, now I shall be remembered. It's something. It's rather nice." Who had said that before?

Another silence. He thought what he felt was probably pity. And pity, in his case, took the form of an inward heaving rage.

"Don't you ever drop your mask?" he asked.

She turned on him suddenly, so that he could see both her eyes. Her voice was no longer controlled. "This isn't a mask. It's my face," she said. "Besides, the few times I've tried, it hasn't got me very far. Do you remember that scene in the banqueting hall?"

"Don't you ever forget anything?"

She looked down at the animals again. "Only the

good things," she said, and they were silent again. But she did not draw away when once more he touched her. "No beautiful woman will ever accept pity," she murmured.

"It isn't pity."

She tipped the basket over the balcony and turned savagely on her heel. "Come," she said, and led the way through the palace to her own apartments, with a furious disdain for appearances. Her apartments overlooked the garden. There he went to bed with her. It was not a pleasant experience, and he found it dismaying. For it made him realize that locked up inside and way down in her, beneath all that cautious and now utterly ruined beauty, too late to escape, or even admit that it was there, was a young impulsive girl whose tenderness had never found anyone and now knew it never would. Often, alone, she must catch glimpses of that drowned self, thirty feet down, so concealed by the glaucous heave and swell of time, that she would never be able to tell whether it was alive or not.

She cried out, at that sudden, futile glimpse of pleasure. It was so fugitive.

And in the garden Ikhnaton heard it.

For these days he wandered restlessly about the exterior of that half-deserted palace, unwilling, at night, to go within. He had been alive again such a little while that he found the later summer odorous sweetness of the dying garden almost unbearably kind.

And even he, who had imitated everything, now found that there were moonlight nights when he looked across the lonely rooftops of the city, through that quiescent blue which is the magic of moonlight, and wished that life were otherwise. But life was not otherwise. Who had he been, he wondered, when he had still lived with the Queen?

And so, though he would not come to see her, he did sometimes steal through the garden, part the shrubs, and look towards her apartments. Tonight he found them blazing with light. That in itself was unusual, and he paused uncertainly, shivering in the quick breeze off the river. The spore of a dandelion floated aimlessly in front of him.

Then he heard her little scream, and moving closer, saw them together. Illness had left him slightly unbalanced. He had always been curious as to what ordinary people did together. Leaning against a tree, he watched until they were through.

Now why had he never been able to do that?

At last they stopped. Everything was still, except for the low baying of the wind. Horemheb left. After a long time Nefertiti came to the end of the pavilion, and stood beside one of the pillars. The expression on her face was appalling. Then she withdrew, without bothering to unfasten the pulled-back curtains, and one by one the lights went out. He heard her stir once, and then she must have slept.

He blundered out from behind the tree. Something brushed against his face. He swept it aside. It brushed against his face again, like a thousand furry fingers. He sobbed and ran away, hurrying, half-bent, down one of the garden paths.

It was the end of summer. The flowers were over. The sudden gusts of wind detached every winged spore from the naked pips and they rose in a vast whirling cloud from which he could not escape, moved this way and that, until he waded in them, darting as they did in and out, up and down, higher, sweeping downward upon him, until he was overwhelmed. He ran faster.

They strung out behind him, and though seeming to whirl away, in another gust returned, hovering maddeningly around him, and feinting away when he batted at them, until angry with tears he saw they rose from everywhere, like mocking stars soaring up to their proper places in the sky.

He sat down on the cope of a pool, protected by rushes, and wept. Then, by caprice, the wind drew them off, to drift and settle some otherwhere, and so take root. Only one or two drifted before his vision now, the little lost ones, too weak to go anywhere else, who must do the best they could here.

And there was nothing he could do to them, absolutely nothing at all. He could banish Horemheb, but Horemheb would not care. Horemheb had the army. And to abolish Nefertiti would be to abolish one-half the Aton, and have even that crumble away.

He had lost them both, a friend and a wife. He could not banish them. Nor could he go on alone. There must be someone left to him, there must be something that was not an appearance.

On the other side of the pond the rushes parted. A figure stood on the alabaster cope, almost naked, and wistful. It neither saw him nor spoke. It was Smenkara.

To have no one was better than to have Smenkara. He returned to his pavilion.

There he saw staring at him his own life-mask, with all its foolish confidence. It was true, unlike his father, he had not died. He had survived. But for what? For what?

Picking it up, he dashed it down, and smashed it, and left the pieces where they were.

Part Three

Fifteen

But even the God cannot destroy God. Once he has revealed himself, his worshippers will not let him. They have too much at stake.

He had almost died, he was worried, and there was no one with whom to share his worry. Our characters cannot sustain so much weight. Too much worry eventually makes us cave in on ourselves, like a summer roof packed with winter snow, with a splintering roar that in our own ears sounds much like a giggle.

And a giggle it should be. For the scales had fallen from his eyes at last. He saw things as they were. And why, then, should he not snatch this last secret game for himself, in a savage parody of faith?

For he saw now there was not one here who believed. Not one. Well, perhaps a foolish few, who had not the wit to see through anything, but of these loyal, devout, these sedulous courtiers and high priests, not one. It had been nothing to them but a game with Pharaoh's vanity.

Very well then, now he would have a game with theirs, beginning with the Queen, for to give him credit, yes, he saw now, Horemheb had never pretended anything. He did not even think of Ay. No one ever thought of Ay, which was as Ay wished it.

He prepared to enjoy himself.

For once more he had discovered something new. A sense of humour they had in those days, and some verbal wit. But a sense of comedy had nothing to do with either of those. The subject matter of humour is man taken on his own terms at the wrong time, the subject matter of wit, a game with language merely. The essence of wit is to pretend that the words we use to describe each other also define us. But your comedian is a zoologist with a genius for classification. That special form of deceit called honesty particularly appeals to him. Ma'at is only a vanity.

Your man of humour strangles whole towns in the name of justice. Your comedian destroys nothing. He does not have to, for he knows it will destroy itself, given the time. To him futility is not even futile. It has not even that much dignity. It is merely meaningless. So your true comedian will not die for his beliefs. He would much rather let his beliefs die for him, which is more natural, and besides, they would die in any case, so they may as well die to some purpose. If anyone else goes on believing in them, that only improves the comedy. Any horse can say haha in the midst of battle; but it takes a firmer strain to say haha in the midst of peace. This is what it means to be mettlesome.

While he had believed in it, it had never occurred to him that this new faith of his was so ludicrous. Now he began to see the possibilities. One could laugh at it all day, and he proposed to. Others did. Why not he?

Once discovered, and the trick was very easy. And yet was it, for alas, no matter if one laughed all day or not, even so, one cried all night. All his life he had craved understanding, and now, instead of receiving it, he was ready to give it. It was called comedy. Whether he cried all night or not, he was at least beginning to understand what a blessing it was not to have anyone there to watch. It was better so. It had more dignity.

He was very glad that Smenkara had not seen him in the garden. Smenkara would have the crown now, and much good might it do him.

He took the Queen up again at once. As the one person at court more disfigured than he, she pleased him very much as a public spectacle, where all had to worship her. No ceremony, not the slightest, so long as it was public, should do without her from now on. He was careful, too, always to behave before her with the proper gracious sweetness.

While he had been bemused, she had taken part of the religion to herself. If she believed in it so truly, why should she not take more? The idea pleased him.

But really, she must not be allowed to look sideways. She must face the world head on, so that the world could see the good eye of faith and the bad eye of disbelief. This required a small rearrangement of the ritual, but that was soon done.

And at banquets, on the balcony, and at receptions he put her once more on the other side, not only so that he might see her corruption, but also so that she should not see him smile. He gave her credit. She did not flinch. But surely her smile became a little more fixed?

In truth she was too busy to smile. If ritual was what she craved, why then, she should have a thousand details to attend to.

Then there was Meryra to tease. He was a very old man, and rumour had it, that though high priest of the Aton, and thus the truest of all believers, he had images proper to the Amon, Osiris, and Ptah cults in his tomb-house. Rumour was true. He sent workmen and had these post-mortem safeguards either smashed to pieces or hacked out. It was not a matter to which Meryra could very well refer. Pharaoh could. He publicly deplored the vandalism and stated that at his own expense he would restore all those stuccoes, reliefs, and paintings in which Meryra had petitioned Pharaoh for eternal life for ever in the Aton. Meryra need not therefore tremble. His future life was now eternally assured.

Meryra shook from head to foot. It could, of course, have been paralysis agitans, but Ikhnaton rather thought not.

Oh, it was very bland. He did it all with a completely straight face. Only he avoided Tutmose's studio.

Only alone in the broiling whitewashed sanctuary of that remorseless temple he would stare up at the sun, until his vision turned black, and say, "Oh Thou, why hast Thou played me false?" Outwardly, of course, this merely looked like another contracted spasm of devotion.

There was also his pride, his joy, his pleasure, the balcony of audience. That also became suddenly once more agreeable. It was truly dizzying, all that fervour, all that loyalty, all that belief, all that self-interest down there, mewling for favour from the street. Favour he gave it gladly.

All those men he had raised up from nothing should have it first. Hatiay, overseer of the royal building programme, a common contractor and now a noble, whose house they said was richer than Pharaoh's out of pilferings: if that was what he wanted, why should he not have a golden collar, like the rest of them? Mahu, chief of police, whose men carried about them amulets of Bast and Thoth, and yet who managed to appear fervid in the Aton temple when he appeared among them, why should he not have his collar, too? To Sutau, Overseer of the Treasury, for peculation, five farms; and to May, Prince, Royal Chancellor, Overseer of the Soldiery, and Bearer of the Fan on the King's right side, who wrote a secret despatch to Thebes every week, a donation of twenty gold bars, to pay his runners.

And even to Horemheb, who had not one tomb at Aketaten, but another, richer, finer one at Memphis, a gift of furniture from the palace, specifically for his tomb at Memphis. Horemheb clearly did not quite know what to make of that. Let him puzzle it out for himself.

There were others, too. They should all have their reward. These days he went round the city with new eyes and saw everything. He had given them palaces, very fine palaces, but now small details were clear to him. Wood was the most expensive thing they had. A good solid beam two feet across was worth the price of five or six slaves. The nobles had brought their pillars with them from Thebes, but instead of trimming them to fit the new rooms, had instead raised the roofs. This was because they might have to take the pillars back to Thebes again. And the same was true of doors. They were saving their doors for the empty sockets waiting for them at the old capital.

He said nothing, but wondered that he had not noticed such things before. He had founded the city for ever and ever, but that had not prevented his court from camping out in it for thirteen years. No doubt, after he had gone, they would pull out the wooden pillars of the balcony of audience, with as little compunction as they removed their own. Which one of them, he thought, would think to do so first? And in the palace, too. There must be hundreds of columns in the palace. He had taken them as a matter of course, and never thought of them as valuable. But of course they were valuable. Who would get those?

He looked round at the wine-flushed faces of the court, at night, when they were drunk, and could almost believe that he knew. Certainly Smenkara would not stop them.

Oh yes, there was great amusement to be derived from that sort of thing. All the same, sometimes, before dawn, he would whirl out into the desert, alone, in a chariot, climb one of the high altars that stood there, between the city and the cliffs, and face the oncoming sun, while the wind whipped around him.

"Are you truly not there?" he would say.

And sometimes, on some mornings, when the first rays of dawn struck him, he was reassured that yes, no matter what anyone thought, that glorious power of the sun was still there. It still had the power to warm his hand. It was only the cold and the wind and the sharp sudden crystal chirp of a bird that made the tears stream down his face.

So he fooled all of them, but Nefertiti. She had grown thoughtful and perhaps devout, and so she could sense his interior change.

Sometimes now he shook. He was growing feeble. Someday he would die, whether he admitted it or not. Someone would have to take over, once that event occurred. She laid her plans accordingly, and sent for Meryra. She knew she must defend herself, and she expected him to help, for as the official high priest of the heresy, he could not look forward to much should that heresy collapse with Pharaoh, and she put no faith in Smenkara. Together they planned what they would do when once Pharaoh was dead. They had Pa-wah in attendance on them, but saw no harm in that. Not only was Pa-wah second in command, but he was actually a fanatic believer. They knew they could trust him.

He was a fanatic believer, but for that very reason he coveted Meryra's place. This interview gave him the weapon he needed, but it took him a while to decide how to use it. Pharaoh would not grant him an audience, and besides, Meryra would be there to speak before him, even if he did.

In his own way Pa-wah was canny. There was one person Pharaoh would believe, precisely because she would use this supposed plot as an argument against the whole cult. He sent off a messenger to Tiiy.

He had not understood what he had overheard. They had talked so elliptically that he had thought not that Pharaoh was dying, but that they were planning to kill Pharaoh. So he expected a long possession of power in Meryra's stead, and he would indeed make the religion glorious.

He was an utterly wretched creature.

Sixteen

Tiiy, when she received the messenger, of course knew better, but saw no point in saying so. She now had to her hand the exact instrument she needed, and not a moment too soon.

For there had been political developments. Everyone of us must put by some altruistic vanity, against the day when we might otherwise be tempted to accuse ourselves of unjustified self-interest. Hers was, as it had always been, that she, and she alone, guarded the country over an empty throne. People have invented worse, and at least she was quite sincere. As for Pa-wah, she dismissed him from her mind. He was unimportant, though his evidence was useful. First she summoned the Amon priests to a conference. Then, without sending any courier ahead of her, she set sail for Aketaten.

She arrived, as she had wished, unannounced. Only Pa-wah expected her, and him she swept aside. She was transfigured. This time she meant to have her way.

Ikhnaton was making a tour of the glass factories with Smenkara, Meritaten, and the three smallest daughters. Now that he saw less of Nefertiti, of Meritaten he saw more. It was pleasant to be able to give the children these little bright beads to play with. They had reached the age, except for the youngest one, when they had begun to develop a touching young vanity for such things.

On the whole it was one of his better days. He felt almost healthy, and the sun, thank God, had slowed down his brain to a pace at which it was almost comfortable to think. Smenkara and Meritaten were oddly alike, and she was a dumpling version of the Queen, amiable, and yet harmless. The smell of the works, with its smouldering chemical fires, was far from displeasing and just acrid enough to keep him awake.

They were watching a craftsman make a sort of milleflori vase by putting different coloured strands of hot glass on a core and then rolling the result around on a sanded table, when the messenger arrived.

His first reaction was panic, and his second anger. There had been much unrest recently, even at Aketaten. This unrehearsed commotion in the streets, with a hasty impromptu guard, would do nothing to make things any quieter, and there were already rumours enough. She could at least have had the decency to come in a closed litter, as a middle-aged woman should, instead of rattling by for everyone to gape at.

It ruined his whole day and brought back his heartburn. Nothing like this had ever happened before. It shook him out of his mock comedy. He sent at once for Nefertiti, instinctively, and then returned to the palace as publicly and as leisurely as possible, in order to re-establish public confidence.

But, though he smiled and patted the children, and even turned twice, very deliberately, to wave at Smenkara and Meritaten in the two chariots behind, he could scarcely hope to restore what wasn't there, and the effort proved too much for his strength. When he dismounted in the palace yard he was trembling. It took two attendants to hold him up.

He tried to tell himself it was only with rage. That was what he told everybody else. But he knew it wasn't. However, in a few moments his circulation returned to normal and he was able to walk. He found Tiiy in the state hall.

He felt so ill himself that he was not prepared to find that in the past two years she also had aged rapidly.

Her paralysis agitans was quite real, and in a woman so small and tight-skinned, even at fifty-eight, the effect was horrible. Amenophis had had it too. He wondered if he would be next. Perhaps that tremor in his hand was the first warning. Had he not diseases enough already? He could not possibly control them all. He felt a muscle twitch in his cheek. Whatever had happened to the morning? Why only an hour ago he had been in the best of health.

She looked beyond him, at Smenkara, Meritaten, and the oddly silent children. "Get them out," she said.

He did not bother to argue. She was still a considerable actress. One look at the expression on her face convinced him. He got them out.

"Who is this person Pa-wah?" she demanded.

He blinked. It took him a moment to remember. "Assistant to Meryra."

"But not, it appears, fortunately for you, in everything," she snapped. Then she unloaded her bile.

She had added an embellishment here and there, and almost believed the story herself, she had made it so credible, but really, she could see, he was no longer worth killing. He would not last long. All the more reason, then, to force him to act.

He believed her. She could see that. It wouldn't have mattered what she said. Secretly he must have been expecting something like this for years. Besides, he could not have many illusions left, and at least this was a new one. It relieved boredom. In a way it must be some outlet for the frustrations of several years. It even seemed to bring something erect into that slumped, proud and yet defeated posture.

It was not the best of moments for Nefertiti to arrive, but then nobody had bothered to tell her Tiiy was there. She swept into the room blandly, with Tutankaten and the third daughter, Ankesenpa'aten, whom these days she took everywhere with her, as someone secretly timid, though outwardly firm, would walk two dogs.

When she saw Tiiy her eyes widened with astonishment, but she said nothing. She only held the children by the backs of their dresses and stared.

He accused her, in a monotone, repeating Tiiy almost word for word.

"It is not true," she said quietly, but she was breathing fast. "It is only that when you die, someone must carry on. The man Pa-wah is spiteful, and a little deaf. Perhaps he did not understand."

"I am never going to die," he shouted. It was the first time he had shouted in his life. He repeated it, this time quietly and thoughtfully. It was then Tiiy made the mistake of calmly smiling at her daughter.

That was too much. Inside Nefertiti something snapped. She turned on Ikhnaton the whole deadly insight of that one blind eye.

"Not die?" she said. "You stink of corruption. You died a year ago, in that pavilion, when you lay there for fourteen days. Do you think I was not there to watch? Do you think I did not smell it? Have you never seen yourself? Do you dare to scorn me, for this, when you are like that? Your eyes are sallow. Your jaw trembles. Your belly is distended, and you can scarcely walk. Your skin sweats and your touch is revolting. You are four-fifths water, or the sun would shrivel you up. And what else do you think you ever were?"

She stopped. She knew it was something she would never be forgiven for saying, that Tiiy had goaded her into saying. She looked pitiably at them both. It was only anger, pent up too long. But she could read in his eyes that what people say in anger is always the truth. It is only when they are trying to make themselves agreeable that they sometimes have the skill to be able to lie. For the most part of human virtue is based upon an ineptitude for vice. The clever alone are honest, for only they know how to conceal the truth. And yet it does not make them kind.

What she had said was true. He would never forgive her. Again Tiiy smiled. And yet Tiiy was not deliberately cruel. It was just that, in her opinion, for the good of the kingdom, one of them had to go. She did not even want revenge.

Ikhnaton did.

He could not strip her of all position. Public peace would not withstand that. But he could banish her for ever from his sight, to that north palace at the end of the city, from which she was forbidden to emerge, except to worship. And he could strip her of her throne name, then and there. As co-regent with himself, she had been called Nefer-neferu-Aton. He would reduce her to the rank of no more than a discarded minor priestess. The name he would give to the most despised person who came to hand, who in this case turned out to be Smenkara. Smenkara was always at hand when there was something to be given away. Let him receive this highest honour then, as a sign of the contempt in which Ikhnaton held it.

Nefertiti understood his reasoning all too well. She retired as she was ordered, to the northern palace. But at the same time she was careful to take Tutankaten and Ankesenpa'aten with her. She said this was to protect Tutankaten. Actually it was to protect herself. Smenkara was frail and shallow, and with the second heir under her domination, she did not think she would have much to fear. His adherents would have too much to gain by protecting her. For herself she had no love for Tutankaten. However, she was always careful not to show this.

Unfortunately children see more than they are shown, and very little of what they are. Tutankaten at nine was an opportunist. If he consented to go with her, it was only because he was afraid of Smenkara and had to seek shelter somewhere.

Tiiy had had her way in one thing. Now, it appeared, she would have it in another, too.

Ikhnaton made her wait. He brushed her aside, summoned the court, and stripped Meryra of everything. He revealed the whole plot. And since he had to edit Nefertiti out of it, therefore he made Meryra sound the worse. There was some satisfaction in that. The courtiers managed to look both horrified and loyal. He then raised Pa-wah in Meryra's stead. The courtiers managed to applaud virtue and to bow low to this, their new Eminence. Well, that was only to be expected. The chameleon imitates the colour, not the plant.

Pa-wah would have spoken. He sent him away. The man was a fool. Tiiy would have spoken. Her he could not send away, but he could go away himself. He retreated to his own rooms, posted a double guard to prevent her entering, and went to bed.

Tiiy did not try to enter. For the time being she had gained what she wanted. No doubt he was tired. For now he deserved his sulks, and while he sulked, she had much to do. She must consult with Ay and Horemheb.

He was not, however, sulking. Even the bitterest of men must search the bottom of an empty well, for some last scum of water to refresh him. And since he is bitter, then only bitterness can refresh him. For now there was no one left to him. He had fallen into a trap. He should never have sent Meryra and Nefertiti away, even if what Tiiy said was true, for he knew he had not the strength to oppose her alone.

He must find someone.

"To whom can I speak today? I am laden with wretchedness for lack of an intimate friend. To whom can I speak today? The sin which treads the earth, it has no end," said the prophet Nefer-rohu when the Old Kingdom fell, eight hundred years ago. Of course that could be dismissed as pessimism. After all, Egypt was still there. On the other hand, Nefer-rohu wasn't.

"Every mouth is full of love for me, and everything good has disappeared," he had said further. And that alas was not pessimism. That was merely the truth speaking, as usual, out of turn, not too early, as some might like to think, but on the contrary, and also as usual, too late.

But perhaps not utterly too late. If one cannot have anything else, then one must face up to the matter, and have what one can. In the morning he sent for Smenkara.

Alas, Smenkara at twenty-four, Nefer-Neferu-Aton or not, had no resemblance to Nefertiti at fifteen, nor was the year fifteen years ago.

Smenkara, anxious to please, succeeded only in being faintly unpleasant And yet the boy meant well. The boy meant very well. But the ease with which he said what he meant sounded very like the most affable of lies. Smenkara believed in everything. He had no ability to ease the turmoils of a reluctant doubter, for he had never doubted anything since, at the age of five, he had told his first spontaneous lie. Truth, like everything else to him, was merely ornamental.

And yet he was some comfort. At least he was there, he was soothing, and Ikhnaton badly needed rest.

Tiiy would not let him rest. She appeared with Horemheb and Ay, and Smenkara slipped unobtrusively away. He hated scenes.

The political developments were certainly serious. The Syrian Empire was evaporating. Byblos had fallen. Old Gaza, an administrative centre, was undergoing siege, and most assuredly would fall. It was Aziru again, with the Hittites behind him. Ikhnaton must take action at once.

Very well, he thought. Anything to get rid of her. He took action at once. He wrote a letter of admonishment to Aziru. It was all he could do.

For Tiiy also must face realities. There was not

enough money in the treasury to pay the army, even if it should march. He wrote that he would come and kill Aziru if Aziru did not behave. Since nobody in Egypt believed it, it was unlikely that Aziru would believe it either, but what else could he do? It was too late.

Tiiy told him there was much that he could do. He must marry Smenkara and Meritaten and accept the boy as co-regent.

Why not? He had it done at the Aton temple, with Pa-wah to officiate. When the crown first settled on his head, a light muslin pschent for summer wear, Smenkara gave a smile of shy pleasure. Apart from that he seemed totally unaffected. He continued to live in the palace, with Ikhnaton and his wife.

For Tiiy that was not enough. A coronation in Aketaten was no coronation at all. Smenkara and Meritaten must return with her to Thebes.

Ikhnaton refused, though even Ay and Horemheb advised the step. When he demanded why, they told him why.

The Empire was in such peril, that those in Thebes would have to be reconciled. The Amon priests might be disbanded, but they made mischief in a thousand ways. Ikhnaton grew stubborn. The Aton religion was all he had left. He would not give it up.

It was Ay who subtly pointed out that he need not give it up. The two religions could flourish side by side in Thebes, but with Aketaten as the religious capital of the country. This proposal made even Ikhnaton smile. That truth and dishonesty should be worshipped side by side was, to his present mood, both symbolic and agreeable. Was it not ever so?

He let them go. He tried to think it was because, as Ay had pointed out, he could not rule without a full treasury, and that this effort at a reconciliation would replenish the treasury. A practical excuse for what we do is always more convincing and more comforting than the real reasons.

And the real reasons were that he was tired. He longed to rest. And he knew that everything, even the affections, must be paid for, if not with cash, at least with expensive bait. And the reason why everyone became so angry when one said this, was that it was true and they knew it. They might be sorry it was true, but that would only make them the angrier. The giver was always hurt. The taker only sometimes.

Now Smenkara was Pharaoh too, he wanted a nest of his own. Ikhnaton understood. It was what he himself had wanted. He gave in.

"Anything," he said. "Anything. Only leave me alone."

They left him alone.

A week later they departed for Thebes. He even went down to the jetty to watch them go. Tiiy carried Smenkara and Meritaten about as though they were no more than the symbols of her own office. Perhaps that was all they were. He did not envy Smenkara. And as for Meritaten, it was better not to have any feelings about her at all, since seemingly she had none.

Horemheb and Ay also returned to the old capital. From now on they would alternate between the two cities. As the boat moved out into midstream, Smenkara seemed frightened. He looked back out of startled eyes, and waved. It was the last Ikhnaton ever saw of him.

Ikhnaton returned to his own quarters, slowly and reluctantly. It was now only a matter of keeping up appearances, but once one has seen through appearances, that is not so difficult to do. One has only to hold them from the back, like a shield, and they protect one quite well.

He had sworn never to leave this glorious city of the sun, where he would live for ever and ever. But that had been a matter of choice. Now he saw that he could not leave it. He did not dare to do so.

He moved through time as though suspended in some fluid preservative. The months went by. It a little restricted his movements, but it kept him alive. No doubt he could have learned what was happening in Thebes, but he did not wish to. Horemheb and Ay came and went, but had rather less time for him than before. When he gave orders, they obeyed them and carried them out, but with something like impatience. He saw that look on the faces of the palace servants, too, and on those of the courtiers.

For he went on seeing the same familiar faces. It was merely that now he saw fewer of them. That was only reasonable. Not even Egypt had enough nobles to stock three courts. There was not only Thebes and his own, but Nefertiti had gathered a considerable party around herself and Tutankaten, mostly of those new nobles whose fortunes would stand or fall with the Aton cult, the nobles he himself had raised up, until they were big enough to leave him.

He would almost have called her back. It was ridiculous that they should be at opposite ends of the city, with the neutral, sleeping slums between them. Her speaking in anger he could have forgiven, but her speaking the truth in anger he could not. For truth is the worst lie of all. It brings down all our illusions.

He heard of her only through Pa-wah.

Recently Ikhnaton had slighted the temple ceremonies. He had not felt up to them. Now he exerted himself. He asked questions. He asked Pa-wah questions about her. He would never see her again, but he did want to know what she was doing.

Reluctantly Pa-wah told him. No one than she could be more devoted to the Aton. Even Tutankaten and Ankhesenpa'aten accompanied her to the ceremonies. He had had to ask her to moderate her zeal, on the grounds that so much fatigue was bad for the boy. But she, too, it seemed, was dedicated to the Aton. While she lived there would be no backsliding.

"To the Aton?" asked Ikhnaton blankly.

"To the supreme, all-knowing, all beneficent disc of the Sun," said Pa-wah.

"Oh yes," said Ikhnaton hastily. "Yes, of course."

He had only to look at the man to know that Pa-wah believed every word of it. For some reason this glimpse into rabid belief was not encouraging. He wanted to say: "My dear man, what on earth can you possibly know about it?"

Of course, from the gleam in his eye, Pa-wah knew everything about it, and not even Pharaoh, his own god, was any longer in a position to tell him otherwise. Ikhnaton could only wonder if when he himself had had that fervour, he had looked like that. The thought was sobering.

And could it possibly be true that the Queen was devout? No, he gave her more credit than that, for she had started at that point of amused indulgence that he had now reached only after the fatigues of a long journey through disillusionment. Yet, when your favourite doll is battered and broken, you do not throw it away. Instead you love it more than ever, for it has been with you for a long while, and you can still remember how it used to look. It gave him a certain pleasure to listen to the ravings of Pa-wah.

Indeed, perhaps it was better this way, with Smenkara and Tiiy in Thebes running the country to suit themselves, and he here left in peace. Why was it, then, that moving through the dusty rooms of the palace he sometimes found himself walking on tiptoe? And in the inner sanctuary of the temple, where even now he went to lay his flowers, he looked round that whitewashed emptiness and sometimes had the illusion that Nefertiti was there. He could almost hear her voice, and he

213

still, from force of habit, used that perfume special to them both.

His strength had rallied, and he was able to take chariot rides again. He no longer took them through the crowded noon city, for the cheering got on his nerves. Instead he would leave at night, preferably very early, just before dawn. One of his real pleasures was still to see the dawn come up. That still moved him deeply, as the first warm rays touched his face. Indeed, it was something to move the entire world, if the world were awake to see it. It had been his great fault not to know that the world prefers to sleep in.

It was on such a morning, clattering through the unweeded and still nocturnal streets, that something in a side alley caught his eye and he reined in to watch.

It was the servants of some noble, carrying their master's household furniture through the furtive streets. And those cloaked figures, surely they must be the master and his family? He could not recognize who they were.

He galloped to the docks, got down to the ground, and leaning in the shadow of the door to a warehouse, watched. Yes, there were five boats being readied. And while he waited, not one, but three processions began to converge upon the jetty, amid the hushed orders of sailors and stevedores. He remained quite motionless. He watched it all. The three families had pooled their resources, no doubt.

As dawn began to seep over the cliffs, the boats put out to the middle of the river, very quietly. Why on earth did they bother to be so clandestine about the matter? he wondered. A light breeze stirred along the water, the sails ran up, and the boats tacked towards the south. Thebes.

With a wry smile he went back to his chariot and returned to the alley. He recognized the house, now. No doubt they had left a caretaker. The door to the garden stood open. He stepped inside, with a glance at the small Aton temple beyond the pool, and went into the house. The hieroglyphics on the door lintel told him the place belonged to Tutu, a noble in the Foreign Office. No doubt Smenkara or Tiiy had made him a better offer. The house was a shambles. He kicked aside a wine jar on the floor. The wooden columns alone were left. Perhaps they had not dared to take them yet, but they would call for them in time, of that he was sure.

He thought it fitting that the first man he had ennobled should be the first to go over to the other side. He could even admire his courage for having been, if only in this clandestine manner, the first to leave.

He returned to the palace and slept all day. When he woke, it was with caution, for the beautiful child of Aton was not very beautiful any more.

Once he had asked Tutmose why he preferred to do only masks. Tutmose had thought for a while, and then said, "One morning you will wake up and discover your face is only a mask. We all do."

Well, he had, and it was.

None the less, there were deceptive mornings when he felt quite healthy, mornings when the sunrise could be believed in. He persuaded himself then that life was as it always was.

Death was getting closer, all the same. In Thebes, after a short and unforeseen illness, Tiiy unexpectedly died.

Now it was Horemheb's turn to discover that loneliness is the greediest guest at any feast, the one who stays on after the others have sensibly gone home. It was something he could not mention even to Ay, the way he felt. But wandering a little lost through the palace at Aketaten, he came at last to the household magazines and saw on the shelves the rotten fruit they no longer had the time to eat, that sat on the shelf and spoiled. Idly he picked up an apricot that dissolved in his hand. Why, of all fruit, is it the most rotten that has the most tantalizing smell?

Angrily he flung it down against the wall.

Seventeen

They lived on that way for another six months.

We think the upper air is inhabited no higher than the most ambitious hawk, the one with the keenest vision and the swiftest pounce, who likes to fly alone. But much higher than that, in the thin violet world between the atmosphere and that space which we like to believe contains nothing, there is a complex society of ancient bacteria.

These are the inert husks of quite a different life, frozen out there, a crew of diseases in suspended animation, in order to survive the long voyage to their destination. Then something happens. We do not know what. Something thaws them out, and a new kind of darkness falls from the air, like the invisible ashes of a plague. And thus, after all, the sun which not only gives, but also takes away, and has given the world so much, now gives the thinning gift of a new disease.

But we do not know this. It takes some time to learn that the enemy has landed.

The city was already a little unreal.

Horemheb and Ay were in Thebes, and it was they now, more than Ikhnaton, who kept Aketaten going. The others all went on tiptoe through the neglected streets.

Yet from a distance the city still looked much the same.

But, if a city may do such a thing, it looked thinner, and somehow defenceless at sunset, under those angry red cliffs. The sun ebbed away from the entrances to the rock tombs quite early in the day, and one might look up and see the black doorways, like small square samples of the night.

It was a little restless. With less to do on the public works, the workers roamed the streets, followed closely by the police and army. The nobles seldom appeared in public any more, and then only on their way somewhere. The passage of the day was marked by three or four habitual processions. Nefertiti left her new palace in the northern suburb, accompanied by a sleepy and resentful Tutankaten, at dawn, moving to the Aton temple in a tight knot of nobles and guards, to celebrate the sunrise. There were also two new cermonies invented by Pa-wah, the kindling of the divine fire, and the perpetuation of the divine fire. These over, and the toy white procession moved back to the northern suburb, not to re-emerge again until sunset. Though it was difficult to find new acolytes, and several of the old had disappeared already, presumably to Thebes, Pa-wah was always busy.

Ikhnaton did not appear. He was ill. The court did not quite know what to do, but was not unduly worried. The dynasty, in the person of Smenkara, was safe. But they moderated their adoration of the Aton. Service in the palace was slack. It was hard to find the servants, let alone to get them to do anything. In the zoo the great cats snarled restlessly, or lay under the trees. Sometimes now they were not fed. But the inertia of the installed officials was enough to keep the machine in operation, and they were as busy as ever, indulging themselves in last-minute peculation.

Then, it was impossible to keep the matter secret, it was found out that Pharaoh had a new disease. He had Asiatic cholera. He was unable, any longer, to give orders.

Pharaoh's illnesses, like the headaches of a major prophet, were well known and bothered nobody. One had merely to loiter outside the closed doors of his apartments, with an ironic smile, waiting to be told what to do by the invisible presence. It had become a regular part of the day, and everyone enjoyed it, for you met your friends there, and could talk over the current gossip. But Asiatic cholera was another matter. It was neither a pretty nor a strategic disease. And now, of course, there were no orders.

The courtiers prowled the corridors in anxious gangs, like greyhounds without either a rabbit or a master. They had run this track so long that they had almost forgotten how to run in any other. It was the absence of a rabbit that bothered them most. Automatically, at the correct hours, they found themselves tugging towards the same mechanical bait, and now it wasn't there. The wisest of them, the most independent, retired to their own houses to await developments. And no one had seen the three princesses for days. A few, perhaps, looked at their wooden pillars and estimated the cost and trouble of shipping them to Thebes.

In the absence of anyone else of authority, decisions rested with the chief household steward, a harassed man who had not been out of the palace for ten years. It was he who remembered to have the princesses fed. Pa-wah should have been consulted, but was not. And since Nefertiti represented an opposing faction, with her own court, it was to nobody's self-interest to notify her.

The chief household steward called in Mahu, the chief of police. But Mahu would do nothing. The mobs were beyond his ability to control. He did, however, post guards around the palace and sent a despatch to Horemheb, at Thebes. Then he retired to his own household and bolted the doors.

A great many bolts shot home during that anxious four days. For that was how long the crisis lasted, four days. The chief steward caught a glimpse of Pentu's face, as he left the royal apartments, and being a methodical man, sent for mortuary workers. These, unknown to Ikhnaton, were installed at once.

Behind the palace, at one end of the store-houses and magazines, was the mortuary yard where Maketaten's funeral furniture had been prepared. Work was resumed, on a day and night shift, for there was much to be done in a hurry. At night the adjacent courtyards were lit by the uncertain fury of the workers' torches and flares.

Cholera is a contagious disease. It was remarkable how suddenly that palace became empty.

But Ikhnaton had a wily body. Weak and diseased from birth, he had learned a thousand ways to stay alive, of which epileptoid fits were by no means the least. Now, unexpectedly, he seemed to rally. Indeed, one symptom of that disease is a last-minute impulse towards wandering.

He had been comatose, but not altogether unconscious. He saw his body subjectively from the inside. It was an echoing flannel tunnel, hollow the way a broken, fallen bronze statue is hollow. Through the tunnel a heavy plush water was ebbing away, with the illusion of running faster than it was running, constantly speeding up, until the surface, if it had a surface, became an oily blur. He did not watch this from his head, or mentally, because his head was stuffed up and wadded with the white-yellow-green offal of a lobster. He watched it from some hummock inside there, about where his lungs would be. He knew of course that this had to be stopped, because it meant that he was dying, but he did not want to stop it. Bits of the roof of the tunnel seemed to be caving in, and the echo was not so much a sound as a texture. Though he knew he should panic, his consciousness felt too humid and heavy, with a dangerous placidity that prevented him from turning to flee. The process was too inevitable not to be fascinating, and he could not help but watch it idly. Besides, it had nothing to do with him. It was just something he was watching, with a completely absorbed incuriosity. It had nothing to do with him in any way. So this, he realized cosily, was dying. He had never expected to watch the process and still live.

He felt no panic, though he was dimly aware that he should feel panic. When he got back he must set down the process in detail, and he felt rather pleased with himself on the whole, because no one else had ever been able to report it before. It was being watched, but it must look very different from the outside.

Then he realized it had touched him. It had lapped round his will, until he had no desire to do anything but go along with it, like a log, safely rooted to the bank, that of its own volition abruptly, with a sort of comic sigh, shoots out into the main stream, and is sucked away even as it at last realizes what is happening. It was like being lapped by a tight, viscous honey, full of drowned midges, up to his ankles. It was pleasant; and then, frighteningly, it took hold.

In that moment he knew that he had only the second between the grip wrapping round him and tightening to escape. Otherwise he would be swept away with it. But there was nothing he could hold on to. He couldn't raise his body. The connective muscles would not respond. The luxury of that vertigo was too intense. He was covered with fur and couldn't move. He knew the only way to escape was to feel frightened, but he couldn't feel frightened. It was too much of an effort.

But that part of his will which was untouchable even by his will got him to his feet. There was a sort of wrenching plop, and he was standing up. He noticed that though he was now vertical, his consciousness was still somehow rushing unconsciously through those horizontal tunnels. If he could get his body away from there, perhaps it would be all right.

It did not occur to him that he could not get his body

away from his body. He did not know what part of him was directing what part of him. Perhaps his muscles were more tenacious of life than he, but since, having lost his brain, he could no longer communicate with them, he let his body go where it would, only impersonally concerned with whether it would win out this time or not, but inwardly smiling, because he knew it wouldn't, he had caught it out at last, but still, you had to admire the stubbornness with which it was trying.

At the last moment, it was said, you were overwhelmed by light. He knew perfectly well what was happening, but had been so busy to prevent its doing so that he had not had the time to think. Now, abruptly, his head was almost clear. He opened his eyes.

For a moment the room was unfamiliar. Egyptian bedrooms were too strait. He needed space. His hearing, for the first time in his life, was acute. He could listen to the contented, snake-like slither of the flames in every lamp, echoed from the cornice of golden uraei beneath the ceiling. He struggled to his feet, swaying and bald without his wig, and lurched out into the corridor. He moved automatically through swirling shadows, towards the light, and so came out into a garden courtyard.

Why was everything so restless? It was as though death were everywhere, quietly stalking him through the reeds. Here and there he seemed to catch the glimmer of its plump, sturdy, bare calves. The wind was warm and blew every which way. He could hear a snarl from the zoo, the fretful piping of a thousand birds who had had the feathers on their bottoms stirred. And there was another sound, quite dreadful, an echo of the sound he had pretended to hear years ago at that temple up the river from Thebes, and now really heard, the sighing sound of the desert, as the

222

sand danced over its surface like beige snow. And how it mocked.

He felt weak. He vomited. Clutching a pillar, he forced himself on, towards a glow of light somewhere in the distance. For he had been wrong to doubt, he never had doubted, he never now would doubt, the glorious power of light. His eyelids were granulated and painful. He had always believed. It was only the other believers of whom he made mock. He had only to live until dawn, to reach that light ahead, to be well again. He would live for ever.

But why was he alone here, and why were there not more lamps? The light seemed closer now, brighter, higher, and soon the sun would be almost visible, and he would be safe. His vision had narrowed to that oblong of light ahead, and he struggled towards it. He had to reach it, and he did reach it. He held on to the doorway and peered out.

It was the mortuary yard.

The workers looked up, saw who it was, and dropped their tools. For what they saw was the very image of the death they were carving. He saw the row of ushabtis, tightly bound in, like Osiris, with his head on each of them.

Their sweaty unshaved faces stared at him in shocked disbelief. "And the dead king, Amen-em-het, said to his son: hold thyself apart from those subordinate to thee, lest that should happen to whose terrors no attention has been given." It had happened. He turned and fled. He called out for Pentu, for Nefertiti, for Smenkara, even for Ay and Horemheb. There was no answer. For the things of the mind are irreversible. They go right along their road to the end, right to the end of the night. Even his own god had failed.

It was the death of a grasshopper. And ants are sanctimonious. Grasshoppers suffer horribly. For to be amusing and to give generously is not the same as credit. Our debtors have no charity. Their only mercy in the winter is to tell us how foolish we were to have given them anything. No doubt they are right, but there is nothing to be gained from a lesson in morality after the act has been done.

He had reached the shadowy banqueting hall. There stood the throne. He lurched towards it. For after all, God or no God, he was still Pharaoh. He swayed up the steps of the dais. Vision narrowed down. He turned to confront that empty hall. The first thing he had thrown away was now the last thing he wanted, for it was the only thing he could have. He smiled.

And then, at last, it was dawn. The light lapped and caught at the gardens and the pillars of the hall and slid smoothly across the painted floor and up his face. It might have been a benediction.

His only mistake had been a slight confusion. Pharaoh had always been worshipped as a god, and he was the glorious child of the Aton, so why should they not worship him? But men do not worship the source of life. They worshipped Pharaoh only for what they worshipped in themselves, the source of favour, wealth, and power. For men do not adore anything. Men who do we avoid as absent-minded fools, worthy of our hate because, after all, there is the uneasy suspicion that they may have something we cannot lay our hands on, and nothing is so infuriating as intangible wealth, for it cannot be stolen. Real men worship only what they fear, and what they fear to lose. Religion is not insight. Religion is only a system of bribes and indulgences, rewards and benefits, a matter of making ourselves comfortable at God's expense, as we do at Pharaoh's. Insight is something we should do better to keep to ourselves, otherwise someone will find a way to take it away from us. For men are clever. Give them time and they will pull anything down, including the roof over their heads.

He did well to die there, on the throne.

And there they found him, early in the morning, crumpled up at the foot of the dais, dead and fallen from the throne, and what he had spewed up was like plump white maggots, who had eaten him away from within.

As soon as they heard the news, the mortuary workers struck at once. It was what they had planned to do all along. In that hot climate a body could not wait. It was what they always did. Each new death always meant slightly higher wages.

And in Thebes, even before they knew he was dead, for the course of cholera was certain, at the temple of Amon, with solemn seriousness, the priests rolled out that horrible jointed doll again, and freshened up their vestments, too. For them it was a great victory, and as they had known, they had only had to wait.

There was not even enough money in the treasury at Aketaten to bury him.

In the palace everything was chaos. It was not only the endless, undulant wailing of the professional mourners, or even the anxieties of Pa-wah, caught without a precedent or a ritual and incompetent besides. Nefertiti appeared with a small guard and her own corps of nobles, but even they were loyal only by circumstances. It was that everywhere everyone was packing up, prepared to take refuge with Smenkara at Thebes. He was a weakling. They would swiftly overpower him with loyalty, seize the government, and make their peace with Amon afterwards. Nefertiti could do nothing. It was all very well for Pa-wah to hold processions in the streets and swear to the eternal life of the Aton. He found no compurgators, even among his own priests. The Aton was no more·than a foible of Pharaoh's. Naturally being loyal to Pharaoh had meant humouring him in this. But the nobles already had new arguments ready. With Pharaoh dead, loyalty to his foibles would be disloyalty to his successor, and that meant disgrace, dishonour, and confiscation of their property.

Unfortunately no matter is so easily solved, for even an empire takes a while to die.

Horemheb, already on his way back from Thebes in any case, arrived, took over the police, paid the mortuary workers, and established order. Ay remained at Thebes. Until some answer came from Smenkara, everyone was to stay where he was. To make sure that they did, Horemheb closed off the harbour and set heavy guards to patrol the streets.

Meanwhile Tutmose had appeared at the palace. He had taken their faces for almost twenty years. He would also take this one, since the mortuary artists needed a model from which to work. That was not, however, his real purpose.

He had grown older himself. It made him sympathetic with death.

Pharaoh had been carried back to his own apartments and deposited rather unceremoniously on his own wooden bed. It was late afternoon and the room was deserted. Tutmose's slave put down his master's tools and withdrew. Tutmose went over to the bed and looked down.

Ikhnaton dead was not agreeable. He had the distended belly of a dog drowned in the river, and the body stripped, one could see that pathetic little penis was the black colour of a shrivelled artichoke. But while he watched the face became beautiful. Pharaoh had not lost faith after all, for we never lose what we are born with. We slide back as easily as we slide away, for some things are bred in the bone, and though the flesh may engulf them, they show up again quite readily, when the bones show through at the end.

It was like the difference between playing the harp and performing on it. About a performance there is

226

always something hard and brittle. It is the thing exhibited from the outside, for public view. Thus the parody of the last years. But if the performer is also a player, he never quite loses his contact with the music, no matter what he may do to it extrinsically, parody it though he may be forced to do. Understanding and virtuosity are poles apart, but precisely because they are, they manage to co-exist.

And if you know the musician in that late virtuoso stage, as Tutmose had done for many years, you may still come upon him unexpectedly and find him actually playing. He will not then play very well, for he is not trying to impress anybody. But he is totally selfless and intrinsic with the work. He plays then with love and understanding, until one realizes that he doesn't believe in the concert version either, and never did. From a sort of admiring scorn one is thus forced to turn to a genuine admiration. For what he believes in, in private, behind all that flashy and necessary cynicism and rubato, is becoming one with the work. And so, idly listening, one understands it too, for after all, the point of any composition does not reside precisely either in the notes or in the accuracy with which they are played.

Looking down at Ikhnaton's already withdrawn face, Tutmose could see that very well, and it did not displease him. It only made him sad. For he himself did not share that certainty. When you come right down to it, though other people may believe in the integrity of the artist's beliefs, the artist knows that he has no beliefs about anything. All he believes in is the validity, indeed the paramount importance, of the quality and process of the act of believing.

So the artist whose subject matter is religion itself is always the victim of scepticism, for he alone knows it has no object, but is only a process. In the circumstances he has nothing ahead of him but disillusion. So Tutmose had the more rewarding task, for as a different kind of artist, he did not have to concern himself with ends. To him everything was merely a means.

And yet, at these ultimate moments, one believes in something. He had a lifetime filled with faces to show it forth. But he was very glad that, unlike Ikhnaton, he had never had to be certain as to what that something was.

Having taken his cast, he went back to his studio. Insight is very dangerous. It disqualifies one for the immediate concerns of life. Unless one has the strength always to remember that what is true in one world can never be true in the other, one is apt to break oneself to pieces on the sharp edges of the incongruities between them. For this reason the Orientals are wise, to put off meditation until middle age, when the immediate involvements of life are usually over, for having become a physiological spectator, one is quite willing to admit that, after all, we do live in plural worlds, through which we most wisely proceed as the body shuts behind us one door after another on the now discarded physical delights. For one cannot furnish an altar with chairs and tables appropriate to a bedroom, or a bedroom with the bare walls of heaven.

It is only reasonable. One cannot breathe until one is born; one cannot talk until one has learned to breathe; one cannot take action until one has learned to move; one cannot think until one has learned that action is limited; one cannot concentrate until one has learned to think; one cannot meditate until concentration has taught one how limited is thought; one cannot perceive until one learns that meditation is not concerned with perception; and one cannot die until one has been reborn. And one certainly cannot have eternal life until one learns that it has nothing to do with mortality. And to do anything backwards, or at the wrong time or position, causes severe cramp and often deformation.

Nor, unfortunately, does the artist create. That is an illusion of the non-creative, who still believe that all things are made somewhere and had a moment when they did not exist. But an artist, in seeing that things are and are not simultaneously, knows he can only set down the appearance of one or the other at a particular moment and from a particular angle from which, perhaps, it may be true, since we call him creative, no one else had thought to look.

So he made a mask from the mould and set it up with the others. He had now the whole family, or almost the whole family, and the others would come with time.

That afternoon Nefertiti came to the studio. She had not set foot there for two years. He did not find her older. On the contrary, he found her congruent with that statue he had never shown her, the one behind the curtain, in a niche of its own.

She looked at the mask intently. "What does it mean," she said at last.

"What difference does it make? I never judge. I let my hands do that."

"You've collected all of us. Why?"

He stirred uneasily, for she had moved him. "Not all art has a meaning. Sometimes one plays, and that is when one does one's best work. When one forgets one is playing. But as for being earnest about it, ah, you will never do anything that way. It is our great secret, we so-called artists. You know how it is. The incompetent like things they have to admire to be a little difficult. They've gone to all that trouble to admire them, even asked someone what they should admire, which is humiliating, it may have taken them years to see what you're getting at, and naturally they want it to be hard for you, too. You can't blame them. They never understand that the inconsequential is such hard work. It takes a lifetime.

"One has to be alone, you see. Oh not to think. Nothing as serious-minded as that. But it is such an effort, you know, to learn how not to think. One needs quiet for that. Sometimes I sit here all day and nothing happens. The sun comes up and goes down. Or sometimes I listen to the fish. And then my fingers get hungry. They feed on plaster, you know. And then they show me what I have to say."

"And what do you have to say?"

"Nothing. Oh, always nothing. But that sound when the fish jump, like a fifth and a second on a harp. A sort of plonk, and yet a sort of silence. You can find it between the eyelid and the eye, that little fold between the eyelid and the eye couldn't have happened on any other face, though I don't even remember whose face it was. Perhaps neither does he. So that is what one does, you know: work every day, watch as much as you can, and wait. For the artist isn't a mystic any more than the mystic is a mystic. They're both too busy looking to go to the bother of living up to a name. And these aren't portraits. They are just the faces one always needed, and a face is only a mask for what we mean."

"You've never talked that way before."

"My subject matter never died before, either."

She glanced round the studio and smiled slowly, but with such a different smile from the smile on her bust up there, on its bracket above them.

"You'll wait to do me now," she said. "You'll need that."

For that he had no answer.

On the bench the mask of Ikhnaton seemed to glow and shift. It was a trick of the still wet plaster, and that was all his work was, really. They owed their immortality, and he his life, to nothing more than the properties of plaster. But it was a pity that she had grown so wise.

"What's behind it all?" she asked.

Again he could not say anything helpful. "One goes through reality like a series of rooms," he said. "Always looking for what is behind appearance. And then, when one is tired, one thinks one has found the ultimate door, opens it, and comes out on the other side. Then one looks back, and sees nothing but the opposite façade, and one wonders what is behind that, the habit of searching is so strong, forgetting of course that one has been through the rooms, otherwise one would not have seen that the back façade and the front are identical. So it's easy to become confused. All one can say is that at last one has seen both. That's all we can ever hope to do. To see both."

That made her wistfully angry. "Do one's servants always turn out to be one's masters?" she asked.

"Yes, usually. They're interchangeable, like everything else." He gave her an ironic bow, simply because he did not feel in the least ironic, and knew she would never come to see him again. As before, with the slave to hold his tools, he would have to go to her.

But it was a pity. From disliking her, he had come to like her very much. And that, too, come to think of it, fitted into the parable of the two façades.

Pharaoh was buried the proper eighty days later, under a heavy army guard, in the unfinished Royal Tomb, in the room beyond that where Maketaten lay sealed up. The last thing they carried into his tomb was his bed. He had never been very happy in it living. Perhaps he would be more comfortable in it now. And so, having laid away the beautiful child of the Aton, the rest of the world turned to its own concerns.

It was difficult to know what to do. The city was already almost abandoned, and yet they dare not leave. No orders, as yet, had come from Smenkara and Thebes.

So life went on a little longer, like a turbine in an abandoned generator house, breaking down, but still with a few revolutions left to go, before the lights suddenly flicker and go out circuit by circuit, as the power is withdrawn closer and closer to the source, so that it at least may continue to burn bright, even though there is not enough to go round.

And then, just as they were all packing anyway, the news came that Smenkara had died in Thebes, of the same disease as Tiiy. It did not mean much. It was like the darkness of an exhausted candle. It would have snuffed itself out soon in any case.

Eighteen

Nefertiti moved at once. Of course she could not win, and yet for a while it seemed as though she could. For three years chaos was to have a director.

The northern palace was altogether a makeshift affair, splendid, but unfinished, and much too small. That end of the city lay across a wadi and at the far end a wall had been built from the cliffs to the shore, with the northern customs house on the other side of it. Living there, she could control the revenues of the northern customs house. Those and the temple lands supported not only her, but also her court. For she had a court, chiefly by design, of needy nobles who could expect nothing from Thebes, and whose loyalty to the Aton was therefore as desperate as it was assured.

She did not bother to send for Ay or Horemheb. She went herself to wake Tutankaten, at three o'clock in the morning, and led him by the hand to the central hall. There Ankesenpa'aten was waiting. The girl was now thirteen. Nefertiti had them married at once and Tutankaten proclaimed Pharaoh and Lord of the Aton. The business was done almost before her nobles were roused and assembled. Then, with Pa-wah to help, and what else could Pa-wah do but help, she had runners sent through the city, to announce the news. It was cried everywhere, and before the citizens, or more important, the army or the police, had time to recover from the announcement, heavily defended by guards and priests, the entire party made a state progress through the hostile city and gathering crowds to the Royal Palace. She had had the priesthood turned out everywhere. They were to hold rites, processions, anything, to keep the streets and temples clogged with some sort of ostentation and order. She was shrewdly sure the others would fall into line.

Tutankaten was then ten. He too fell into line. He did not protest. He too was shrewd and he knew far too much. He was also sufficiently worldly to realize that she was quite capable of having him murdered and herself proclaimed in his stead. For the moment, until he had a court of his own, he would obey. Besides, it was exciting to stand there unblinking, in the dawn streets, his bony knuckles tight on the rail of the chariot, and to feel on his head, for the first time, the weight of the double crown.

There was no one to bar their way at the palace. By the time Horemheb was up, and as for Ay, he never rose early any more, she had him firmly seated on the throne. She had brought it off. There was nothing for even the more powerful nobles to do but sigh heavily and unpack. For he was the legitimate and only male heir, and if he was also a child of ten, and she had taken advantage of the situation to have herself created regent, there was nothing, for the time being, that anyone could do about that, since with Tiiy dead, neither was there any other legitimate regent.

She knew exactly what she meant to do. She meant to rule. After all, had she not ruled, more or less, for years?

It was not her fault if she underestimated the intelligence of a virtual child. For she made the same mistake with Tutankaten others had made with Ikhnaton. It had simply never occurred to her to ask what he thought about or what he knew.

He knew, as it turned out, a great deal, and what he chiefly knew was that he hated his sister Nefertiti, was afraid of Ay, and loathed Horemheb on sight, all of which he kept tactfully to himself.

What on earth would have happened if he had not been so frail, for like all the rest of them he was obscurely clever, adroit at intrigue, and so tutored in cynicism from the cradle that cynicism had become a way of life. For cynics also have their blind spot, which can be played upon. They would have us be cynical only about those things they are cynical about, but he was cynical about everything and knew exactly what he wanted. He wanted his own way.

The problem was, how to get it.

He waited three years, quietly, but there was very little that missed that suddenly divine eye. He had nothing against Aton worship. The ceremonial was pleasing, he was at the centre of it, and it was only a little boring. He did have a great deal against Nefertiti's devotion to it. She insisted upon temple ritual, when what he wanted to do was to go hunting on the cliff-top deserts. He went to hunt on the cliff-top deserts. If she wanted the religion to herself, let her have it.

This attitude pleased her. She thought that her dominance over him was complete, and it was refreshing once more to be in the public eye. She took over most of his temple duties and intrigued with the cabinet while he was off to snare a rabbit.

She overlooked the truth that at any moment, once he had some power behind him, he could fling the cabinet out overnight and bring in a new one. She thought instead that she had cleverly consolidated her own power. And so, for that matter, did Ay and Horemheb. It never occurred to them that he knew enough about government to supplant them.

As a matter of fact, they were quite right. He knew nothing about government. But then he didn't have to. For as Pharaoh he was the government, and the government was whatever he chose to call it. But not until he could find some power to put behind him, and certainly he had none where he was.

It was, he saw, a paper city. He could see at a glance how makeshift the palace was. It was certainly gorgeous. But he had only to take a walk to discover that they lived only in part of it. At least two-thirds of it now were walled off, and at the southern pleasure palace of Gem-Aton the water had drained out of the lake, so that dead bulrushes stood rigid in a tight vise of cracked mud as solid as cement.

Also the building had its anomalies. He discovered them one by one. The female harem he found interesting, and Nefertiti amiably kept it restocked. But it did seem to him that the older women had grown slovenly from disuse. He had them shipped away and redistributed as household servants.

But what of that other harem? That was indeed an oddity. The machinery of the palace administration still maintained it, but here and there in the corridors you came on a mummified mouse that nobody had bothered to sweep up. And who were all these ageing young men who used too much kohl and rouge, seemed to have such faith in the rejuvenative powers of musk and sandalwood, and who now had a frugal little orgy once a week on three bottles of Ikhnaton's very best wine of the Royal House of the Aton, saved out of their daily allotment? It made him giggle, but it was not for him to make economies. He left them where they were, as a pious monument to his regal brother, whom he hadn't liked either.

Like so many people in frail health, he thought nothing so much proved his own virility and stamina as a few drolls, dwarfs, hunchbacks, and cripples to serve as skulls at the highly enjoyable feast. Except for the replenished harem, those at court obediently managed to grow uglier. And when he was bored or depressed he could always look at his guardian's white eye.

His first petty act of revenge was to have her pet

great cats hauled off in cages and released in the desert, for him to hunt. He had the pelts made into rugs.

Unfortunately the cats had ceased to amuse her the night she had gone to bed with Horemheb. She walked over the new rugs without comment, complimented him on his prowess, and even said they looked quite nice.

At the same time he was forced to alter his opinion of Horemheb. Though out of condition, the man knew everything about hunting and proved a good companion in the chase He was respectful without grovelling, and besides, as head of an army loyal only to himself, he had great power. In short, he had to be won over. Besides, no less than the chase, and in exactly the same way, military prowess was something enjoyable. It was impossible to consider Syria. Ay always bored him with talk of Syria. But he saw no reason why tame Nubians should not be as exhilarating to kill as tame great cats. The danger was equally slight, given one went out with a sufficient number of beaters, and the counterfeit equally exciting. And then there was glory in it. Glory was what he wanted. Therefore he was always careful to take Horemheb's advice.

On the other hand, there seemed to be something between Horemheb and the Queen. Not exactly an intrigue, of that he was sure, but something. They seemed to respect each other, and though Horemheb was stupid enough to be loyal to the throne, he was more loyal to the throne than to its present occupant. He would do what was best for the country, and what was best for the country might not necessarily be best for Tutankaten.

He solved that problem neatly by ignoring Ay's fears of further revolts in what was left of Syria and sending Horemheb north to Memphis, to reorganize both the internal and external defences of the country at that strategic administrative capital, and also to prepare the coming Nubian campaign.

It made him breathe easier to have Horemheb gone. Now he needed a tool to use against Nefertiti.

He was not in the least taken in by Aketaten. There were more priests than ever and they swarmed everywhere. The rituals went on all day. But grass grew in the streets and he could not help but notice that, though it was true, the Aton was all powerful and he was its living incarnation, and therefore all powerful too, the priests never left the boundaries of the city; and come to think of it, except for his wild animal hunts, neither did he.

If he was all powerful, then he must be all powerful somewhere else. But where? Horemheb was safely at Memphis. That left him Thebes.

He was then thirteen and a half, and though that was not the legal age of manhood, he had something better to bargain with than manhood. He was Pharaoh. He undertook negotiations with Thebes at once. Because they had to be undertaken in secret, they took six months.

He could not help but smile. He saw again familiar faces he had not seen for months, and they were now happy faces. It was as though he had suddenly joined a secret fraternity, which met at the throne instead of at some private house. And a few concessions to one religion were certainly to be preferred to total concessions to another, and that one moribund.

In Thebes there would be a new coronation. They would roll out that doll again now, for good. But though that might sober him, he was not one to be afraid of dolls. He had played with them all his life, and like all thoughtful children, he knew very well how terrible they could be. He was quite prepared to have one reach out and touch him. And a fear of the dark is small enough price to pay for the pleasures of the day. Besides, unlike other terrifying things, a doll can in the last resort be put away once we are strong enough to remove it.

Since it was necessary to reconcile one greed with another, he would first take away the army's gold monopoly, and then give half of it back, leaving the other half to Amon.

That done, and he was almost ready. He had had enough of the tyranny of women, first from his mother, then from Nefertiti. But he moved with care. Though Nefertiti must know something was going on, she must not know what that thing was, until it was over. There was, for instance, the transportation problem to be solved. He solved it.

And then his moment came.

On the 10th day of the month of Athyr, year 1366, he rose particularly early and went to the temple, to celebrate the rebirth of the eternal Aton disc. Nefertiti was there, and he would not have missed the occasion for anything. The weather was cool and there was a stiff breeze. He said a few words to Pa-wah, congratulated the Queen on her appearance, and was just leaving the temple when news came that an immense flotilla was appearing round the bend of the river.

Of course it was. It had been hove-to over night, with instructions to appear at this hour. He had himself driven immediately to the wharfs.

To tell the truth it was thrilling. Over and over again, one behind the other, in a solemn wedge, the boats appeared from behind the cliffs, the air lifting happily at their sails, water birds screaming and wheeling over them, as the prows rose and fell on the almost motionless water. There must have been two hundred of them, chiefly the gold and ebony state barges of the nobility, some of them sailing for the first time in twenty years out of their berths at Thebes.

As the sun grew stronger, there rose up from them the faintly mocking rejoicing of a hundred orchestras, to mix with the crying birds and the unintelligible hymns of as many choruses.

The other boats held back, hovering, as the first of them drove forward with a smooth majestic glide towards the jetty attached to the palace. This was the barge of the high priest of Amon, who had been restored to all his offices, and as it drew close to the stone stairs, one could make out the immense black statue of Amon, its shell and silver eyes staring forward over Aketaten from a gilded shrine on the prow, with its own indestructible proud look of idiot certainty.

It was even the same high priest as twenty years ago, who astutely prostrated himself before Tutankaten. Together they went to the palace.

Now anyone might know the matter who chose. He was quite prepared for Nefertiti when she appeared. He was even willing to be alone with her.

"Why was I not told?" she demanded, and she was furious, and yet dangerously calm.

But some things may be dangerous without being in the least able to do us any harm. "Because you are not coming," he said, and left her standing there.

That afternoon the boats set sail again. The jetties were crowded. The nobles had prudently taken what was most valuable with them, left caretakers behind, and would come for the heavier goods later, at their convenience. The wind had blown so many ways in their lifetime that they could not be sure, even of this almost certain departure for good.

Tutankaten was quite sure.

The royal barge had been readied a month ago. Now it emerged from its boat-house. To the sound of trumpets, Tutankaten and Ankesenpa'aten left the palace for the last time, without a backward glance, and crossed the plank to the barge. Nefertiti did not appear. The plank was thrown carelessly into the Nile, the hawsers were loosened, and the barge moved out into midstream, at first ahead of the high priest's barge, and then, more prudently, or perhaps because of an idle riffle of the current, behind it. The music once more struck up. The fleet manœuvred into assigned order of precedence, and then, with some shouting from boat to boat, settled down and moved smoothly off.

Looking back, Tutankaten's eye was caught by the figures on the rudder. It was the old royal barge, and the figures were those of Nefertiti and Ikhnaton, since no one had thought to remove them. The sight of them startled and displeased him, but then he saw it did not matter, for this time the boats were headed upstream and not down, and they were going the other way, back the way they had come.

It was ironic, if you liked. For they were all leaving. Not even Ay, in particular not Ay, had been left behind.

Nineteen

It was incredible.

At dawn it had been the centre of an empire. Now, at evening, it was not. Yet, even though this had happened, it was to keep up a shadow life, after all. It was precisely that it had been left so suddenly, that made one believe in those shadows.

For three weeks one could go through the royal magazines and still find edible vegetables and fruit prepared for the royal table. There were 15,345 bottles of wine still in the cellars, but waiting now not to be drunk, but stolen. That evening, in the royal banqueting hall, an overturned amphora still noisily dripped wine on the painted floor. On one of the food stools lay three bitten figs.

Where were the servants? Why had they cleared nothing away? Those who were left were in the kitchens, not knowing whether to hang themselves or gorge on the royal banquet they had been cooking all day. Being human, they wiped their tears and ate, for the food was undeniably as good as ever. For a few weeks they even fed the goldfish, the greyhounds, and the zoo.

But then Nefertiti withdrew to the northern palace, alone, for her three remaining daughters had been taken off with Tutankaten. In the course of the next six months the servants had either been dismissed, called to Thebes, or had drifted away, since no new foodstuffs came into the commissary now.

The palaces were the first to fall into disrepair. Workmen from Thebes stripped them to the walls, and what the workmen did not take, looters did. The guards made a half-hearted attempt to stop them, but it was only half-hearted. Mahu had gone to Memphis to join Horemheb, and there was no one left to pay them. They, too, drifted away and left the population to itself.

People entered the palaces timidly at first, out of curiosity, to see how a pharaoh had lived. But with all the rich furnishings gone, they found what they saw disappointing.

Goodness knows where the creatures left in the royal harem went. No doubt they either found places or died. As for the male harem, that was not pretty. Some had become castrati and sphinctriae to seek favour, and all to no purpose. Because of the reason for their maimed condition, not even the temple eunuchs would have them. What could they do? They drifted away and no one remembered them.

Decay is too stealthy to have a historian, and few people realize that buildings, like history, have a physiology. No one saw or heard the first piece of plaster fall. No one could date that event. But the floors were soon littered with the chips.

There was no one to draw the curtains now. They grew rotten and the wind pulled them down. The wind was everywhere. It blew through corridors and courts, and burst exultantly into chamber after chamber, as the roofs fell in.

The gardens left to their own devices went back to natural law and choked themselves to death. The animals in the zoo starved. Those greyhounds in the kennels who could make their escape did so, and now slunk through the city in ravenous, shuddering packs, until even they were thinned out, for being overbred, they were no match for the common curs. However, a few of the wilier ones survived.

Mice came out one by one and then in bolder, hungrier groups, to scurry across the painted floors. And spiders, too, spun desperate webs among the columns, all to catch a single fly.

The merchants left next. It was no longer to their advantage to stay. And with the merchants gone, who was to pay the workers? The glassworks were the last to close. Tutankaten, who was called Tutankamon now, did not care for glass, so neither did his court. Those in the Delta did. The glassmakers migrated there.

The craftsmen were siphoned off, ordered to Thebes, for the new temple works Tutankamon undertook to placate the priests and to please himself. Even those sculptors cleverest at the new style went back to the old with a sigh of relief. The old had been so much easier.

Tutmose remained. He had no desire to go anywhere else. He had enough to live on, and his work was still here. He had always worked for himself, and now he did not even have to flatter his sitters, for there were no sitters. It was better that way. He liked the peace and quiet of the deserted city, and he had much to do.

The guards left. Without any traffic at the customs house, Nefertiti lacked the money to pay them. The priests went last. They belonged to a heresy and were interdicted. But even they had to eat, interdicted or not. A year later and there were only fifty left, where once there had been thousands, fifty to rattle about in three major temples of vast proportions and fifty or sixty of more modest size. So one by one the temples were shut off, of course, for the time being, until only that smaller one was left, in itself too vast for merely fifty, where Nefertiti worshipped, fifty, of course, and Pa-wah. There was indeed nowhere else for Pa-wah to go.

Tutmose never saw her. But he wondered why she bothered to go through that mockery of a service. Perhaps she needed the discipline.

Soon there was no one left in the city but the caretakers, a curious body of taciturn creatures, never to be seen outdoors. In the second year, however, there was considerable activity. Hammers and chisels did not make a cheerful noise in those abandoned streets.

The nobles had at last settled down and sent to Aketaten for their precious wooden pillars and doors. However, that excitement was soon over, and nobody, as yet, except Hatiay, Ikhnaton's Royal Contractor, had so far dared to remove wood from the public buildings. He, it was true, had taken four royal pavilions and six peristyle halls for resale, secretly, in the Delta, before he left.

Often now, with a cane to protect himself against dogs, Tutmose would wander through the grass- and weed-strewn city, and one of these ambles brought him to the temple of Hat-Aton, where Nefertiti persisted in holding services. Attracted by the thin sound of one harp, he went inside.

Though smaller than that of any of the other great temples, the outer courtyard was sixty feet long. Its raised ramp was lined with small sphinxes alternated with withered trees in tubs. The whitewash, though dazzling on that hot day, was now grubby. Formerly the way would have been lined with priests. Now they were spaced out thinly. They did not notice his presence. Nefertiti was half-way to the inner shrine. She seemed feeble, and leaned heavily on Pa-wah. She reached the inner pylon and disappeared from view. The others sighed, turned around, and marched to the priests' houses near the outer gate.

Tutmose hesitated and then walked through the inner pylon, around the baffle, and stood in the shadow of the platform, to watch.

The inner shrine was barren and glaring. All but one of the offering tables were empty. Some of them had cracked, so that the tops had slid off the bases. She was not worshipping. Twitching her robes nervously to her,

245

she was talking earnestly to Pa-wah, as though asking a question. On the immense silver slab of the altar lay a small wilted bouquet.

Watching her, Tutmose realized suddenly that she believed it. That was understandable enough. What else was left of that city in which she could believe? But it was terrible to see her reduced to the nagging superstition of an old woman, forced to believe in a fool like Pa-wah, and to beg him for an answer to anything. It was too soon. Was it to this that the folly of that inspired child had reduced her?

Yet from this distance she was still beautiful, or worse, one could see that she had once been. He was deeply moved and very angry. He turned and slipped away.

That afternoon something happened that had not occurred in Egypt in all the seventeen years of Ikhnaton's dominion. It rained, and did not merely rain, but poured down, with the helplessness of a cloud-burst.

It was magnificent. The light caught the rain, so that one stood in a mesh of silver threads. But no one had repaired anything in that city for at least ten years. One-fourth of the buildings simply washed away. Stucco gave. Parts of those royal murals of Nefertiti, Ikhnaton, and the children came loose and fell from the walls, so that where they had been sitting, now no one sat at all.

As rapidly as the water had destroyed everything, beating down even the plants in the deserted gardens, it drained off and the earth was dry.

But the temple of Hat-Aton was wanly changed. Part of the outer wall had fallen away, and much of the stucco had come loose, revealing a mass of dingy mud-brick. And the sheen of the silver altar top was gone for good. It was now dull and patchy.

Under these circumstances he was not surprised to notice that Nefertiti did not go there any more.

But sometimes, early in the morning, or late in the evening, he would catch a glimpse of her in the distance, a lean, uncertain figure, halting, but still erect and proud, moving this way and that, or merely standing motionless, watching. Sometimes she seemed to be calling on someone, or searching about for something.

He was relieved when one day a greyhound trotted up to her, and he saw that at least she had a companion, and had been searching for only that. The few maids who still paced behind her were certainly no company.

Nor, though she still had one or two petty nobles around her, did he ever see them. He had no idea what went on up at the northern suburb. Supplies, however, were becoming harder to get. He was forced to send trusted servants up and down the river for them, until he hit on the device of starting a private farm on the other bank.

The supply of plaster, though, was inexhaustible. He had merely to regrind the stucco on the walls. That was convenient.

Then, too, he was growing older. He did not go out much any more. No doubt most people would have found the deserted city eerie. To tell the truth he found it eerie, but he also thought, in a contrite moment, that it was just about what he deserved.

Unexpectedly one day Pa-wah arrived on his doorstep. The man was beside himself with terror and said the Queen had died. Tutmose gathered up his tools at once.

He had never been in the northern suburb. He found it a shambles, and utterly silent. Apparently everyone had fled as soon as she died. He entered the palace, if palace it could be called, only to find it had been sacked.

He sent Pa-wah out of the room and did what he had to do. He took this last mask. But he could scarcely bear to see her. In a corner of her bedroom, on the floor, lay something the looters had overlooked. He picked it up, and found it was the head of Maketaten he had sent her long ago. He looked at it thoughtfully and put it in his pouch.

Only then did he dare to look at her. In death she was still beautiful, more beautiful indeed than she had been for years. But what had she wasted all that beauty for? She simply lay there, and she was still there. And yet she was not. It was a little more than he could stand.

He went out to Pa-wah. Someone had to do what was necessary. There was in the house only the greyhound, and even it shied away from him. He never did find out what became of it. But Pa-wah was worse than useless. The man was a helpless fanatic hysterical with self-pity.

It was not surprising. One man may worship an abstract principle, but ten people hoping for somewhere to take their troubles, never. Beneath the level of meditation, religion is nothing more than the sick man's efforts to keep on a really good nurse. Pa-wah turned out to be despicable. He did not even know how to dig.

Tutmose left him shivering against a wall and buried her himself. Somebody had to keep that body from the dogs, and as for the meaning of it, that was how they buried the poor, in a sheet, in the desert sand. Besides, there was no funeral furniture to bury with her. She must have lain helpless, with Pa-wah in the house, for a week, and during that time the furniture had been carried away, down to the last stick.

He returned to his own house, and after some deliberation, wrote a letter to Thebes, to Tutankamon.

There was no answer. Nor had he expected one.

Indeed, in these two years Tutankamon did nothing notable. The Amon priests had begun to grow overbearing, so while rewarding them amply, he had annoyed them as well, by keeping up the Aton temple at Thebes. Perhaps Pa-wah went there. Certainly Tutmose never saw him again.

Tutankamon did give orders that Ikhnaton's body was to be burned, and this a party of silent workmen came to Aketaten, went up the valley to the Royal Tomb, and did. But even that could not be laid to theology, either his own or anyone else's. That was idiot spleen and nothing more.

But why had Ay or Horemheb not done something to help Nefertiti?

The answer was simple. She had left their letters unanswered. Alone of them all, she had stayed on, out of pride if nothing else, until it was too late for her to go anywhere.

And yet, in a way, she survived.

Part Four

Twenty

In Thebes, inevitably, while Horemheb was absent at Memphis, Tutankamon sickened and died.

There was considerable disorder as a result. Even the priests of Amon were upset. They need not have been. For though Tutankamon had no children, there was still one heir left.

Ankesenpa'aten, but of course she was Ankesenpaamon now, for the titulary was changed, did something pathetic, that no one would have guessed she would have had the courage or the wits to do.

She despatched a letter to Suppiluliumas, King of the Hittites, saying she was a defenceless widow and asking him to send one of his sons to marry her and assume the throne of Egypt. Thus the power of the Hittites had made its impression even on that stubborn, watchful, girlish head. She almost succeeded. Suppiluliumas actually did despatch one of his sons.

Fortunately Ay discovered the plot and sent word of it to Horemheb in Memphis, with the result that the prince was murdered as soon as he crossed the Egyptian border. Whereupon the Hittites marched into Syria, captured the murderers, and sent them to Boghazkoy, which they would not otherwise have seen, to be hanged, drawn, and quartered, or something worse. But of that no matter, for though the Empire had fallen, at least the throne was safe.

Ay quietly took it for himself.

For Ay was such a very old man that there was one thing about him that everyone had forgotten. Royal Father Ay was quite literally that. As he had opened the period, by siring Queen Tiiy, in whose image they had been made, so should he close it. He had served them all for such a long time, and to such little point, that he saw no reason why he should not now serve himself in this, and be Pharaoh, too.

He would die soon, and for that he was not sorry. After all, the real question is not whether there is life after death, but whether there is death after life. If we knew for certain the answer to that, then our lives might be easier, and we, too, might stand on the balcony and watch, with a free conscience, without fear of consequences. But, as it was he who had first brought scepticism into the family, and so destroyed the faith of an empire, so it was only fitting that he should be the one to answer that question for certain by quietly slamming a dynastic door in the faces of the curious.

As for the little princesses, they simply did not count. For the rest, he was satisfied that in this life there was nothing to be done but to make the best of what could not be helped, to act with reason himself and with good conscience towards others. And though that would not give all the joys some people might wish for, yet it was sufficient to make one very quiet.

This was what one earned by being wily. But wiliness is not incompatible with a sense of what needs to be done. So after he had buried Tutankamon, and with him every stick of furniture and personal memento of the whole sorry succession, until the palace was stripped bare of every reminder of what they had been and were now no longer, he had the tomb sealed and sent for Horemheb.

To Horemheb he explained exactly why he had taken the throne and exactly what remained to be done.

"I shall live only two or three years," he said. "But that should give you enough time to bring the army into position and between us to satisfy the priests. And then, when I am gone, you must restore order as best you can."

He looked at Horemheb with some satisfaction, for though time had taken away much from Horemheb, it had left his sense of responsibility, and a sense of responsibility was what was needed now.

So it came about that in the year 1360 Horemheb lost a real father, and became, he, a commoner, Pharaoh of Egypt. It cannot be said that he regarded this as any accomplishment, though he understood the irony well enough. But something, as Ay had seen, had to be done.

He was then a man of fifty, and of good sound stock. He was to rule until he was older than Ay had been, until he was a man of eighty-two, for thirty-three years.

And he was to be a good administrator.

When they rolled out that jointed doll in the Holy of Holies, he took the matter with equanimity. But he also took it firmly. When the god spoke to him, he in turn spoke back, for he knew very well how to manage such things, and in particular a high priest.

"Come out from there," he ordered. "For we have much to do, and we cannot waste time on these dumb shows, you and I. You may save that for my successors."

And so to Pharaoh, from the priests, because he gave them what they wanted, Life! Prosperity! Health! and from the army, too, since he was careful to keep the gains of twenty years and play the two factions off against each other, for the country's good, as strong men have always done, throughout history.

Twenty-One

$\mathbf{H}$e never gave a thought to Aketaten, which was a pity, for in a sense certain things still happened there.

Not a great deal, of course. Workmen came and razed the temple of Aton, pouring over the ruins a smooth sheet of cement, as though to seal the god in for good. This was what the Theban priests wished, and if such petty acts pleased them, after all, why not? Workmen also removed all the wood from the royal buildings and from the palaces of the nobles, which meant that even the caretakers at last took their departure, to search for some other silent, mole-like sinecure.

The props of the balcony of audience were taken out, though it did not at once collapse. It stood up for a while of its own weight, so that anyone curious to view life from that vantage point could have done so. But since nobody any longer wished to do so, in time it too fell down, and Tutmose found its ruins, in the course of one of his morning walks.

When he returned home he did the last of his works, and it was by no accident that it was about the one of them that the others had forgotten, the one whose reputation, alone among that crew, was still glorious.

It was at the death-mask of Amenophis III he looked, and then, taking a little plaster, he summed it all up and himself as well.

What he did was a face of Amenophis at forty, a face that outstared posterity, simply because it had no choice but to stare it down, a young face, a permanent face, a transient face, and a very old one; and a face with some capacity for feeling and even for love of a sort, though that capacity was small.

Then he laid down his tools.

Whether he was dying, or whether the time had come for him to die, the outcome was much the same. His turn had come.

He had nothing to complain about, since beyond our own motives, existence has no reason. It is merely phenomenal. Once we have realized that we are free to turn to other things.

Looking round his studio he could see, as he had always felt, that art was a branch of metaphysics, older, more diverse, infinitely more subtle, tougher, and much better suited to meditation and the indication of the nature of the ineffable than any theology or eschatology, which, no doubt, was why theologians and mystics affected to despise it. At least Ikhnaton had not made that mistake. Besides, art survives, and of what theology can that be said? Theology outlives its worshippers always, but those to whom it might be of some use, never.

Again he looked round the studio, but now for the last time. What did he believe in? This was what he believed in. And by an odd trick of patronage and neglect, he was able to leave it all behind him. From the shelf high above, the bust of the Queen stared down the future with one eye, poised and assured. But was it the Queen? Who could say? It might as easily be something that lasted, skipping from face to face, in the human animal. But to be able to transmit even that much of insight he found singularly comforting.

So much for theodice, that science of justifying evil in the good, which like so much of science, was devoted to the justification of something that did not

257

exist in the name of something that did not exist either.

It was not so bad to die.

But it is harder to kill a building than a man. Of course properly speaking a city has no thoughts: a city is only an aggregate of men. If it has any consciousness at all, it has only the group consciousness of those who lived there. So says reason. And yet an abandoned city is full of thoughts.

For the world is strewn with our abandoned dolls. More even than our idols, they attest to our belief. A dead city is as sad, as futile, and as empty as a rusty suit of armour. Everything we do outlives us. It has always been so. It always will be so. Each man is only a skeleton within this accreted shell.

Yet standing on the cliffs above Aketaten, one can look across the faint mounds and the excavated streets, towards the sluggish river, at dawn, and face all that emptiness with some assurance. For after all it is not dead. It lived once. It has been imagined. Or perhaps, come to think of it, it imagined us. Every valley and empty plain of it is haunted. It is only that we do not know the name of what it is haunted by, which is just as well, for give the ghost a name and it vanishes.

For the rest, it smiles, like those forgotten gods standing about in jungles and museums. And we recognize that smile. It is the same smile our own gods will have when we are gone, the smile of survival, of perfect knowledge, the smile people always have when we have left the room. The city waits.

In the past it had to wait quite a long time.

Then, in 1335, when Horemheb was a vigorous man of seventy-five at the peak of his powers, it happened that he passed Aketaten on his way down to Memphis.

From the river the city almost looked real, and he decided to go ashore.

He wandered for a while through the decaying streets, empty except for a single greyhound, which would have nothing to do with him. It feinted in a wide circle always ahead of him, and must be the descendant of one of the royal ones, but what on earth had it found to breed with here?

So, at last, he came to Tutmose's studio, and after some hesitation, entered it. Tutmose had never taken his face, nor had he ever wished Tutmose to do so, but now he was curious.

To see dust and sand piled up here and there against the floor, and in the studio itself, open to the sky, almost as high as his thighs, was not unexpected. But to find all those masks there was.

Tutmose had not outlived his art. His art had outlived him. From four walls these faces jeered Horemheb down, and he thought it better to leave. Merely by their existence he found the place disturbing. It brought them all back again.

Before going back to his boat, he paused to look over the desert outskirts of the city. And from somewhere out there, as he had heard it fifty years before, came the voice of silence. It was only a delusion, for nothing stirred. And yet he had heard it. It was there.

But he had not caught what it had to say, and the voice of silence can never be repeated. It can only be heard once, and in the works of a few artists, seen. Besides, it does not really speak. It only sighs and says, "I know".

Nor had those masks told him anything. They were not really the people they depicted. They were only what Tutmose had learned from the people they depicted. And as for himself, he was not sure after all that he had learned anything from them.

It upset him. But he continued on his journey, after

a last look round. For after all, even there, too, at Aketaten, it had only been a game. The voice of silence was only a game, as the emotions were only a game, sincerity was a game, and even Man was only a game that something else was playing. As for the voice of silence, it was only the sigh of something that had found the game a little long. And that was all it meant. But that meant a good deal, for to tell the truth, he found it a little long himself.

For no, it was not difficult to be a god, but it was very hard to be worshipped, when one knew one was not one, and even harder to be loved personally, if one's capacity for love was small.

He should never have set foot there again.

For he was a very old man, and was to become even older. It made no difference. From the moment of birth our life grows daily a little shorter, and we soon grow accustomed to that. But his thoughts could not help but turn back to that long ago time, even without this unforeseen prompting. And he could remember very well how as a young and eager body, he had wanted also to stand naked in the rain. The patter was reassuring. It was like silver fingertips in the middle of the night. Feeling it, we want to say: I am. But those who need us will not let us be. And so we come to say: farewell, I am never now, I was; which alas is true of all of us, except that some of us cannot even say that much.

He could have used the convenience, right then, of Ay's amused philosophy, as the boat drifted down towards Memphis and responsibility.

For it was all very well for the priests to shout Life! Prosperity! Health! but just by inconveniently believing, Ikhnaton had robbed his successors of all the comforts of convenient belief.

Who more than Horemheb, who had restored the public power of Pharaoh, could more see through that fiction that Pharaoh was a god? And yet he was still worshipped as one, he who believed in no gods, and yet still believed in the power of Pharaoh, which in part derived from that worship. So more than anybody else, more than any of them ever had been, he was left with the worst question of all, the one that can never be answered.

Twenty-Two

Who was this Horemheb, this God?